I WAS STARING THE MU[illegible] IN THE EYE.

"You've got guns on you," I said. "Make your move first."

"Slow," he answered, "you're a brave man. You could've gunned me down anytime, but you waited to face me. I hope I don't have to kill you now. I'll try to let you off with a broken leg, or a smashed shoulder."

I looked him back in the eye. "I'm going to beat you, because there **is** a God, somewhere!"

The killer started to speak, changed his mind, and suddenly his face froze in ugly lines. His hand flashed inside his coat for the draw. It was a beautiful move. It was as fast as lightning, and even as my hand jumped for my gun, I knew I'd never beat him. He fired twice before I dropped the hammer on my first cartridge.

I felt the whir of the bullets past my head: he wasn't playing for the body after all—it was my death that he wanted!

Warner Books

By Max Brand

Man From Savage Creek
Trouble Trail
Rustlers of Beacon Creek
Flaming Irons
The Gambler
The Guns of Dorking Hollow
The Gentle Gunman
Dan Barry's Daughter
The Stranger
Mystery Ranch
Frontier Feud
The Garden of Eden
Cheyenne Gold
Golden Lightning
Lucky Larribee
Border Guns
Mighty Lobo
Torture Trail
Tamer of the Wild
The Long Chase
Devil Horse
The White Wolf
Drifter's Vengeance
Trailin'
Gunman's Gold
Timbal Gulch Trail
Seventh Man
Speedy
Galloping Broncos
Fire Brain
The Big Trail
The White Cheyenne
Trail Partners
Outlaw Breed
The Smiling Desperado
The Invisible Outlaw
Silvertip's Strike
Silvertip's Chase
Silvertip
The Sheriff Rides
Valley Vultures
Marbleface
The Return of the Rancher
Mountain Riders
Slow Joe
Happy Jack
Brothers on the Trail
The Happy Valley
The King Bird Rides
The Long Chance
Mistral
Smiling Charlie
The Rancher's Revenge
The Dude
Silvertip's Roundup

MAX BRAND

Slow Joe

WARNER BOOKS

A Warner Communications Company

WARNER BOOKS EDITION

This Warner Books Edition is published by
arrangement with Dodd, Mead and Company, Inc.

Cover art by Roy Anderson

Warner Books, Inc., 75 Rockefeller Plaza, New York, N.Y. 10019

A Warner Communications Company

Printed in the United States of America

First Printing: June, 1972

Reissued: February, 1981

10 9 8 7 6 5 4

CHAPTER I

SAN WHISKEY was the American of a Spanish-named town on the border. I never found out the real name, or else I've forgotten what it was. San Whiskey is all that sticks in my mind, and yet I was down there at least half a dozen times, for long or short visits.

This time I came in by night. There were a lot of reasons why I should stay away, Marshal Chip Werner and his jolly boys being one. There was only one good reason why I should go in. That was because I wanted to stretch my legs under a table and smile at a pretty waitress, and eat red hot frijoles.

The last reason won, of course. You try two months of flapjacks and bacon and see what even the thought of good chuck does to you!

The last time, I had come in over the desert stretch north of the town. This time I went down to the river, and followed the winding up it. My pony stuck knee deep in a muddy bog just outside of the place. He pulled out his forefeet with a sound like the popping of guns. But after that, we came right in, and I went to the house of Mike Doloroso.

Yes, he had another name, too, but I can't remember what. That was all quite a while back—what I'm talking about.

Mike was as Mexican as grease, but he had red hair, so we gave him a new front name for himself. It used to make him get mad and show the white of his teeth.

I went the back way to his house. A couple of pigs got out of their wallows and grunted away from me. Then I banged on the back door. A girl opened it. The lamplight from inside shone on the brown curve of her legs and made a red smudge of her hair.

"Where's your old man?" I asked her.

"He's around," says she.

"Around what?" says I.

"Town," says she.

"Listen, sweetheart," says I, "you ever hear the old boy speak of Slow Joe Hyde?"

"You know Slow Joe?" asked the girl.

She came out a step into the dimness, but I could see her cock her head, and clasp her hands with interest. She was a pretty thing. You take a Mexican girl around fifteenish and they're worth while.

"Sure, I know him pretty well," said I. "It's me they call Slow Joe, honey."

"Go on," says the fresh kid, "you ain't big enough to wear two names!"

It made me mad. As a matter of fact, I stand five feet nine of anybody's money. Only, I sit rather low in the saddle. That's what used to make some of the boys talk as though I were a runt. I reached out and got her by one ear. It was so delicate to the touch that I was half afraid of breaking it off. She began to squeal, softly, dancing up and down on her toes with the pain.

"Go tell your old man that I'm here," said I.

I let her go. She whisked inside, made a face at me, and slammed the door in my face. But I guessed that she would go to tell her mother, or her father, or someone about me, and she did. After a while, the door opened, and Mike Doloroso was standing there in front of me. One hand was behind his back, and he was sticking his jaw out. But when he heard me speak, he grinned. You could see Mike grin on the darkest night, as if he had a light in his mouth.

"You damn gringo," said he.

"You damn greaser," said I.

I got out of the saddle and stretched myself, one half at a time; I'd been riding about twelve hours with hardly a break. Mike whistled; a kid showed out of the dark, took the mustang, and started off. I hollered after him to shove a good lot of crushed barley into that pony's feed box. Hot or cold, you couldn't founder that little rat of a horse no matter what you fed him.

Then I went inside with Mike. He took me into a back room. There was a stained, naked, wooden table in the middle of the place, and four or five wooden stools around it. There wasn't anything on the floor, not even cheap matting. It was damp underfoot. The walls were sweating, and streaked. There had been an overflow of the river about a month before.

"This is pretty comfortable and cheerful, Mike,"—I said.

"Si, señor," says Mike, through his white teeth.

He always dropped into Mexican when he didn't follow your drift.

"I always like," says I, "to drop into a place where there's a good fire on the hearth and a coupla kids turning on the spit, and some jugs of red paint circling around, and the boys putting up a smoke screen around the faro layout. This is just what I'm looking for."

He seemed to tumble, then.

"I been closed up," he said.

"Who did it?" said I.

He made a face that gagged him, for a moment. Then he managed to say:

"That Werner—that marshal."

"He's bad business," I agreed.

"He ruin me!" said Mike. "He ruin Doloroso. Oh, damn!"

It was wonderful to hear Mike swear in Mexican, but in English he was only one-handed; left-handed, at that. It made me laugh to hear him.

"What you got around here?" I asked. "Where's the guitars, and the chow, and the singing."

"That Werner, he take everything," said Mike.

"And the roulette wheel?" I asked.

Because Mike used to have a crazy little roulette wheel, too.

"Roulette? Pah!" spat Mike. "That make me a ruin man, Joe. Werner come in and watch that wheel work and say: 'Crooked, by God!' Then he pinched the place. He pinched it black and blue. Oh, damn!"

"Well," I said, "Werner had a wrong steer. He's not so

bad as all that, after all. Now, you go and rustle me up a meal. I'm sorry that you're cleaned out. But you get the old woman to cook for me. She's got some tortillas and frijoles handy, to begin with, and she can jam some meat on the spit while I'm downing that. You can find some red paint for me, too."

He blinked thoughtfully for a moment, but then he seemed to have an idea, and he grinned and nodded.

"Then you work up some music and singing for me," said I.

"I'm closed down," says Mike, very sad.

"Listen, Mike," said I, "you're closed down to the public, but I'm a member of the family. I saw a red-headed streak of sass that can play a guitar, or I'll eat my hat. She can sing, too. I can't eat in San Whiskey if I don't get my regular music with my meals."

Mike's face was a tombstone.

"That's my daughter, Joe," said he.

"Listen, Mike," said I, tapping him on the shoulder, "I don't steal horses, either."

He blinked his eyes again and swallowed hard on the idea. But then he managed to nod.

"All right," said Mike.

He went out, shuffling the heels of his huaraches; he'd begun to hum before he reached the door, and then I stopped him with: "There's another fellow down here in the house that's waiting for me."

"There ain't nobody but my family in this house, now," said Mike.

"Look, Mike," said I, "he's about that high. Blue eyes. Corn-colored hair. A smile on both sides of his face. He wears two guns, rides a fast horse, and wears high heels and golden spurs, with bells in 'em."

"I never seen him," says Mike, shaking his head in a bewildered way.

"You're lying," says I.

"I never seen him," says Mike.

"Well," I told him, "if you should happen to see an hombre of that cut around the town, you might tell him that Slow Joe Hyde is in here, waiting to see him."

"Sure," said Mike. "If I should happen to meet him—"

He went on out, forgetting to hum as he went, and I sat down on one of the wooden stools and leaned my elbows on the table, and did a little quiet damning.

Werner was making too much trouble. It's all right for a marshal to be honest, and devoted to duty, and all of that, but why should he be a hog and skin a poor little fellow like Mike Doloroso?

I made a cigarette, lighted it, threw it away. Made another, scratched a match, and put the match into my mouth instead of the cigarette. That made me spit and damn for a while. I wanted to kill Werner before I was through.

I never had had much use for the law. I hated it worse than ever, now. Just then the door opened, and a fellow with golden spurs and blue eyes and corn-colored hair came into the room. I forgot my troubles.

CHAPTER II

He came over and gave me a hand and a smile. He had the sort of a smile that soaks right through to the heart, in a jiffy.

"Mr. Lew Ellis, if I ain't mistaken," says I.

"Mr. Joseph Hyde, I believe," says he.

"That same," says I. "Will you sit down, sir? No, take the armchair. I'll ring for scotch and—"

"Thanks," says he. "Brandy, if you please. How are you, you old wall-eyed son of a gun?"

"I'm pretty good," says I. "How are you, Babyface?"

"You don't forget nothing, do you, Runt?" says he, darkening a good bit.

"I was always too big for you," says I.

"You picked on me when I was a kid," says he, sticking out his jaw.

"That's because you can't grow up," I told him.

All at once he grinned at me, and the blue-gray of steel went out of his eyes.

"Old Slow Joe Cactus," said he. "I'd kind of forgot about your thorns. How's things, boy?"

"Just turning green," said I. "We look for ten sacks to the acre, out our way. What does you pa say about your section of the country?"

"Bumper crops," said he.

"Grain?" said I.

"Yeah, yellow grain," said he. "How are you raising your crops, boy?"

I made a puffing, popping noise with my mouth.

"Soup?" said he.

"Yeah."

"Where?"

"Oh, around the corner," I told him.

"Going to freeze up on me, Joe?" said he.

"Why should I tell you where I've been cracking safes, handsome?" I asked him. "I'll tell you, though, after I get something between my backbone and my belt. What's your yellow grain?"

"Guess," says he.

"Chinese," says I.

"Yeah."

"Are they running free?"

"We've been sliding a lot of them across the border," says he. "But things are tightening up on me. Werner is around a good deal. That gopher is under-ground getting information all the time. That's why I sent for you. I want you in the job, son."

"You don't get me," I answered him.

"Where not and why not?" said Lew Ellis.

"Werner is where not, and the Chinese are why not."

"Are you scared of Werner?" said he.

"Yeah, and so are you," said I.

He stopped. He didn't want to boast, of course. But as a

matter of fact that yellow-headed kid was afraid of nothing in the world.

"Well," he said, "I think you could let Werner ride. He's smart and he's deep, but he's not as smart and as deep as all of that. We're working a big plant, son, and if he closes one door, we've got plenty of others."

"That's all right," says I.

"While it lasts, you make about a thousand a week for your split," says Lew.

I whistled.

"It must be a cinch of a job," says I, with a sneer, "if you come across that big."

"It's not a cinch," he admitted, "but it's pretty hot while it lasts. Do you want to cut in?"

"No."

"What's Werner done? Tied a tin can to you, sometime?"

"I'm scared of Werner," I admitted again, "but that's not all. There's the other part of it. Running in Mexicans is all right. They got almost as much right to the Southwest as we have, I suppose. But the Chinese are different. I don't want to run in no Chinese."

"Why not?" he insisted.

"Because," I said, "a Chinese and his five kids can live on five cents worth of rice a day, and they get fat on a rabbit once a week. They can undersell your white men every time."

"They crowding into your line of work?" asked Lew Ellis, making himself a smoke, as he gave up his argument.

"Yeah. They'll be puffing a few safes, too, before long," I suggested. "In the meantime, when do we chow?"

"Right now you chow," says he.

And in comes Mike Doloroso with two plates. One was tortillas, a foot deep of them, each as thin as a cigarette paper. The other plate wasn't a plate at all. It was a platter. And it was piled with red frijoles, steaming. Those beans were so full of peppers that just the steam from them set me to sneezing.

"Mike," I told him, "sometimes I love you just like a father. Where's that music?"

"Alicia," says he, licking from his thumb some of the

red sauce that had spilled on it, and looking at me pretty thoughtfully.

Well, she came in, with all the sass out of her, and her eyes on the ground, and a new dress on, and her hair twisted into a knot at the back of her head, and little bright slippers on her feet, and a big guitar in her hands.

"Alicia," says I, "you're a honey. Take that stool there in the corner. Imagine that you're the whole damned orchestra, and let's have a song out of you."

She gives me a curtsy. Mike Doloroso stood in the doorway. First he narrowed his eyes at the girl, then at me. But he wound up considering yellow-headed Lew Ellis. Ellis hadn't said a word. He was just looking, but he was one of those fellows who can look their way out of jail.

I was wrapping up beans in tortillas, not tidy, but fast. Don't bother me with forks when I see a chance to feed myself frijoles. Leave me to a couple of stacks of good, cold, thin tortillas, and I'm the boy to show you how the morning paper wraps its mail orders!

Alicia, while she was tuning up, managed one look over at the table, and she was so interested in watching me eat that she forgot what she was doing. She just sat and opened her mouth and her eyes. She was only a baby, that kid. But she was a sweet thing to look at.

"You sing a good song, beautiful," I called to her, "or the devil will catch you while you ain't looking."

I hooked a thumb at Lew to show her where the devil was sitting.

"You save your mouth for beans, will you?" says Lew to me, very cold and deliberate. Then he adds: "Where did you find this around San Whiskey?"

"She's the red-headed streak of trouble that belongs to Mike," says I.

"The devil she is," says Lew.

"The devil she ain't," says I. "And she may be the devil, too, for all I know. Mexicans don't have to go to Sunday school to learn about things."

She began to sing and play. Her playing was all right. It had the rip and the swing to it. Her voice was small, but pretty good, also. Only, it was all full of wobbles. This was her first public appearance, anybody could see.

So I gave up my platter and plate, for a minute, and put a bend in my neck, and helped her out on the chorus.

When I got through, Lew says: "You damn Caruso!"

He was ready to slam me with that whole platter of beans, what was left of it. But the girl was laughing. I don't mind being laughed at, mostly, if it puts people at their ease. And she was eased, all right.

Just then, there came in about ten pounds of roast kid. I sliced off a chunk of it and swallowed.

"Old son," says I, "this is the only kid that ever was raised on milk and honey. Go get me some of that red wine of yours. I love you, Mike. I'm gunna make you my heir!"

He gave me a satisfied grin and went hurrying out. There was that good thing about old Mike Doloroso. The money he made out of his guests never fed him as fat as the pleasure that he saw them getting. God bless a man like that, I say!

The girl began to sing again. And she let her voice run right out into the song, and she tilted up her head, and she opened her mouth, and by thunder, she was the only human I ever saw that looked as good stretching for a high note as she did making a silence. And, all the while that she sang, she twinkled through her eyelashes, and the twinkling was for me! I pretty near fell out of my chair.

"Look, Lew," says I. "You don't know it, but you ain't in the room."

"I can't talk the tortilla-bean language as good as you can," says Lew, pretty disgusted. And he smoothed down his hair. Well, he was a handsome kid, all right, and I didn't blame him for being sore.

"Good old Lew," says I. "You're a bright lad, but you're only a lad."

"What aged you, son?" says he. "A sea-trip, or being tied up in a tree, or was it the wrinkle that the greaser cut into your face, or the frown that the mule planted between your eyes, or the cock of your chin where the flatty socked you with his club?"

"Age," says I, "is a thing that you take on in different ways. Me, I'm soft and simple, and little things like knives, and kicking mules, they make a lot of difference to me. But long-whiskered hell-fire is about all that'll make you seem to need a shave, youngster."

He took this pretty well. He even grinned at me.

"You still got your lingo with you, boy," says he. "Now, talking about that Chinese business—"

"Try my other ear, kid," says I.

"Aw, listen, Joe," says he. "Outside of the money, I need you."

"Quit it," says I.

"I need you, honest," says he.

"To build a happy home?" says I.

"Just," says he.

I forgot the roast kid, for a moment. I just sawed my knife absently on a bone and stared at Lew Ellis.

"Try again," says I. "You mean you mean it?"

"Yeah. That's what I mean. I've found her. I want her. She wants me. I need another five grand, is about all. Then we stop!"

"You mean, you mean marriage?" says I.

"How do you think I was raised?" says he. "Didn't we both go to the same Sunday school? Listen," he goes on, leaning across the table a little. "I'm crazy about her. She's crazy about me. My God, I'd wade through fire for her!"

"Is that why you were watching Alicia so hard?" says I.

"Oh, go on, boy," says he. "You know that old habit is the last dog to stop barking."

"It's all right," says I. "Only I was just curious. This girl of yours, what would she think about the business of running in Chinese? Would she want to found a happy home on that sort of tripe?"

"She don't need to know a thing about it," says Lew Ellis. "Now, Joe, I'm putting it to you straight. I've got a big bundle of work on my hands. I've got a crowd of the Chinamen that'll be velvet. They need a little handling, though, to steer them all by Werner, damn him. That's why I asked you to come down here."

"Wait a minute," says I, "and—"

"Don't you tell me that you're afraid of Werner," he argues. "I know that you're afraid of everything, according to you. But the only round the other guy ever wins is the first."

"Shut up, Lew," said I. "You read me by your own light. You couldn't see my print, otherwise. But I'll tell you this. If you really want me to cut in and help you—"

Just then a door closed, somewhere towards the front of the house, with a sort of muffled sigh.

The girl's singing and guïtar stopped for a quarter of a second. She looked across at me with eyes like a cat's in the dark.

"Joe, Joe!" she whispered. "They're coming. Guard yourself!"

And right away, she leans back and pitches herself into her song as though there was nothing at all in the air.

CHAPTER III

THIS fellow Ellis was as cool as they ever came. I'd known that before, but while the icicles are dripping up and down my innards, he slips his hands inside his coat to loosen his guns.

"Who are they?" says he to me.

"God knows," I answered. "Werner, maybe. There's a window behind your back, let's—"

"The lights, first," says Ellis, and makes a pass at the lamp with a long blue-black Colt already in his fingers.

He never finished that swipe. Through the window behind him a pair of guns went blam-blam-blam-blam—just like that, as if they were two-stepping the piece together, and Ellis keeps right on leaning until he hits the floor.

I was on the floor, too. It's usually the best place in a pinch, and gives you a chance for steady shooting; but I saw that the window wasn't the only point of attack. Into the doorway, as big as life steps Marshal Chip Werner, and I see a head over each of his shoulders. I came near potting him as he stepped through the doorway. I would, I swear, because I was fond of Ellis. We'd grown up together, as you might say, and fought our way into a real friendship. But the gun in the marshal's hand was hanging down, and it isn't so sweet to take a pot shot at a fellow who is not on the trigger ready to shoot back.

Just then another pair of bullets come driving from the window. One rips off a big splinter from the floor and throws it in my face. The other slug comes winging and humming like a bird beside my ear.

The marshal ups with his six-shooter and covers the black darkness of that window.

"Stop that nonsense," he says in his gentle, quiet voice, "or I'll slam the pair of you up the river for life."

Somehow I felt that took care of the boys at the window.

I got up and laid hold on Ellis. A pair of the bucks with the marshal ordered me to keep hands off, but Werner was white.

"Let him be," he said, "because Ellis was his friend."

Was my friend?

Well, I turned him over and it looked that way. He was a mess. He was blown to bits, almost. He was all sopping red. He had the look even to the eyes, which were half open, and what I saw looked like the eyes of a dead fish.

I got up and dusted my hands. Dusted the blood off them, I mean.

"This is a pretty good party, Werner," I said. "You'll enjoy the encore in hell, too."

"Shall I sap him, chief?" said one of the bucks with the marshal.

There were four of them in the room, by this time.

"No, fan him, Bill," said the marshal. "And put the stuff on the table."

They fanned me, while Werner took one of the stools and tilted it back against the wall, with himself on the top. He took out a tailor-made cigarette—they were rare in those days—and lighted it, and began to puff slowly and inhale like a fellow who knows what he's about.

"You're letting Ellis die," I told Werner. "I saw his foot twitch, just then."

"Did you, really?" says the marshal. "Well, that's too bad. We don't want to be inhuman. A couple of you boys give him a look. Sam, you're two parts doctor. Take him into the next room. Call somebody to scrub up this mess. I'll keep Hyde here with me."

"Cuffs, chief?" said someone, jingling a pair.

"No, that's all right," said the marshal.

They began to carry poor Ellis out; my heart ached. I hadn't guessed how I had liked that fresh kid. Then the girl barged in and lets her guitar drop with a clangor on the floor. She grabs my arms.

"Joe, what'll you be thinking of us—of me?"

I took her face between my hands. Her cheeks were red hot.

"I think you're a good one out of a bad breed," I said. "You run along."

"What will happen to you?" says she, leaving go of my arm and beginning to wring her hands.

"I'll probably stand quite awhile without hitching, that's all," I told her. "Now you hoof along, Red, and pray for me every Easter Sunday till I come back, will you?"

She got out of the room, with a big sob breaking just as she reached the hallway. Then I heard her break into a rapid fire of Mexican with a mighty dangerous snarl in her throat.

Just after that, her father came into the room, and he was carrying my bottle of red wine! That was pretty cool! He stopped short for a minute when he saw that my hands were free, but then he went on and put the wine on the table.

"Mighty sorry, Joe," said he.

"It's all right, Mike," I said to him. "I might have known what you would do to get the padlock off your front door. I won't bear a grudge. I like to stumble on higher ground than you."

"But," says Mike, with both his hands in the air, "I know nothing. I only hear when—"

I looked him in the face and he couldn't stand it. He went out, closing the door behind him as softly as though he were leaving a church.

That left me with the marshal, and the blood on the floor. He went to the door, locked it, crossed the room to the window, and stood there for a while teetering back and forth, his hands clasped behind his back. I gathered up my stuff from the table and lodged it about me where it belonged. But I was puzzled. His back was still turned when I said:

"I thought you'd been wanting me for a long time, Chip."

"Yeah. I'd been wanting you," said Werner.

I stared at his back, but there was nothing to see except to admire the fit of his coat. He was a great dude, in those days.

He always looked as though he were just about to go to work, never as though he had come in from a job. He was so dapper and neat that I never could see where he put away his guns; but nobody in that part of the West was fool enough to forget that he always wore them.

"I'm glad you've changed your mind about me, anyway," I said.

He smoothed his hair. It was already so slick that I could have seen to shave in it. He didn't answer.

"I'd rather have you absent-minded on the other side of the room," I told him. "You don't think I'm fool enough to try a break through the door, do you? But I could use that window."

He yawned. He still had his back to me.

"We'll have a little chat, Slow Joe," says he.

I eased myself back onto a stool and swallowed a groan. Of course, however, I saw that I never could hope to get away from him without a deal. I had thought, for a minute, that he didn't have enough stuff on me for an arrest. Now I changed my mind.

There was a big, thick-sided glass on the table, with a chunk bitten out of one part of the rim. I filled the glass, drank from the smooth place, and put the glass down with a thump. It was the worst wine in the world, with an after taste like wood ashes in the throat; but it had a body and a kick to it. I closed my eyes while the stuff warmed me.

Then I made a cigarette and lighted it. The blood-stain was spreading on the floor and turning into mud. I had a fool desire to touch the rim of the puddle with the toe of my boot. My foot kept moving a little back and forth.

Marshal Werner came back and sat down on the stool he had placed against the wall. He teetered back in it once more, knocked the ashes off his cigarette, and seemed to measure the length of it. It was about half gone.

He was exactly opposite me. I thought it a queer thing that two fellows as handsome as the marshal and poor Ellis should have been in that little room, one after the other.

He said: "That's a pretty girl, Slow."

"Yeah," said I.

"A cut above her kind," says he.

"Yeah," said I.

"Fire, too."

"Yeah, fire, too."

"They're better that way. With fire, I mean."

He knocked the ashes off his cigarette again, though the coal was still a clean, clear red. That told me that he was pretty excited, behind that beautiful, cold face of his, behind those gray, misty eyes. I felt better. My own nerves improved a hundred percent. I took another whiff of smoke.

"Have a sock at this wine," I suggested.

"A swallow," said he.

I poured the tumbler full. He came over and slid the red ink down his throat in one pouring. He was no larger than I, but even in drinking he was big.

Then he went back to his stool and sat down again, tilting back once more. He moistened his lips even after the drinking. The tip of his tongue was purple with the wine.

"I'm thinking, Slow," said he.

"Yeah. I know you've been to school," I told him. "Take your time. I can wait for you as long as the jail can wait for me. Only, this was a rotten play you made today."

"What play?" says he, absently.

I pointed to the blood on the floor.

"Ellis was my pal," said I. "I don't know what you may have in your mind. Before you start your talk, I just wanted to tell you that. Ellis was my pal. Nothing you can say will cancel that out."

"Oh, Ellis," says he, as though he'd forgotten there was ever such a man in the world. "I didn't come here for Ellis. I came here for you."

"You just slammed Ellis for fun, eh?" said I, beginning to heat up to the surface, even.

"I didn't slam Ellis," said he.

"I'm not saying that you did," I answered, holding myself hard. "But your hired hounds did. That's the same, with me."

"My hired hounds didn't do it," says the marshal, wearily.

"Then I only dreamed that Lew Ellis was plugged four times through the body," I said.

"Outside pair of hands did the trick," he replied.

"Uninvited?"

"I let them come along. I didn't know—"

His voice trailed away; he was plainly thinking hard.

But I got rather impatient. I still was seeing Ellis lean out of his chair as the bullets hit him from behind. I still could see the jerk of his body as each of those slugs went throbbing into him.

"Then I'd like to know the names of the pair!" I yelled at him, suddenly.

He held up a hand to hush my noise.

"That's exactly what I hope I can tell you," said he.

CHAPTER IV

You can bet that I sat down again, fast. I didn't say a word. I pulled myself together, and began to watch like a cat, for I knew that Werner was a deep one, a tricky one, and always playing a game. This play of the cards I could not follow. I had a terrible desire to look up his sleeve.

After about sixty leaden seconds, he said:

"It shapes pretty well for both of us, if you see things my way."

"Yeah. I hope so," said I, reaching into the dark and closing on nothing at all. "Suppose we begin with what you've got on me."

"The Tolosa job," said he.

I took a quick look backward. I only had a tenth part of a second to do the reviewing, but I had always felt that was about the slickest job I had ever pulled. I felt so then, as I looked back.

"I don't know what you mean—Tolosa," said I.

He looked at me in his considering way before he answered:

"You love emeralds, Slow. And that's a pity."

He looked at my hand. So did I. There was a great big flat-faced emerald set in the only ring that I ever wore. I loved that green baby like a sweetheart. It was a blue-green. It was the bluest-greenest that you ever dreamed into.

"Yeah, I like emeralds," said I. "What about emeralds and Tolosa?"

"There were emeralds stolen out of the bank safe," he answered. "I have a description of every one of them. I don't want to press the point, though, unless you'd like to have me examine that one on your hand."

I blew on the emerald and polished it.

"What's the use of bothering about little details, Chip?" said I.

"Yeah. That's the way I feel," said he.

"Go on," said I.

"I'm not thinking about emeralds, just now."

"What *are* you thinking about?"

"Ellis."

"The devil you are!"

"He ought not to have died," went on the marshal. "He ought not to have been plugged. He was only a kid and a fool. Ellis was the kind that could go straight. He never was like you."

I blinked, at this. I suppose every thug always thinks that he has it in him to go straight, sooner or later. But there was something that rang in me like a bell when I heard Werner say that I'd never turn the corner onto the straight and narrow.

"I let them play my hand for me," said Werner. "That's what I don't like. They brought me some information. About Ellis. He was a side line, with me. I wanted to get you and send you up for a long term. You're the sort of a thug that I don't like."

"Why not?" I asked him.

"You haven't got enough vices," he answered. "Booze, for instance. You don't lean on it too hard. You're the kind that keeps learning and covers up better and better. A yegg like you might go on through fifty years and never be clipped inside the ring. That's why I wanted to get you. That's why I framed the job on Mike Doloroso."

I was amazed to hear him talk like this. I began to wonder if he were drunk. Not with booze, but with fatigue, or mental strain, or something like that. He seemed to be putting everything right out in the clear.

He went on:

"Then this pair of strangers comes along and tips me to Ellis. Well, I don't mind taking two birds with one stone. I assign that window to them, and they use it to murder

Ellis. That's all it was. Murder. They used me. They played my hand and played it wrong. Why?"

He got out another cigarette. I thought he would never be done with the rolling and the tapping, and the lighting of it. Finally he said:

"I see this job bigger than you are, and I see you as the man to put it through. I want the scalps of those two sons of trouble. I want you to go and get them for me. For the state."

"Listen, Werner," I said. "I never knew before how fond I was of you. Now I see that I've always loved you practically like a blood brother. Just give me the names and let me loose. I'll get them for you! But what's this stuff about the state?"

"If you get them, you're wearing a cute little steel badge while you work," said he. "It won't be any weight for you to carry."

"A steel badge?" says I, standing up so that the chair fell back against the wall.

"Deputy," says he. "That, or jail for you, boy."

I poured myself out another drink, a full one. I put it down. But still my brain wouldn't clear. I gripped the table by the edge.

"You're a regular wit, Chip," said I. "I certainly love to laugh at what you say. Deputy, eh?"

"Yeah, deputy," said he. "That or the pen."

"Then you and your deputy and your badge be damned," said I. "I'll take the pen, for mine. I'm practically hungering for the pen, compared with what you want me to do."

He nodded at me, not in agreement, but in thought.

"I always knew you had something in your craw," says he. "Let's hear what you've got against the law?"

"Why, hardly anything at all," I told him. "Just begins with a little matter of claim jumping, and then a rich rustler turned loose when the old man had the goods on him. That broke the family the first time. Then my brother railroaded for a killing he was a hundred miles away from. Hardly a thing. But you know. It's just one of my sore points. I'm funny that way. Just touchy on that point."

"The brother?" says he.

He cocked his head over on one side and twisted his mouth and screwed up his eyes. It was a pretty fair suggestion of a hanged man. I wanted to get up and slam Werner on his sneering mouth.

"No, not that," I said. "They just sent him up for life. That was all. Hate to take your time mentioning it."

"How do you know he didn't do the killing?" asked Werner.

"Because I was with him," said I. "But let's get on to the pen. You see how it is. Just a peculiarity of mine that I don't like the law. I'd rather step into hell than to wear—"

He stopped me, holding up his hand, small, beautifully made, like the hand of a woman, almost, except about the lean, hard knuckles.

"Don't say it too hard, Slow," said he. "Many a fellow is tied by his own words tighter than rope. Wait till I finish. You know Kearney County, don't you?"

"Do I know myself?" said I, some of my heat fading a little.

"Those two fellows came out of Kearney County," said the marshal.

"They couldn't," said I. "First because Lew Ellis comes from there, and everybody loves him up yonder. Second, because his cousin, Tom Fellows, just about runs things in the county. Nobody from up yonder would want to soak Ellis anyway; besides, they'd be too scared of Fellows. Tom Fellows is a lion."

"The two killers, they came from Kearney County," said the marshal.

I lowered my head and looked at him. I saw that he had the facts. I looked back into what I knew of my home county, and my old head spun and got dizzy. I couldn't put the things together at all.

"Listen, Chip," said I. "I been pretty wild; they like 'em wild in Kearney County. If they saw me wearing a badge, they'd give me the laugh and the run."

He held out a little steel shield with a pin inside of it; I almost knocked it out of his hand, and then I saw the blood on the floor. I had almost stepped into it.

"Damn you, Chip," I said. "Gimme their names! And when I've got 'em, I'll tear off this thing and step on it."

He put the shield on the table. I laid one finger on it. Then he sighed.

"Their names are Whitey Peyton, and Frank Gregor," he said.

It knocked my jaw down to hear the names.

"Hey, boy, are you crazy?" I said. "Those two would never work together. Whitey is a regular family member of the Peyton outfit, and they've been cattle-warring with the Willow bunch for fifteen years. How could the two of 'em join up on one job?"

"I'm telling you facts. I'm not explaining it," said the marshal. "If I could I wouldn't be hiring a thug like you to work out the burrows of those animals. I don't know Kearney County, and you do. I didn't love Ellis, and you do. You've got the information, and you've got the cause. Your price is a ticket out of the pen. Now you know everything that I know, but still you've got some marching orders to listen to."

I dropped the infernal shield into my pocket. It made me sick to touch the thing. They'd worn shields, too, the swine who pinched my poor brother, Dick.

"Go on with your orders," I said.

"You can't simply go and grab Peyton and Gregor. I've got nothing against them. They simply helped out a United States marshal. So far as the law is concerned, they deserve rewards, not punishment. But I know that they came down here for murder, and I guess there's something behind it all. You find out what the something is. If they belong to opposite camps, why did the two camps combine? You go on the trail and dig up the material. Get something on them, if there's anything to get. But mind you—there's an oath to take first."

"Oath?" said I.

"You have to be sworn in. The oath goes like this."

He repeated it. I told him to take the oath to the devil. I told him two or three ways he could take it to the devil. He only grinned at me.

"You're a conscientious objector, I see," says the marshal. "Well, then, I'll simply get your promise that you'll never pull a gun except in self-defense or to enforce the law."

He stuck out his hand.

"Wait a minute," said I, and I had a little think. But the blood was there on the floor, seeping in. So I took his hand and looked him in the eye, and felt something like a harness settle over my soul and my body.

He took a big, deep breath.

"*That's* done," said he. "Mind you, old son, I know it's a hard job. It's not finding men. It's finding something on them. And there you are!"

The door opened. One of the posse looked in.

"Hey, chief," he said to the marshal, "Ellis is passing in his checks, and he wants to see this Joe Hyde pretty bad. Can he?"

"Hyde is a free agent," said the marshal. "He can go, if he wants to."

"Free what?" yelled the other guy.

But he swallowed it. A marshal is not like a sheriff. He has a bigger hand to play, usually. So this rough in the door blinks at me a couple of times and then swallows what he's learned. He was the one who had asked, earlier, if he should sap me. He didn't seem to feel so good about me, now.

In fact, he made me walk before him, into the room where Ellis was lying on the bed.

CHAPTER V

THERE was only one lamp, and the chimney of that one was pretty much smoked up. It showed me one of the posse sitting in a chair, smoking, not bothered much by what was happening. Alicia was on her knees easing the head of Ellis with one brown arm, and wiping from his lips the blood, as it bubbled.

I got down on my knees, too, so's my ear would be closer. This kid was dead. I could see that. There was only a breath and a half in him, so he didn't waste it all in one or two big words. He just whispered.

"Slow," he says to me, "three mile out of town on the Ginger Pike, there's a bridge, and by the bridge there's three willows, and between the roots of the middle willow there's a new hole, and in the hole there's a wallet wrapped in oiled silk, and in the wallet there's six thousand bucks. Get it."

"Yeah," says I.

"Shall I go?" says Alicia to me.

"Don't be a fool," says I.

She wipes his lips again. He goes on:

"Take that coin north to Kearneyville and find Ruth Edgar. She's the girl. Give her that money, and give her my spurs. She always kind of admired them. Tell her good-by and God bless her. Kiss her for me. And—God—help my —rotten—soul."

He was about all done, but his hand made a little fumbling movement that I understood. I grabbed it and gave it a squeeze, and leaning still lower I said in his ear: "I know their names. I'm gunna get 'em both for you, boy!"

Did he hear me?

Well, that I don't know, but by the way he was smiling and dead when I straightened up, I guessed that he had. I gave him a good long look. Once he'd split my lip in a fight; I seemed to be tasting the blood again. Alicia closed her eyes; her tears were falling on his face; and I thought it was pretty fitting and right that a girl should by crying over handsome Lew as he died. He'd done a lot of heart-breaking in his time. Then I got to my feet and unbuckled the golden spurs that he'd been wearing. I wrapped them in a silk handkerchief that I took out of his breast pocket. There was one drop of blood on that handkerchief. It looked like red ink.

"Look here, you," says the buck that had brought me into the room, "state property—what's on a dead criminal, and—"

The other lad had more sense.

"Shut your mouth before you crack your lip, will you?" says he.

My friend pulled up, and I went out of the room and found the marshal. He was lying down flat on the table where I had been eating. In another moment he would have been asleep, but when I stepped in, he was wide awake in an instant.

"How is Lew buried?" I asked him.

"Federal expense," says he.

"Here's five hundred to do it right," said I, putting the cash in his hand. "Flowers, and everything. Right here in San Whiskey you'll find enough mourners. What d'you say? I can't stay for the ceremony."

"I'll bury him," said the marshal, "as if you were there to see. So long."

There was a lot of common sense about Werner, as you may have noticed before this. He didn't hold out his hand to say good-by and I was grateful for that. I said "So long" to him, and left the house. In the barn, I found Alicia saddling my horse. She seemed to know what she was about, so I sat down on the feed box and had a cigarette and a think, for I needed both. I wasn't trying to puzzle out the

Gregor-Peyton game. There was too much of that. I would have to tackle one thing after another on that trail. I was thinking about Lew Ellis, and the Chinese-running business, and the house he would never build for his girl. Ruth Edgar I didn't remember in Kearneyville, for I'd been away several years, and these girls, they grow out of short skirts into trouble in just a jiffy.

When I looked up, Alicia was waiting with my brindled mustang, so I got up, stepped on my cigarette, took off my hat, and kissed her good-by. She seemed to take it for granted. Then I put a hundred bucks in her hand, five double eagles.

She tried to drop the coin, but I closed her hand over it.

"You're not going to get along with your old man from now on," I said. "If the nap gets rubbed off too much, and you can't stand the gaff, here's something that will give you a start. If you need another lift after starting, send me a letter to general delivery, Kearneyville. Can you write, Alicia?"

She pushed back from me a little and looked up into my face for a moment. I guessed that the red-head was smiling at me in the dark.

"Yeah. I can write," said she.

And then she began to bubble.

"Aw, go on. You may be Mrs. Shakespeare, for all I know," said I.

I led the pony into the yard, forked it, and waved my hat at Alicia until she was soaked up in the blot of the night. Then I took the Ginger Pike and rode like the devil for three miles, not that I was in a hurry, but that I needed the fresh air in my face.

When I hit the bridge, I saw that there were plenty of willows around, and he hadn't even given me the direction, but after a while, I saw three that stood together like brothers. I lighted matches around the central one, found a place where the ground was a little disturbed, and in a few seconds, I had the oiled silk of the wallet in my hands.

I didn't wait to undo it and look at the coin. I just climbed the brindled pony and headed for Kearneyville.

It was ordinarily a good five day trek; I nearly killed

my horse and did it in three. Not that I was in such a great rush, because I knew that my men would be waiting for me, all right, at the other end of the line; but I felt nervous, day and night, and had to take the nerves out on something. You know how it is.

As a matter of fact, when I climbed the ridge and looked north, down into the broad, rolling grazing lands of the valley, I was sorry that I had come so fast. Trouble was waiting for me with a brass band, and I knew it.

A fellow has a funny feeling about going back to his home town. He always wants to put on a little dog at a time like that. I looked down at the faded shoulders of my blue flannel shirt, and the thorn-scarred leather chaps I was wearing, and the old, battered boots I had on, and I was sort of ashamed, for a moment. But I had rubbed against the world long enough to thicken my skin. Besides, I never was a dresser. So I didn't even stand up in the stirrups to brush the dust out of the creases and the wrinkles of my clothes. I just jogged the brindle into the main street and told Kearney that it could like me or lump me, just as it pleased.

It was pretty good, though, to look the old town over. It wasn't much to see. It was just one of those boom frontier towns that get their full growth before they're ten years old, and grow gradually senile afterward. It had cheap frame shacks, and cheap looking stores and a couple of hotels with false fronts. I don't think I ever knew how many people there were in Kearneyville. It had two newspapers, but that didn't mean anything, because everybody bought a copy of each to see how each editor was cussing out the other fellow. But no matter how small and ornery the town might be, it meant to me the place where I had grown up. It tickled me to see the grocery store's new sign. The old one was still in the attic of the house where my family had lived; unless new tenants had chopped the thing up for firewood. Then there were the lots where the kids played football and baseball, and the grove where the boys used to go after school, and fight it out. I could still remember some of the socks that I got in the clearing inside of that bunch of old poplars.

There was always a lot of fighting going on in Kearneyville, and that was because the town split into two factions, according to the two parts in the cattle war that had been tearing up the county for such a long time. It was one of those wars where there's not such a lot of killing, just a cowpoke or a sheepherder found dead by accident, now and then, and some cow rustling, now and then, to liven things up. But there had been a few real gunfights in Kearneyville, too, and the town cut up into alliances. The adults varied in their allegiance according to the way they themselves looked at things. But the kids were divided according to the side of the main street they lived on.

The biggest part of Kearneyville was to the north of the street. The best houses were there, too. And the kids of that side of town held with the Willow tribe. The south side stuck up for the Peytons, and I lived on the south side. We had fewer hands, so we had to fight all the harder and more often. Mostly, though, we got licked. Of course, I remembered those old times, while the brindle was stumbling through the liquid white dust of the street into the rut holes. But I had to remember that I was after one of the Peytons, now. And not being a Peyton, I was nothing, as you might say.

Nothing but a damned deputy marshal, with a shield in my pocket!

I saw nobody except a squalling baby in a front yard, until I got to the old blacksmith shop, and there was old Jud Masters leading out to the hitching rack a horse he had just shod. He looked just the same. Ever since I could remember he had been toothless enough to seem to be grinning. He hadn't changed. He was just as strong in the shoulders. His Adam's-apple was just as big. The soot was just as black in the wrinkles of his smile. He wore his spectacles on the same hump, half way down his nose.

"Hullo, Masters," said I.

He turned around and said:

"Hullo, Runt. When did I stop being 'mister' to you?"

"I beg your pardon, Mr. Masters," said I. "How's things?"

"Fair enough," he said.

He began to look me over. He seemed half mad and he

seemed half glad. Old folks from your home town are generally that way when they see one of the youngsters coming back. They half want them to come back rich and famous. They're half pleased to see that the brats can't beat out the older generation.

"How's things with you?" said he.

"You can see for yourself," said I.

"Kind of greasy, I'd say," said he.

I didn't mind that. It was true.

"What's new in town?" I went on.

"Nothing much. Since you been here, the Thomases and the Edgars and the Sloans and the Wickbys have moved in. All up on the north side."

That was the stuff I wanted. I asked what houses they'd taken, and he told me. The Edgars had moved into the old Gresham house; so I started that way.

CHAPTER VI

THE old Gresham place laid out to be something. Sam Gresham made a slough of money in cattle and he socked a big slice of it into the house he built. He planted a fir hedge around it, and set it a good bit back from the street, so's he could make a driveway and have longer to go home. He put out a garden, too, with pampas grass in it, and a lot of foreign trees. He had an orchard on one side of his house, and he had a vegetable garden behind it. He used to keep two outside men working, all year round, and two women fiddling about the house. It was the biggest outfit inside of Kearneyville, while it lasted. Then it flattened out, and got dusty. It was vacant so long that it got most of its windows busted, and a ghost in the observation tower over the center of the house.

The gate to the driveway was open and hadn't been closed for a long time. It sagged from one hinge and swayed east a bit. So I rode right in. Nobody had done a lick on the garden for fifteen years, so it looked pretty good. It was just a brush tangle, with paths worn through, here and there, and funny looking trees sticking their heads up. The orchard had grown old, and twisted, and thick in the skin. I guessed it gave as much as a barrel of wormy apples every year. But it made a good shade.

In the old days, you hitched behind the house, but now there was a rack in front of the place. I threw the reins over a post, and Brindle was asleep on three legs before I got to the front door.

I knocked, and heard the echo go walking down the hall and washing through the old rooms. I could peer through the screen doors and see that the hall was as hollow as the shell of a bad walnut. All the big mahogany fixings were gone. It was clear that the Edgars were not putting on dog like the Gresham outfit had done. They'd filled in the window glass and let it go at that.

There was no answer to my first knock. I thought nobody was at home, and that relieved me, for the golden spurs inside my pocket were no heavier than my heart when I thought of the interview that I had ahead of me. She was crazy about him. He'd died naming her. For three whole days I had been making up my speeches.

I knocked again. This time I raised a quick step down the hall, and the bang of a door.

It might be the girl. No, there was a shuffle of dragging heels, and a bent, gray woman came and looked at me through the screen. She was drying her big red hands on her apron.

"Well? Well?" she asked me.

I got off my hat and said I wanted to see Miss Edgar. Miss Ruth Edgar.

"Land sakes, how'm I to know where she is?" says the lady. "She might be upstairs. Give her a holler. Or she might be around in the orchard. I can't do your lookin' for you."

So she turned around and went hurrying back to her kitchen.

I walked down the front steps feeling worse than ever. You know, when a girl has that sort of an atmosphere at home, it's likely that when she gives her heart to a man, she gives her soul, too, and begins to sew on baby fixings the day after she's said "Yes."

I wanted to take brindle and slide downtown and get myself a drink, but I figured that I'd sleep a lot better that night if I got the thing over.

I looked up at the second-story windows. They seemed blank, glittering in the sun. It was sort of a fool play to holler to a girl you'd never seen, and when she shoved up the window to introduce herself with: "Sorry to bother you, but your man is dead."

So I walked around the corner of the house into the orchard and saw her. She was lying in a hammock with her arms folded under her head, looking up at the sky through the apple leaves, I suppose. And she had on a little smile, like she was thinking of how she had won the blue ribbon at something, or how good her organdy party dress would look, or how she would furnish her parlor, or nobody's business. She was mighty pretty, blonde; and, even with her elbows sticking out like that, they didn't have a sharp point. Her hair was a fluff; one ray of sun fell on it, and went into the shining mist of it.

She wasn't smiling at the sky through the leaves, either. It was a man-smile that she was wearing. You know when you tell a girl how much she means to you and somehow she is all by herself, to you, and all at once you notice that she's looking off at the horizon, with a little smile breaking the corners of her mouth? Then you know, for the first time, that she's really listening.

Ruth Edgar was listening, all right. There was a big cowpoke sitting in a chair beside the hammock. He was a whale. He had a seventeen inch neck, red mahogany. He was sweating so he shone, but he didn't mind that. In fact, he was smiling, too, and leaning like a runner near the finish.

I rolled a cigarette and lighted it. I felt the golden spurs above my heart, but they didn't weigh so much, just then. When I looked up from the scratching of my match, I saw the pair of them staring at me. The girl was on her elbow. The puncher spoke to her. Then he got up and ambled over to me.

He looked me up and down, real mean.

"Want anything?" he asked.

"Room," said I, and looked back.

He was big enough. He was game enough. But all at once he saw I meant business. And what was the use for him, after all? You know, you can tell iron that's been through the fire, and my mug must have looked that way to him. In those days, sixshooters made for a lot of thoughtful consideration between men. When he got through considering, he calls over his shoulder:

"This fellow wants to see you private, Ruthie."

Then he ambled on around the corner of the house. It wasn't a very good exit speech. It didn't warm up *that* audience, at least. By the time I got to her, "Ruthie" was sitting up in the hammock, cold as a stone.

"Well?" says she.

And I saw that she was related to the old lady of the house. I pulled it on her fast, to see if she would blink. I said:

"I've just come from San Whiskey where I saw Lew Ellis die."

She stood up. But she didn't blink. I saw she was the real gunmetal, and no fooling.

"As he died," I went on, "he asked me to take you his love and kiss you good-by for him."

"Is that all he asked you to take me?" said she, narrowing her eyes at me.

"That and a lot of best regards," said I.

I picked up her hand and kissed the tips of the fingers. It's the only time in my life that I've kissed a hand; though a lot of fists have kissed me. But I felt that one part of Lew's dying request had to be fulfilled.

"How did it happen?" says she, looking down at her hand.

"Through an open window," I told her. "Marshal Werner's men."

"The dirty pigs!" said she. "Look—what's your name?"

"Joe Hyde," said I.

"Yeah. I've heard of Slow Joe, too," said she. "The kid used to yarn about you to me."

"You mean you used to call Lew the 'kid'?" said I.

"Is that all wrong?" says she.

"Not between friends," I answered her.

"Look, Slow Joe," says she, "when Lew was dying, or before, did he say anything else to you about me?"

"Yeah. He talked about a little house and a little cattle, and a little wife. All that old guff. Why?"

Still she didn't blink. I almost began to respect her.

"He didn't say anything else—about the start he was making, I mean?"

"I don't know what you mean," said I.

She seemed to think that I was lying. But why should I give away what I knew—to her?

"You don't know what I mean. Oh, I see," says the girl. "I'd like to know one thing, though."

"It's a pleasant place for talk," says I, looking at the empty chair.

That seemed to rile her. She stuck out her jaw. Then she thought better of it.

"Where'd you get that nickname of 'Slow'?"

"Because thinking is so hard for me," said I.

"Yeah?" says the girl. "Thinking is hard for you, eh? Lemme tell you something, Slow Joe, you've thought too fast, this time."

"You tell me where I've slipped," said I.

"You're holding out on me."

"Holding what out?"

"I don't know how much. You think because a girl just sits in the broad daylight and does a little harmless flirting that she's—"

She stopped, because my grin was so wide.

"I hope you choke on it," says she, stamping.

I didn't know what I was hoped to choke on—my grin or what I was holding out.

I held out my hand.

"It's been a real pleasure to meet you, Ruthie," says I.

She swung back her hand. I saw what was coming but I didn't dodge. She laid the flat of that hand right into my cheek, and jarred my silver fillings together.

"You—!" says she.

"I guess you feel better," says I. "So do I. Good-by, ma'am. Shall I call back your boy friend as I go out? Or is there somebody else in line?"

I wasn't in any hurry. It was a good thing, it was a comfort to me to see the way her breast was heaving. She looked as though she had run a mile; she sounded that way, too.

"I'll tell you, Joe," says she, at last, pulling herself together. "You're making a grand mistake. I'm going to prove it to you, one of these days. You're going to wish that you'd come clean. You're going to wish to the sky that you'd come clean with me."

"Thanks," said I. "When I wish that, I'll come and try to sit in that chair. So long, Ruthie."

I went back to the mustang. The big boy was sitting on the front steps. He didn't meet my eye in an embarrassed way. Instead, he looked me over like something he wanted to know by heart. In fact, when I got into the saddle and jogged down the driveway through that wrecked garden, I had a tickle in the small of my back, as though a gun were lining up on me. And I was rather glad to turn into the dust and sunshine of the street again.

Something about Ruthie stuck in my mind like a thorn. And I was to find out later on that premonitions can be full of good sense.

Then I lined out to find the minister.

CHAPTER VII

THERE was more than one church in the town, but there was only one Reverend Thomas Way. I never knew what he was—Episcopal, Presbyterian, Methodist, or what. It didn't matter. He was himself, and that was enough.

When I got to the church, I saw a wash cloth grinding in circles on one of the windows. When the drying and polishing cloth had been used, I could see that it was Thomas Way who was doing the work. So I got off, threw the reins, and walked in.

He had his coat off, and a sort of Mother Hubbard apron over his clothes, and his sleeves were rolled up and showed his red flannel undershirt, and he was tackling another window with enthusiasm and muscle that seventy years hadn't taken out of him. I watched him for a minute. His thin face was always so set that it looked stern, from a little distance. He had to be pretty stern, at that, because he was always fighting so many battles that were not.

Then I went over and spoke to him. He knew me at once. He dried his hand on his apron and gave it to me.

"My dear boy, my dear Joe," says the good old man. "How happy I am to see you!"

He didn't look at my clothes. I don't suppose that he ever saw anything in his life, except eyes and hearts. I was best pleased not to have him look too close at mine.

"What's the matter with your damned congregation, Mr. Way?" says I. "Can't it lend you some elbow grease for this sort of work?"

"Mother generally tidies up the place," says he, "but she's growing a little rheumatic, now. Besides, I relish an

opportunity for exercise. After I've finished these windows,"
—here he took a look down the remaining half of his job. It's a funny thing that churches have to be so full of light! —"I'll have a splendid appetite for supper!" he winds off, very hearty and bright.

"I hope you don't give it all away," says I.

"What did you say, Joe?" says he.

"I wanted to talk to you about a bequest for the church," says I.

"A bequest?" says he. "For the church?"

"And you," says I.

"My goodness," says Thomas Way, and takes his glasses off, tries to see me better, claps the glasses back on again, and gives me a hard squint.

I laid six grand in his hand, counting it out. It made a stack, now that it was loose. It fluttered and rattled in his fingers as though a wind were blowing.

"There's six years," said I. "Five hundred a year for the church. Five hundred a year for you and your wife. Mind you, you can blow five hundred a year on the poor, out of this money; but if you don't spend the other five hundred on you and your wife, my friend—"

"Five hundred—a year—on my wife and myself?" cries out Thomas Way. "Joe, Joe, what in the world would we do with so much money?"

"Eat meat once a day and get a doctor when you need one," I roared at him. I needed to roar. When I saw the trembling of his hand, I didn't trust myself to talk softly.

"I couldn't possibly accept—" says he.

"Do you want a dead man to get up out of his grave?" I shouted.

"Dead?" said Thomas Way. "Dead?" says he, with a gentle music in his voice. "God grant him rest and mercy!"

"He's going to need a lot of granting," I said. "Lew Ellis is the hombre who sent you this money. Lew Ellis is dead in San Whiskey in a shooting deal. This is his message to you."

"My poor Lew," says Thomas Way. "I often saw him with you. He was a bright, beautiful boy, Joe. I think he was once inside my church, too!"

"I'm moving on," says I. "Good-by, Mr. Way."

He followed me to the door. He laid a hand on my arm.

"Joe," says he.

I turned back in the doorway. I wanted to go. I wanted mighty badly to get away. And he stood there before me, hesitating, seeing only my mean eyes, mind you, and the black heart inside of them, till I looked down. He says to me again, in that voice which only good men have:

"Perhaps some day you'll come to me for a little chat—about old days—my dear boy!"

Well, I got away from him, and fumbled to Brindle, and spurred all the way to the Kicking Mule saloon. There were several reasons why it should wear that name. One of them was the style of red-eye that they pushed across the bar. I elbowed the swinging doors open, put down three shots in a row, spread my elbows on the bar, and looked around.

Fatty Carson was on duty. He had his dimpled fists on his hips and he was chewing a cigar in a corner of his mouth. He never lighted a smoke. He just chewed up cigars, all day long, while a yellow stain crawled around his lips and widened, and widened.

"Nobody changes in Kearneyville, Fatty," I told him. "You're only like the rest."

"Gave up potatoes and bread," says Fatty. "That's why I ain't changed none."

"Makes you feel better, too, don't it?" says I.

"No, it makes me feel like hell," says Fatty. "Have one on the house."

I said no. I had remembered, in time, that I had a lot of work to do. I had so much that I didn't know where to begin.

"Glad you're cutting the stuff out," said Fatty. "Glad to see a boy that won't take more than three in three minutes. That's what I call temperance, practically."

"Same old Fatty," says I.

I went over to a corner of the saloon and sat down in a chair. I took off my old spurs and threw them away. I put on the golden spurs of Lew Ellis and stood up. The bells tinkled sweet and small and far away.

CHAPTER VIII

Now that I was through with the last will and testament of Lew Ellis in the way that I thought would please him best—if his ghost could watch me—I got old Brindle into the livery stable, hired a hump-backed neck-breaker in his place, and loped out the north road from Kearneyville to the ranch of Tom Fellows. It was only three miles, but I had done my share of riding, recently, and I was tired when I pulled up in front of the ranch house.

Fellows was the strongest man in the county, in the head and in the hand. He was the best rider, roper, and shot. He was the surest hunter, the slickest trailer, the most dangerous fighter. There was no more fear in him than there is in a wolverine. Also, he was the handsomest man, the best dancer, the best singer, the best nature, the truest friend, the easiest enemy. He was everything that is "best" so far as Kearney County was concerned. He could elect a man for sheriff by patting him on the shoulder in public, and he could pull anybody out of office by just keeping silent when others were praising. He never said a bad word about anyone. But everybody seemed to know what he wanted, and everybody jumped to do it.

He had a tidy bit of a ranch that ran along well enough. But the one fault of Fellows was carelessness. Sometimes he would be away for four or five months at a time and leave things in the hands of a foreman. It would have busted anyone else, but, along with the rest of his qualities, Fellows was lucky. He never was broke. He always had money to help a friend, subscribe to a school fund, or give the poor a hand. I say that he always had money to do good, but he never talked about what he did. He was the finest man, up to then, that I ever had known. He was what the kids considered god on earth. It seemed to me as though he must have been going on forever. The fact that he was only thirty-five and looked younger, even, didn't matter. It merely proved that he was gifted with a sort of immortality, also!

So you can imagine that I stepped soft when I went into the Fellows house. You never knocked at the front door. You just walked in.

It was a little Spanish house, clean, but not too neat for comfort. The rooms were small, rather darkish, and the hall went through into a little patio, where Fellows spent his time when he was at home, and not riding his range. It was a pleasant little court, with a squirt of a fountain jumping and bubbling in the center. The sun was westering. Half the fountain was in shadow. Only the cypress-shaped head of it was nodding in the sun.

Fellows was out there, sitting like the fountain, half in sun and half in shadow. He had on a broad striped mackinaw jacket which was a lot too hot for the day. But weather didn't bother Fellows much. Neither did clothes. He came home wearing the clothes he had picked up on his latest travels and he kept on wearing them, for a while, until something else came to his hand. Sometimes he would be as flashy as a Mexican dude. Sometimes he would look like an English Lord What-not, with whipcord riding breeches and all that rot.

Once there was a poor fool from Montana who thought Fellows was a tenderfoot and started in to boob him right in the main street of Kearneyville. But that's another story and a mighty mean one.

What do you think the great man was doing, in his patio? Reading? Playing his fiddle or his guitar—which nobody could make music like him? Or maybe talking to some friends?

No, sir. He was sitting there as calm as a ten year old kid, cracking walnuts and feeding his face with them, and sipping cider out of a big glass mug. He didn't look up until I was half way across the patio. And then he stuck out a hand to me and gave me the smile that made the whole county love him.

"Can't get up, Slow," he said. "Got something weighting me down a little."

I saw it. It was a cream-gray cat with a sooty muzzle and ears, and soot on the paws, too. And it had pale gray-blue eyes that looked up at me without fear.

"What's that?" I asked him. "A cross between a coon and a cat?"

"I just got her," said he. "I'm getting her used to me and the place. They call her a Siamese cat. Look at her eyes, Slow. The color of some of that Chinese porcelain, aren't they?"

I didn't know Chinese porcelain from Indian jugs, but I said he was dead right. He was sure to be. Fellows was never wrong.

He told me to sit down, which I did, and eased myself back in the chair and closed my eyes, and listened to the fountain whispering, and felt pretty good, and restful. That's the way you always felt when you were with Tom Fellows. He said:

"You're fagged, Slow. You oughtn't to work too hard. You're always riding, riding. Here, try some of these nuts. Here's a whole handful of 'em cracked. Start in on these, and I'll fix some more. And have a shot at this cider. It's just right, and just cold, and hard enough to give you a glow."

He gave me the nuts and offered me the glass mug. That was Tom's way. I sipped out of my side of the mug, and ate walnuts, and he ate walnuts and sipped out of his side of the mug. We finished it off.

"Will you have some more?" said he.

"You tell me where it is," said I.

"You're a good fellow, Slow," said he. "Right down the cellar, yonder. Right turn at the foot of the steps—well, you know where the ice room is."

Of course I did. Everybody in the county, almost, knew about the ice room. It isn't so easy to get ice, in Kearney, but old Tom, he used to spend a lot of time and money and horse power hauling ice from the mountains in the dead of winter so as to make himself a reservoir that would last through the longest and hottest summer. I went into the ice room and closed the door, and I let the cold soak into me for a few minutes, while I lighted a match and looked around me.

He certainly knew how to live. Whiskey, and wine bottles, blue, green, amber, and stuff packed in straw, and about everything that a man would want. He knew how to live, but he was never a hog. Anyone who could call himself a friend was welcome to everything that Fellows owned. I often wondered why he wasn't eaten out of house and home. I think it was because we all looked after him as though he were a child, in a business sense. If anybody started taking advantage of that open house, half a dozen hard-boiled cowpokes would be apt to call on him and give him some inside information on how hot the temperature could be in Kearney County, even in the middle of the winter.

Well, I found the cider jug, uncorked it, tipped out a new mugful, and brought it back to the patio. Tom was petting the cat, and singing softly to it, and the cat lay out on his knee and closed its eyes, and went to sleep, sound, arching its neck and grinning in its sleep.

When I sat down, he had his smile for me, as usual, but when I offered him the mug, he shook his head, still smiling.

I settled back in the chair, once more. It was one of those things made by the Indians, with supple backs of willow, woven together. It fitted me everywhere, all at once. I put the mug on the arm of the chair.

"Doggone it, Tom," said I. "I'm so happy that I can't budge even to roll a cigarette."

"You stay here a while and soak up some rest—*and* some cider, Slow," says Tom. "You're played out. You're thinner than when I last saw you."

That had been about four years before. And I *was* a little thinner. Maybe five pounds. But how could he remember just how I had looked? That was his way. A hundred people knew him better than I did. That hardly mattered. No one expected to monopolize him. It was hardly a matter of being the nearest. Once inside the door of his mind, everybody was the same to him.

"I'm a little thinner," I said, trying not to smile with foolish pleasure. "A lot of riding."

"Making good money now, I hope, Slow?" says he.

I looked hard at him.

"You know what my line is now, I guess?" I asked him.

"Cracking safes, the last I heard rumored. Is that right?" says Fellows.

"Yes. Cracking safes. I'm a yegg," said I, and waiting, hard and brittle, for the shock of his criticism.

I might have known better. He merely nodded, his eyes as gentle as ever.

"Must be an exciting game," said he, "and take a lot of skill."

It thawed me out at once, to hear him speak in this manner. I was ashamed, too, and on the edge of saying something emotional, foolish.

"It's exciting, all right," I told him. "It's rotten, too. Besides, I make money. Then I blow it. Dirty money. A fellow is sort of glad to get rid of it."

He watched me, steadily, for a moment. I thought he was going to give me advice. He merely said:

"You ought to lie up here for a while, Slow. You're getting nervous. I don't suppose that they have anything on you, up here?"

I laughed.

"Nobody has anything on me, now. Nobody, anywhere. Look at this!"

I fished the infernal badge out of my pocket and slipped it onto the table. He didn't exclaim. He just picked it up, and looked at it, as much at the back as at the front.

Then he put it back.

"That's useful," said he.

"And I'm going to use it," said I.

His eyebrows raised just the shade of a flicker. I broke out:

"You think I'm a hound, Tom. Don't you do it till I explain. I'm on a one-man trail. When it's ended, I'm through. I had to take this to keep myself out of jail, and get a crack at a pair of thugs that cracked one of my best friends. That's why I'm here to talk to you. You'll help me. Tom, Lew Ellis is dead!"

He lifted the cat off his knee and put it on the ground. He leaned a bit across the little table.

"My cousin Lew is dead?" said he.

"Yes," said I.

Calm and controlled as he was, I expected an outburst, then. But I was wrong. He merely stared for an instant in a way that was hard for me to endure. Then he settled back in his chair and began to make a cigarette. His fingers were perfectly steady. I admired him more then, I think, than I ever had done before. And I had a sort of pity for Whitey Peyton and Frank Gregor.

"Do you know who did it?" he asked me.

I gave him the whole story, in detail—the place, the shooting, the marshal, the names—Whitey Peyton and Frank Gregor. He said nothing, till I had ended. Then, merely:

"Through the back, was it?"

The quiet way of putting it didn't fool me. I shuddered a little. Not many men ever had faced Tom Fellows. No one of them had lived to tell how the thunderbolt struck them.

"Through the back," I hardly more than whispered.

I waited for more words, and, when they failed to come, I grew so nervous that I carried on.

"What excited Werner was not the killing of Lew," I said. "You know Werner. He's a fish. There's no warm blood in him. He wouldn't care much about the killing of twenty Lew Ellises. But he smelled something deep and black, behind this killing. He seemed to think that there must be something behind the job, getting one man from the Willow gang, and one man from the Peyton outfit, and putting them together to kill poor Lew. That's why he put me on the job, and turned me free with a badge to do the trick. Because he knows that I understand things up here in Kearney County. I don't think he's so much interested in pinning something on Gregor and Whitey. What he hopes is that I'll unearth the fox that started the trouble. And by thunder, Tom, if there's anything in the idea—and

Werner is no fool—you and I together ought to be able to go a long way!"

"Somebody behind them," nodded Fellows. "Of course there's somebody behind them. No Willow man ever pulled with a Peyton, before. Who could it be?"

He looked up at the fountain head. Only the top hair of it was silver in the slanting sunlight, now. I had such a faith in Fellows that I half expected him to sit there and think the whole thing right out for me. At last he said:

"You were Lew's friend, Slow. You're showing it now. I won't forget! But what's the first thing? To slip onto the trail of Whitey and Frank Gregor. I'm not very familiar with them."

"You wouldn't be," I told him. "They're a low cut. Whitey is the worst of his family. He's done time. He's done it for manslaughter, and he should of hanged for the job. He's a little runt and gets his name from his blond hair. He's got an upper lip swollen and thick. Looks as though he'd been stung there by a bee. Matter of fact, I think it's some sort of a growth."

Fellows shook his head.

"Don't remember him," he admitted.

I didn't expect him to. He either let people inside his house and his mind, or else he didn't know them at all. He was all ready with the smile and the nod that made the whole county love him, but, as I said before, there were not only about a hundred men he really knew.

"Frank Gregor," I went on, "is a different style. He's a foreigner of some sort. Sort of Hungarian or something. Big cheek bones, and slant eyes like a Chinaman. Narrow shoulders, and long arms, and strong as a gorilla. Dark skin. Dark as a Mexican's."

Fellows shook his head again.

"Zip!" he called.

In came Zip. He was a funny one. No one could tell whether he was Tom's overseer, house-mozo, private secretary, or what. Nobody could tell what his blood was, either. He was the build of a Navajo, straight and slim; he had the round face of a Mexican peon of the coldest blood; he grinned like a Jap, more with his eyes than his mouth;

he was a shadow with his feet and a cat with his hands. Nobody could understand why Fellows kept him. He looked like poison. We all thought Tom kept him on to keep him from starving. Nobody else would have given him anything but the door.

But, because of Tom, we all had to treat Zip as well as we could. I had to get up and shake hands with him, while he asked me in his pretty good English and very funny accent if I were well, and hoped that I had enjoyed happy years since he last saw me, and admired the way my shoulders had broadened.

He was as polite as a woman, or a minister soliciting funds. I gave him a couple of grunts. It was all that I could find in my pocket, just then.

"Zip," said Fellows, "you know everything."

Zip opened his hands and turned them upside down. That was his way, I suppose, of indicating that he didn't know much of anything at all.

"You know Whitey Peyton and Frank Gregor?" asked the boss.

Zip looked toward the fountain. It had lost the sun and was just a streaking of dull gray pencil strokes against the wall. His forehead wrinkled like the forehead of a cat.

"Yes," he said. "Now I remember them both."

"Where did you see them last?"

"Peyton was in Kearneyville. I saw him going into the First Chance saloon when I drove out with the groceries this morning."

I don't know how to spell out the sound of his lingo. The "ing" of morning was really more like "eeng." "Him" was "heem," and there were a lot of other funny pronunciations.

"And Frank Gregor?"

"I pass him on the road, too. He is riding out from town. He turns off on the road toward the Willow ranch."

"Thanks, Zip," said Fellows. "This cider is prime. Have some?"

"It is too early for my drinking," says Zip, and, seeing that he's not wanted any more, he backs out, bowing. He always made his exit like that, damn him!

CHAPTER IX

When Zip was gone, Fellows stood up and said we might as well be starting. I asked him where, and he said to collect the pair of them. We could get Whitey Peyton, first.

I said:

"We can't touch Whitey. We can't touch Gregor. Not till we've got something on them. I'm a deputy. This is no private job. I gave my word to Werner, and you'll play with me, Tom?"

"Certainly, Slow," said he. "Whatever you say goes, of course. You were first on this job, after all. I'm only to help you where I can."

"I know you'll do two thirds of the work before the end," said I. "But first, there has to be a little detection. I don't want you to dirty your hands with it. But you might let Zip find out something—without telling him why. Just tell him you're curious about the past of Whitey and Gregor. I know that they're both thugs. You stay put out here. I'll go into Kearneyville and hunt up Whitey and see what I can see."

Fellows agreed to everything. But he insisted that he should drop in on me at the hotel that evening, by ten o'clock, to learn what I had discovered. Then I left and rode back.

I can't tell you how differently I felt, now that I had Fellows with me, in spirit, at least. For, when the pinch came, I knew that wise head and those wise hands could carry me through the crisis.

I got into town, put up the nag at the livery stable,

damned the stable man for the gait that horse wore, and went to the hotel.

Sam Guernsey was behind the reception desk. The first thing I noticed was that he was getting too old and tired to smile at new business, any more.

"Hullo, Sam, how's everything?" says I.

"Hello, Runt," says he. "One night stand?"

A fine way to welcome a guest.

"I dunno," says I. "I just stepped in to see what your dump could offer. Everybody says that the Criterion is the only decent place in town, now. But I thought I'd see if you'd gone that far down hill."

He pricked up his ears a little, and the ears were red. "The Criterion is a rat-hole. If you're a rat, that's where you'll fit," he remarked.

He began to drum on the top of his desk, and look away from me, absently. But I saw where to slam him. I said, pleasantly:

"I suppose I'll have to go back to the Criterion, all right. They certainly keep a cleaner lobby than this. I just wanted to drop in and tell you I'm sorry, Sam. But after all, a hotel can't stay young forever, no more than a man can. Hotels, and hotel keepers, they get tired out, after a while. Well, so long, Sam."

I got nearly to the door, when he yelled after me:

"Come back here!"

I went back.

"Who's been talking to you, Slow?" said he. "Who's been lying to you about me and the hotel?"

"Why, nobody," said I. "It's all around the town. That's all."

He looks at me pretty bitter, his head down, peering upward. He keeps on tapping on the desk.

"I don't suppose you know," says he, "that I put on a whole new roofing, two year back?"

"Did you, Sam?" says I, very innocent. "Then it was old history, what they told me about the rooms getting flooded all the time. They said that the guests in your house always went to bed wearing life preservers."

"They did, did they?" said Guernsey, turning from red

to purple. "And you don't know, neither, that I got in a new range in the kitchen, and the slickest Chink cook in Kearney County to fit with the range?"

"No," said I. "They all told me that the cooking here was what kept so many doctors going in Kearneyville."

"They don't know nothing!" yelled Sam. "Neither do you!"

"Why, Sam," said I, "I'm just repeating what I heard. That's all. I didn't mean any harm. You know the way that people talk. I guess they've just exaggerated a little when they said the Guernsey Hotel was just a sort of a stable, now, and a drafty stable, at that."

"They ain't three men in this town," bellows Guernsey, "that deserves to bed down in nothing better than sawdust, and wet sawdust, too."

He banged on the desk:

"Did they tell you that I got seven bathrooms in the house, and running water in every room, and the damned Criterion ain't got one?"

"No," said I, "they only told me that the chambermaids, at the Criterion, was a hand-picked lot. That's all they told me."

I thought he would choke. He had to close his eyes for a moment before he bawled:

"And who picked the girls that work here, I'd like to know? And am I blind?"

"Why, Sam," said I, "you know how it is. People just talk."

"And fools stand and listen to 'em!" roared Sam. "Come up here, Slow, and I'm going to show you what the Guernsey Hotel offers. Old, is it? And me old, too, is it? Damn my eyes! The low-down bohunks! The Polacks! The Greasers!"

He took me upstairs, and showed me the best layout he had, a big double room on the corner, overlooking Fourth Street. There was a candy shop across the street; they were cooking some stuff then, and the sweet of it came thick on the air. That room had a bath connected. There were two beds. There was a rug between them, and three chairs, and a bureau and dressing table fit for a king. I told Sam Guernsey that the people who had been knocking his hotel ought to be shot, and he agreed, and he said, furthermore, that he would do the shooting. He got so hot and happy about the way he was going to massacre some of those hounds, that he up and offered me the room for half price. I told him he was an old friend.

I brought up my pack and slung it in a corner. Then I undressed, and filled the bathtub half full of hot water, and slid into it, and just lay there, corked.

After a while, the heat got through my muscles to the bones. I had been trembling like a terrier in a cold wind. Now the heat smoothed me out like an iron. I felt such a lot better that you wouldn't believe it.

Then I scrubbed myself off, climbed into the bed and lay there, spread-eagle. That's the best way to rest. I took a look at my watch and told myself that it was an hour to sundown. I would give myself that much sleep. And sleep I did.

When you're out on the range a lot, as I've been, you learn to time yourself without a clock, even in your sleep. Punctually in an hour, I woke up, groggy till I ducked my head under a cold water faucet. That pulled me together. I shampooed my hair dry, and gave my clothes a couple of shakes, like a rug, before I put them on. The dust certainly flew!

When I was dressed, I felt like a new man. All the weariness that had been building up since I left San Whiskey seemed to be scoured away. The tarnish was gone, and I felt fit.

Then I sat down with a cigarette and tried to work out a plan of campaign. I couldn't find a plan. I rarely can. I'm one of those stupid hombres that can't find a way out of a corral without breaking down a bar. So finally I gave the thing up and started out to find what I could. I found plenty that wasn't exactly what I wanted.

First of all, I wrapped myself around a couple of steaks with eggs on top of them, and plenty of French fried on the side, drank three or four cups of coffee, and smoked a cigarette on the veranda waiting for the grub to settle.

It was a pleasant time of day. Betwixt sundown and down, I mean. The day had let up. So had the men. It was the women's turn, now. You could smell cookery on the wind; you could almost hear the hissing of bacon in the pan. Screen doors were slamming with a jingle. Four or five batches of kids were playing, far and near, and the sound of them put a sad tingle in my blood. This was the very hour for kids to enjoy. And many such an hour I had lived through and fought through there in Kearneyville. It made me feel old and wicked. One of which I was, plenty.

After a time, a teamster comes out and starts telling me how he can put a sixteen mule team around the curves of a mountain road, so I decided that I'd get up and drift. There's nothing worse than a teamster. And the more mules he skins, the more lies he can tell about himself and his nags.

I went up the street, wondering where I would begin, and the first thing that I turned into was the Hard Cash saloon. I asked if Whitey Peyton had been there. The bartender was scrubbing down the bar, and he scowled at his work before he answered:

"You a friend of his?"

"Sure," said I. "Known him for years."

"Then you've gone and wasted a hell of a lot of time," said the barkeep.

I decided that Whitey had been and gone, in this dive, so I barged out and navigated around into the First Chance. Whitey had been there. He was accumulating a pretty long lead, it seemed. They didn't know where I'd find him. They advised me to sit down anywhere in town and listen for a noise like a big wind rising, and that would be Whitey, all right.

I went out and tried the Kicking Mule. Fatty Carson was still behind the bar, and spinning out drinks to half a dozen cowpokes all in one party, each of 'em trying to drink the other under the table inside of half an hour, and all of them succeeding, it looked like to me.

I asked Fatty if he had seen Whitey Peyton, and Fatty looked at me none too pleased.

"Is he a friend of yours?" he asked.

"Not at all," said I, remembering. "I just heard that he was around."

"Yeah, he's around and about and in and out," said Fatty. "Just now, most of him is in there!"

He pointed toward the back room of the place.

As he did so, the door opened, and a fellow came out with a burst of cursing and yelling behind him. He had his coat almost torn off his back, one eye was red and puffing fast. The other one was full of trouble; trouble coming, trouble on its way.

He said nothing to anybody, but walked straight across the barroom and bumped the swinging doors open with his chest.

"That cowpoke has gone home to get a gun," I said.

"Why," says Fatty, "you must have been around quite a lot to be able to see a thing like that."

"Is that one of Whitey's jobs?" I asked.

"Yeah. It looks like it."

"He must be spending a lot of money, if you put up with that sort of a playmate," said I.

"I ain't the boss, here," said Fatty, through his teeth, giving a real wicked look at the door to the back room. "You'll find your friend Whitey in there, all right."

"He's no particular friend of mine," said I.

"Well, he ought to be," says Fatty.

CHAPTER X

It seemed to me that Kearneyville was pretty sour on me. Nobody seemed very glad to have me around, and I wondered how many stories about me had come floating back to the place.

However, there's no use accepting every fight that's offered to you. I make a point of dodging everything except what

I have to take. So I let Fatty's remark slide and went into the back room of the Kicking Mule.

It was pretty well blurred with tobacco smoke, though there were only half a dozen people in it; but these were all around the roulette wheel, and six at roulette are usually equal to sixty at any other game. The wheel was giving them bad breaks and good breaks. They whooped one minute, and they groaned the next. I pushed into the circle and spotted Whitey at once, with his puffed mouth. He was going great guns. He'd unbuttoned his shirt half way down his throat, so he could get more air. He was a hairy little devil and the arch of his chest showed where he got the power he was famous for. In the face, he looked sort of sick. But he was never any sicker than a mean mule.

He had in his hand an open mouthed little canvas sack, and out of this he ladled whole handfuls of coin and dripped it around on the numbers, odd or even, or combinations. I saw him bet two hundred. He lost. He bet five hundred on top of that and cleared a thousand. He ordered everybody to get out to the bar and drink with him so I went along.

Whitey was illuminated, but he wasn't groggy. Groggy was what I wanted him to be before I tackled him, if I had to. Because I knew he would be a handful. It made me ache to think of the fight I would have if I landed on him before he was ready to bend a little.

I pretended to drink my shot, and watched Shorty toss off his. I kept on watching for the effect of it, when we went back into the other room, but pretty soon I saw that there wasn't going to be any effect. He was just getting red-eyed and sour. He wasn't even rusty with the stuff he had put down, and he wouldn't get rusty, either. Sometimes the poison hits a man like that. He stands up all the way through a long night. The next day he gets the jumps, however, and that's worse than passing out.

When I saw that Whitey Peyton was not going to wilt, I was worried and pretty downhearted. The point was that I knew I had to work pretty fast. Bad news works fast along any trail, and it wouldn't be very long before both Whitey and Frank Gregor would realize that I was on their trail. Before that time came, I had to have some sort of an inning—before the shoot-at-first-sight period began, I mean.

Well, I edged into the circle again, and watched the play, and Whitey dropped a whole grand; and won half of it back.

Pretty soon he turns on me and howls:

"What are you doing, elbowing me?"

"Don't you know me, Whitey?" said I. "I'm your friend. I'm here to take care of you."

"Hey, listen," says Whitey, to the rest. "He's here to take care of me. Whacha think about that?"

He was the big winner, and he was treating. They were all his men. They roared at me. They pointed me out and roared some more.

"Whitey, take another look," said I. "You know Slow Joe Hyde, I guess."

"Yeah, I know you," says Whitey, "and what of it?"

"I'll tell you what of it," said I, as the others bawled with laughter again. "The fellow that you threw out of here is coming back with a gun."

"Is he?" says Whitey, dropping a couple of hundred on the nine, for the next whirl of the wheel. "Well, he won't be packing his gun when he leaves the next time."

The fools around him roared again. I saw that I would have to take this bull by the horns, much as it hurt my hands just to think of it.

"If you won't be a friend to yourself," said I, "I'll be a friend to you in spite of yourself. You're going to leave here, and come home."

He waited till the roll stopped. He'd lost, of course, on his single number, but that didn't improve his temper a bit. He said:

"Look here, son, I dunno who made you my grandfather. Get out of here, will you? You ain't playing, and you're spoiling the play. Get out before I spoil you."

"You're drunk, Whitey," said I. "And I'm not going to stand by while you throw your money away."

"Ain't you?" said he. "Maybe you'll lie by, then!"

With that he slammed me. It was an overhand wallop. I had seen it work before, in the old days. When it landed, it tore a man's face off. I managed to get my head out of the way, but the punch landed on my shoulder and almost broke the bone.

The other boys scattered, yelling with joy. They told Whitey to break me in two.

He was a bull, all right, that sawed-off chunk of dynamite. He exploded himself right at me, but a good straight left is better than a wall of stone, if you know how to use it. I'd learned how to use mine in the old street fights around Kearneyville. I'm not the greatest boxer in the world, but I've always known that a straight left is better than money in the bank. Whitey nearly caved his face in against the first one.

He fanned me with a couple of full swings, backed off, and slugged his chin with all his might against my left a second time.

That time he felt it in his knees. His guard went down a little. His legs bent. He shook his head to clear his wits, and now that I saw an opening a cart could drive through, I stepped in and let him have the right where it would do the most good.

It rang a bell in his brain, all right. He dropped on his heels. The boys didn't feel so good, when they saw that. I was thanking the Lord, but I tried to look as though this was the way I knew the thing would turn out. So I stepped to the table and gathered up Whitey Peyton's canvas bag.

"I'm Slow Joe Hyde," said I. "I'm staying at the Guernsey House, if anybody wants to find me. And that's where I'm taking this fool drunk before he throws his coin away and gets himself admitted to the hoosegow. Here, a couple of you, give me a hand with the blockhead."

They did as I told them. We picked Whitey up under the armpits and half dragged and half walked him through the barroom.

Fatty looked a little bit interested, and a little bit regretful. I suppose he had been hoping that things would ripen and blossom until he had a good excuse for sloughing Peyton with a black jack.

Anyway, Whitey, even after he got his legs under him, was still in a dream. Now and then he raised his hand and felt his chin, but all he could say was:

"It's a doggone funny thing—"

There he would always stick.

When we got to the hotel, I handed Guernsey the canvas sack to keep for Whitey, and I could see all worry vanish off the faces of the boys from the saloon. I suppose they thought I had meant to roll Peyton when I had him to myself. Now, they helped me up to my room, and would have stayed around a while, but I told them that Whitey was coming to himself fast, and that, when he woke up, the explosion was apt to shake the roof down.

They saw reason in this, and left. As they walked out, Whitey was teetering around the room.

I locked the door, grabbed him, and fanned him. The little son of a gun had a whole arsenal on him. I took away two Colts, a mean little double-barreled derringer in a vest pocket, a knife that looked like one of the kind the greasers love to use for throwing, and a real bowie that could open a man up to the backbone with one swipe.

By the time I got the last of this stuff away from him, Whitey stepped right out of his trance, saw where he was, and made a run at me. So I poked one of his own guns under his chin and told him that silence was golden.

He seemed to see some point in that. He shied a look at each of the windows, and said nothing. I ordered him to sit down. He did, and I tied him into that chair by the most effective method I know anything about—one thin strand of baling wire turned around the throat and twisted to the back of the chair. That leaves a man with his hands and his feet all free. He can talk, too. But the minute he starts cutting up, the wire simply chokes him. Besides, if you give the wire a twist with pinchers, no fingers in the world can undo it. Then I stepped back and looked him over. He was gray, but he was steady. He locked his jaw, and didn't peep. I saw it was going to be a mean go.

"Your money is safe downstairs with Guernsey," I told him. "You know he's straight. I'm not going to take a penny away from you."

He thought for a moment before he answered, then he said:

"You came to get me, eh? What for?"

I wondered if I ought to beat about the bush. I decided that I wouldn't. The shock of the sight of my cards, face up, might jar some words out of him.

"San Whiskey," said I.

I saw his jaw muscles bulge. He turned a little more gray. I couldn't make up my mind about him. It might be that he was really steel. It might be that he was only cast iron. If the latter were the case, then he would crack under a strain. I decided that I'd supply the strain.

"Ellis was a great friend of mine," said I.

He started to nod, but the thin arm of the wire throttled him. He sat stiff and still.

"Take a rope, if you want," he said. "Don't use this damned thing. It's choking me."

"That's all right," said I. "Ropes make a bad mark, when a man struggles. But that wire works too fast. It kills a boy before he has a chance to work much, and the mark of it rubs out right away."

His breast heaved once, and was still. I handed him a flask of brandy. He put down half of it, and gave the flask back to me.

"What do you want?" said he.

"Talk," said I.

"You be damned," said he.

"That wire is only a symbol," said I. "Guns are quicker."

"They'd hang you damned quick, for murder."

"No, not that. I'm a friend, doing you a friendly turn. I take you home with me. I leave your money at the desk. But you're drunk. You make a jump at me with your gun. You fire; I have to drop you. All I need to do is fire your gun into the wall, and shoot mine through your head. I untwist the wire from around your neck. They find you dead on the floor. And that's a pity."

"You mean murder!" said he, suddenly.

"That's what I hope I mean," said I, and all at once, I did!

CHAPTER XI

WHEN I felt the real conviction steaming up in me, I glared straight at him. I made myself think about Lew Ellis. All at once, I wanted to cut his throat as he sat there, just give the wire an extra turn.

"You wouldn't do it," argued Whitey. "You're a rough. You're not a murderer."

"I saw Lew shot from behind," said I.

He was quiet for a moment.

"Words are all I want," said I.

"Who gave you the tip?" said he.

"About what?"

"Me."

"You got too close to the window," said I. "The lamplight glinted on that bum mug of yours. Nobody else has an upper lip like yours, Whitey. The other fellow was farther back. I couldn't make him out."

"I wasn't in San Whiskey at all," says he.

"That's all right in the courtroom," said I. "But I saw you. You can't get behind that."

"What do you want to know?" he asked.

"Who was the fellow who was with you?"

He paused, then he said:-

"If I talk, we'll both be dead inside of twenty-four hours."

"You will be," I said, "if I can catch you again after you're on the loose."

"How do I know you'll turn me loose, if I talk?"

"You know me, Whitey," I said. "You know I'm a thug, but I'm straight in these things. You'll trust me."

"If I talked," said he, "it wouldn't be you that I'd worry about afterwards."

"It would be your partner in the job, eh?" said I.

"Bunk!" says Whitey. "I'm not as soft as all of that. You dunno nothing. I tell you straight. We'd both be dead. We'd both be dead quick!"

He sawed the air with his fist to give weight to his words. He tried to lean forward but the wire choked him again. It pleased me to see him choke.

"I'll take that chance," said I.

"Fools always do that," says Whitey. "They play single numbers, the way I started to do tonight. And they always lose—everything."

"I hear you argue," said I. "Now I want to hear you talk."

He stared at me. He was so desperate and enraged that his eyes were bursting from his head.

"Go pull the window curtains together, then, will you?" he asked.

I got rather the creeps, when I heard him say that. I went over and pulled the window curtains together, glancing down and seeing that the street was as bare as the palm of my hand.

Then I turned and saw Whitey reaching for a gun. He had picked up the chair under him with one hand, to take the weight of it off his throat. Even so the wire almost was throttling him. Then he had sneaked across to the table and was stretching for a gun when I turned around. I never saw such a face as he was wearing. The wire had shut off his wind. He was swelling and turning purple. But he was a game one—the rat!

When he heard me speak, and saw my gun steady, he eased his hand slowly away from the table, and sat down in the chair. The sitting down, before he got himself rightly adjusted, almost finished the strangling. It was five minutes before he breathed right, to say nothing of speaking. I enjoyed those five minutes more than cocktails. After a while, he was settled.

"What was Ellis to you?" he asked.

"My partner," said I.

"You worked apart," he argued.

"We used to fight it out together like brothers, when we were kids," said I.

This seemed to convince him. He gave as much of a nod as the wire permitted him to do.

"All right," he said. "You ask your questions."

"Who was your partner?"

"A fellow by the name of Creval. Hank Creval."

His eye was as steady as a clock. I love to watch a good liar at work.

"What sort of an hombre?" I asked.

"Not so very good. He's a Canuck, to start with. The mean kind. He's big, raw-boned, and he has a cast in his left eye. You can spot him a mile away. He has sort of narrow shoulders, but he's strong. He likes knife work better than a gunplay, but he's handy at either. And all that you need to buy him is money."

It was a good line. He'd leaned a little on the facts that Frank Gregor's description supplied to him, but on the whole it was as good a job of free-hand lying as I ever listened in on. His eye was clear and frank, like a baby's. Your real, born liar always has an eye like that when he's at work in his profession.

About this time, I thought I heard a ticking sound in the hall. But when I stepped to the door and listened, I changed my mind about it being the creaking of a step. You take an old building like Guernsey House, and it's sure to be so full of creaks and stirrings that it always seems to be wind-shaken and crowded with sneak thieves.

So I went back to Whitey.

"You and Hank Creval, the Canuck," I said to him, "who was behind? Who hired for the job?"

"I did the hiring," said Whitey, steadily. "I always hated Lew Ellis. He cut me out with a girl, up here. I wouldn't stand for that, so I decided to put him out of the way. I knew he was a shifty hombre with a gun, so I got the Canuck to go along."

"Who was the girl?"

"Ruth Edgar," said Whitey.

"Whitey," said I, "you're a good liar. The Canuck wasn't

with you; you didn't hire him. You never would hire help to tackle any *one* man in the world, not even a Tom Fellows. I know what you think of yourself and your gunplay!"

He didn't blench. He had a set of nerves all made of steel. He was shaking a little, but I knew that was because the alcohol was wearing off. Rotten stuff, booze is. You think it's giving you a good time. It's only making you a fool and a beast. And when it wears off, it can turn August afternoon into December.

"Now I want the truth and the whole truth!" said I. "I told you before, Whitey. I mean what I told you. Your life, to me, is no more than a handful of dead leaves. I'd as soon crumble you as not. Will you talk?"

He kept on watching me, thinking. I pulled out my gun again, lifted the muzzle—and then he spoke, not hurrying even then.

He knew that I had some information, by this time. He guessed from what source.

"That dog of a Werner, he double-crossed me," he said.

"I don't know anything about Werner," said I. "I want to know about you and your friends. Start in!"

"Frank Gregor was outside the window with me," said Whitey, talking with the expression of one who has a lot of wood ashes in his mouth.

"Who hired you?" I insisted.

"You don't want to know," said Whitey.

I was amazed by his stubbornness.

"You don't want to die," he kept saying.

"I want to know," I told him, "even if it was the devil himself! So you come out with it."

He closed his eyes. It was not the gray of booze-exhaustion that I saw in his face, now. He was scared to death. And his shaking was not alcoholic nerves, either. He was shuddering with an enormous fear. It made me rather sick, to watch him.

"God help us both," said Whitey Peyton. "You're tying us both to a boulder that will roll us a mile down hill and drop us into white water. You're asking for a cup of poison, Runt. You'll know it as soon as I say that the name of the gent who hired us was—"

Crash! went the door.

They had jimmied it open, fitting in the bar so cautiously that I hadn't heard a sound. And in came, with a rush and a lunge, Sheriff Wallie Blue and a couple of others. They all held their guns on me. They looked like shooting, right off.

Wallie was the boy I had my eyes mostly on. Wallie was elected to office mighty young. He was only a boy, really. But a few years back he'd been cornered by three thugs, and he'd killed one and drilled the other two, and brought them all three into town in his buckboard. All I need to say about Wallie is that he was sheriff because he liked that kind of fun. He loved it. And his face was beaming with the hope of pulling the trigger at me a few times. Well, I didn't enjoy that kind of a party. As I've said before, I never hunted trouble, and particularly with a hardy hombre like Wallie Blue. I just dropped my gun to the floor and hoisted my hands with no more remarks.

"That was a fool move," said Wallie. "That gat might have gone off when it fell. You got no sense, Runt. You never did have much."

They took my wire cutter off the table, and clipped the rung that was holding Whitey. He got out of the chair, stretched himself, fingered his throat, and took a free slam at me, while my hands were still in the air. I side-stepped, and he fell on his face.

When they turned him over, he was out, cold. That was one of the funniest things I'd ever seen. He just took a paste at me, and when he missed, he kept on lunging till he whanged the floor. I suppose he had burned up the last of his nerve power while he sat there in the chair and faced my questions. Particularly, that last one about the fellow who had hired him and Frank Gregor. He had energy for one more effort, and that was all.

Like a bull-terrier, he fought till he was out on his feet!

"You've doped him," said Wallie Blue, to me.

"No," said I, "he only—"

"Don't talk back to me," said Wallie. "I got a mind to bash in your face with the heel of a gun, you dirty side-winder, you!"

I was minded to flash the badge on him, but I decided not to. I would rather go to jail, almost, than to have to show I was an officer of the law.

Damn the law!

They rushed me right down to the street and off toward the jail. When the cold night air hit my face, I inhaled some new ideas and saw that it would never do for me to go to jail, really. I said:

"Wallie, who put you after me?"

"Ask me again," said Wallie, a sneer on his round, boy's face.

"Well," said I, as we got near to the front of the jail, "suppose you reach into my right hand trouser's pocket and fetch out what I've got there."

"A bear trap?" says Wallie.

But he did what I said, brought out the shield.

CHAPTER XII

BELIEVE me, I wished the next instant that I had not used the infernal thing, for the bell began to bang out ten o'clock, and around the next corner slanted a big man on a fine, long-striding thoroughbred. There was only one man in Kearney County who rode horses of that cut. I knew him, before he knew me. Then he cut to the side and leaped down to the ground from the saddle. That horse was so well trained that it came to a stop and turned itself into a statue, just as I began to expect that it would run over me.

It was Tom Fellows, putting a hand on the sheriff's shoulder.

"What's all of this, Wallie?" said he.

Wallie looked uneasy, and then angry:

"I gotta do my duty," he said, "when I hear that this one has picked up a drunk that has a sack full of dough along with him, you know that—"

"Tut, tut, Wallie," said Tom Fellows. "You know that Slow Joe Hyde is one of the best friends!"

"I *didn't* know that," says Wallie, more uneasy than ever. "How could I know that you'd take up with a—"

He nearly bit his tongue off, abbreviating that sentence. No one in Kearney County ever *presumed* on the personal dignity of Tom Fellows. Not that Tom was a draw-gun type, but because there was something about him that froze the tongue of the fools, even of the drunkards. Men raving and frothing, suddenly grew calm when that big, gentle, straight-eyed man came near.

"I wouldn't of touched a real friend of yours, Tom, if I'd known," said the sheriff. "Only, we found him up there in his room at the hotel, with Whitey Peyton *wired* to the back of a chair. Wired by the throat! And—"

A crowd was gathering, piling up fast. Tom Fellows held up a hand and stepped out from the little tight circle of us who were the center of interest.

"Will you boys drift along, please?" he asked.

Mind you, that was to a lot of half-drunken cowpokes, ready to jump their horses over hell-gate and back again for a two-bit bet. But only one voice bawled out:

"Who the hell are you, Big Boy, to—"

His voice stopped. I heard, I almost felt the solid thud as a fist went home in his face. The others were calling:

"All right, Tom." Sure, old man."

"And that street emptied—the boys just washing back into their places of amusement. I never saw a greater power of one man over others, considering how much exploding power per man was represented by those hellions.

We were alone, now, the three of us.

"I'll answer for Slow Joe, when you want him," said Fellows. "Will that do, Wallie?"

"Sure it'll do," said Wallie, eagerly. "Your word goes a mile and back, with me. You know that, old timer."

He was really scared; he followed Tom a step as we turned away together.

"I wouldn't of touched Slow Joe, if I'd known that he was your friend. Or that Marshal Werner's name was written on the back of his badge!"

Tom thanked him, but I was none too happy, in spite of the jail delivery. I would have given anything to keep that badge concealed, for I knew what Kearneyville would think of me wearing such a chest protector.

We left Wallie and went down the street toward the hotel, Fellows leading his thoroughbred, which followed like a dog, its muzzle right at his shoulder, the reins hanging loosely. He asked me what had happened, and I told him.

He could have called me a rash fool. Instead, he merely said:

"Perhaps it would have been better to trail Whitey and Gregor a little while. Now they know someone is after them."

"I know it, Tom," said I. "I'm an idiot. Worse than that. Take any word you can find for me. It'd still be too weak. But one thing is sure. Werner was right when he said that something big was behind those two. Something so big that even Whitey Peyton was almost ready to have me blow out his brains before he'd name the man."

"Is it one man?" asked Fellows, deeply interested.

"Yes, one man."

"And Whitey as scared as that? Whitey has plenty of nerve, I hear."

"Full of it. But there's some one man able to throw a chill into him. Some one man who hired him."

"I'd give a good deal to know the name," murmured Fellows.

"So would I. A lot! And inside of five seconds, I would have known it. But that fool of a Wallie Blue broke in on me! I know that I failed. But in five more seconds, I would have succeeded, Tom, and then I wouldn't seem such a jackass."

"You're not that," said Fellows. "But I'll tell you why I have a new and personal interest in this case. The same man, or men, who were after Lew Ellis, will now be after me!"

I stopped short. Then I laughed.

"After *you,* Tom? Not in this world—not in this county, at the least!"

"You think that I'm strongly posted here, Slow," said Fellows. "I know that I have friends. They're the better part of life to me, in fact. But a power that can throw such a chill into Whitey Peyton, a power that can take both a Peyton and an adherent of the Willow crowd and make them work together—such a power is enough to make me lose a good deal of sleep. Besides, that power now has the same motive against me that it had against Lew Ellis. Read this!"

He gave me a letter, unfolding it for me. I stopped in the light that streamed from a lamp onto the street, but the writing was close and crowded.

"Tell me what it's about, Tom," I begged him. "It's hard for me to read this scrawl."

"Lawyers always write worse than first-graders," said Fellows. "I'll tell you in short. It's word from Doc Newsome, the lawyer right here in town. He says that he has a long telegram from a New York lawyer. It seems that my cousin, Lew Ellis, had just come into a very good estate. Since his death, I'm in line for it. You see what that means?"

I was pretty well baffled.

"You're a lucky man, Tom. How much is it?" I asked him.

"I don't know. I never knew of any rich uncles or aunts or cousins in the offing. All the Ellis and Fellows tribe I know of are only middling well off. But this seems to be the fact of the case. There was money somewhere. And someone knew it was coming. And that is the only reason I can think of under the sun why anyone should have wished to bump off Lew Ellis. He didn't make enemies. He made friends. There's another angle. The only person in the world with a direct motive for the killing of Lew would be myself."

"You, Tom?" I cried at him.

His calm voice went on, unruffled. What a man he was!

"You see for yourself, Slow. With Lew out of the way, it appears that I'm the next heir. To how much, I don't know. But any detective would be very glad to work up a case against me."

I could see that. It made me grind my teeth.

"Tom," I told him, "there's some horrible cur at the back of all of this. You and I both know it. Well, we're going to watch. I see one thing. You're right. Whoever knocked off poor Lew did it because of his coin. And whoever did that, will come after you, too. It's a rotten business. It runs underground, like mesquite roots."

"Yes, it's a bad business," said Fellows. "But it's a problem we ought to be able to solve. Whoever is behind the deal is not so very far away."

I looked around over my shoulder with a chill.

"Why do you say that?"

"Whoever it is, is somebody that Whitey Peyton knows."

"That's true."

"And Whitey," pointed out Fellows, "is never very far from home."

I nodded again.

"No farther than San Whiskey," I said.

"Yes. Now, then, who is there somewhere near by who is strong enough to make Whitey shake in his boots?"

I couldn't help saying:

"You are, Tom!"

He laid a hand on my shoulder.

"Don't laugh about it, Slow," he said, gravely. "This is going to be a matter of life or death. I'm involved. I'm afraid that you've committed yourself so deeply out of the goodness of your heart that now you'll be in almost as much danger as I shall live in. Let's put our heads together. Who could be such a danger? Who is the most dangerous man you know of in this part of the world?"

I ran my eye through my memory.

"Outside of Lefty Townsend and his gang, who could there be, Tom? And Lefty is a good fifty miles from here, tangled up in the mountains, they say, and dodging the posses every day. He has his hands full."

"Yes," nodded Fellows. "It couldn't be Lefty Townsend. Besides, Lefty is not likely to be the next heir in case I'm killed." He laughed softly: "I don't want to be overproud,

Slow, but I don't think I'm in any danger of having to call Lefty my cousin!"

I laughed, too, remembering the black-haired, twisted mug of Lefty Townsend. Then I jumped.

"But suppose, Tom, that the next heir, or the next to the next, had hired Lefty to do this job, and get both you and Lew Ellis?"

I saw him straighten with a start.

"Come, come, Slow," said he. "That's pretty far-fetched!"

I rushed ahead.

"You know that Townsend has his wires stretched out everywhere. He pays for information. He pays high for everything. He's just the man. Whitey swore that if he named the man behind the gun, in this case, he and I would both be dead inside of twenty-four hours. He swore it with a white face, too. He meant it. Well, you know that murder is almost second nature with Townsend!"

Fellows sighed.

"Well," he said, "I would rather think that it's Townsend than any other man."

"It's Townsend," I insisted, inspiration coming over me. "Townsend is a dirty crook, a killer, a thug; and he's just the sort that Whitey would know well enough to be afraid of. Whitey's a plain rough. Townsend is a great rough. Whitey would look up to him like a regular tin god. I know that I'm right!"

We came to the door of the hotel.

"You'd better come home with me, old son," suggested Fellows. "If we're both in the same boat, we might as well use one another."

I yearned to do as he said, but still I hesitated. If I went with him, I'd be only a sort of clerk, doing what he told me. And how could I be that, with Lew Ellis dead, and his golden spurs jingling softly at my unworthy heels?

I told him I would spend at least that one night in the hotel. When he saw that I meant it, he didn't argue, but mounted, and rode away at once.

CHAPTER XIII

WITH Fellows gone, I felt as lonely as a ship without a crew, or a crew without a ship. I was wrecked in the dark among rattlers and gila monsters, you might say. Mighty weak I felt, and all of what they nicknamed me in that town—the Runt! For one thing, I was afraid to go up to my room. I didn't want to look at the chair where Whitey had been sitting with his ugly face. The ghost of him would be waiting for me there—if not Whitey himself, with a gun in each hand!

I thought of Brindle, and decided that I would go to see how he did. Not that I wanted to. Just because it was a way of killing time.

In the back yard of the hotel—the stable yard—there were half a dozen youngsters shooting craps. They had a shaft of light out of a back window of the building, and they were talking soft, so as not to be overheard and the game broken up. It made a queer sight and a queer sound:

"Seven—come on, Eleven!" "Little Joe, you know your papa!" and all the lingo that the niggers talk.

They were as dark as niggers, too—just silhouettes, crouching and moving like jungle cats. And then the dice would roll on a bit of tarpaulin that had been put down in the place of a blanket. And I could hear the quiet chattering of the dice in the box again, and then the clinking of silver as the bets were laid or taken.

I drifted a little nearer. They were all fourteen to sixteen, I should have said. Just the age when a boy's fingers begin to itch for man-sized mischief. And I waited there by the fence, a good deal amused, and relieved to have my mind taken off myself.

Pretty soon one of the kids began to make a run. You know how that happens in craps. Suddenly all the luck seems to be in one pair of hands. A few passes are won, and then the others are sure that the next cast is sure to lose. But it doesn't. And then the next one *must* be a flop. But it isn't. And so the bets begin to double, treble.

Some of those brats had quite a pocketful of coin—they were all old enough to work, you see—and they began to haul out their last dollars to break that run of luck.

The kid who was having it was a slim brat with close-cropped, red hair that frizzed out a good deal, and shone in the lamplight. And he had a pair of slender, fast working hands. After I'd watched him for a moment, I decided that he was crooking the dice. The next moment, I decided that he wasn't. He kept laughing. His teeth kept flashing. He was having a grand party, crooked or not crooked.

Then one of the other lads pipes up:

"That bird's switching the dice on us! Cover 'em!"

They grabbed the dice of the last roll and examined them, their heads bunched together. The winner just sat back on his heels and still laughed.

So did I. I like to see a boy that can laugh when the pinch comes.

Then one of the losers said that this set of dice was all right but he was willing to bet his shirt that the winner had a crooked set on him.

"Let's fan him!" says another.

Maybe it was the grown-up word that tickled and caught the fancy of the rest. They were all for the idea in a minute. Up they got. The winner jumped up, too.

"Keep your hands off me!" he calls, his voice a little shrill, like a boy's voice before it changes.

"Yeah—we'll show you how we'll keep our hands off you!" bawls another.

And he makes a diving tackle at the red-head.

But he only jumped through thin air. Red-head dodged like a jerk of lightning and ran for the fence. He left them behind him. He ran like a scared cat, and when he reached the fence, he made a jump and hooked his hands over the top edge of it.

But one of the youngsters, ahead of the rest, catches hold of him before he can swing himself up and hook a leg over the top of the fence.

What does he do then?

Why, it was as neat as I ever saw. He lets go with one hand and shoves himself around in the air with the other. Then he drops and hits that other lad with knees and elbows at once.

He drops that kid as if he'd been hit with a club. I hear a groaning sigh, and there the boy is down, and Red-head is standing back there against the fence.

The one who had missed the flying tackle is on his feet again, by this time, and he gasps out to hold Red-head till he gets to the place for the fight. He comes up in time. They're holding Red-head. They've formed in a semicircle in front of him. But they don't dive in to grab him and search him. The reason is that a little streak of knife is dripping out of his hand. He's pulled a knife!

When I saw that, of course I eased up closer, ready to take a hand, because it was plain that the winner was game to draw blood rather than be manhandled.

The other boys were growling like angry dogs. They didn't like the sight of that knife, but they were ready to fight it out. In another moment, I knew they'd take a chance of getting stuck, one of them, while they dove in and beat up the winner.

Then says Red-head:

"You're a lot of cowards. Pick out the biggest of you. I'll take him on. You think because I'm a stranger that you've got a right to mob me. I'll show the pack of you. You edge in closer, and I'll cut your throat, you frog-faced pup!"

I saw one of the boys literally jump at the threat.

And he jumped backward!

Says Red-head:

"Who's the best fighter of the lot of you? I'll fight him. But I won't be mauled. I'll stick one of you, first, and I'll stick him so's his mama won't ever have to worry about him again! You understand?"

They understood. There was so much ring to this talk that it gave even me a little shiver. One doesn't expect a half-grown brat to be so full of the real steel, ready to take an edge and cut.

Besides, there was a sporting proposition here, and when have boys been able to resist such a thing? Not Western boys, at least, not when there was a chance to see a good fight.

They picked their champion. It was the lad who had missed his flying tackle. He might not be graceful in the air, but he was a burly brute of a lad. He had bowed legs, and swaggering, big shoulders. He looked able to punch holes in Red-head.

"Knock the tar out of him, Pete," said one of the circle. "Stand out, here, Red-head. We won't search you. Not unless Pete licks you."

They broke into deep laughter, subdued, lest it should draw attention from the hotel, and they be scattered. They reminded me of a lot of alley cats, sneaking out from their houses at night to claw and fight and screech. And, after all, I suppose that boys are about as much beasts of prey as wildcats, anyway!

Now their circle was formed. Pete tore off his coat. Red-head had none—only a blousy shirt, much too big for him. When he doubled up his fists and squared away at Pete, he looked too fragile for words. I was on the verge of stopping the fight, but then I noticed the poise of the kid, and the high way he held his head. You can judge a horse by his head alone, almost. And I think you can judge men the same way.

So I held my hand and got closer, and nobody noticed me, for Pete started a little speech, in which he told Red-head that he was going to knock his head off; then he jumped in, feinted with his left hand, and, like a good boxer, drove his right with a chug against the chin of Red.

That boy went down in a heap. The others raised a shout which they had to muffle, so that it sounded almost like a groan.

I saw Red shuddering, writhing. Presently he got to his hands and knees, and looked around him.

"Get up," invited Pete. "G'wan and get up. I'm gunna balance your fine face for you. I'm gunna sock you a little harder on the other side."

As he was finishing off this speech, Red-head jumped off the ground from all fours, with a sort of screech, and drove his fists like lightning into the face of Pete.

Pete went backward. He didn't seem to be stunned by the punches. He was simply blinded by the lightning speed with which they rained into his face, stinging and cutting. He shook his head. He swung his arms. And Red-head danced away to a distance.

Pete let out an honest roar of rage and came lunging blindly forward. Red, at ease, watched him coming, and, just as he was reaching with a hard swung right, Red dropped to the ground on hands and knees. I never saw anyone move so fast.

Pete hit the thin air, rushed on after his punch, and tumbled over Red flat on his face.

It was like being hit with a hundred pound plank, I expect. Anyway, Pete lay still. He did not even wriggle; he did not even groan. His friends picked him up. He was a limp rag. His face streamed with blood.

And I saw Red-head standing back, still laughing, his hands on his hips.

Those hands were so small that I looked at them twice. That laughter was suddenly so musical that I cocked my ear to hear it. I stepped up and took Red by the nape of the neck.

"Get out of this!" I commanded.

"Oh, go jump in a creek!" invited Red, impolitely.

He twisted his head around until he could see my face. Then he subsided—grew almost as limp as Pete, who still hung lifeless in the hands of his worried friends.

"You come along with me," I directed, and I conducted Red straight across the yard and into the stable.

There was one lantern burning in the harness room. No one was there, so I took the kid inside, and closed and locked the door behind us.

Then I turned around and gathered up my best frown.

"Look at me!" said I.

I was obeyed.

All the fire and the sauciness had gone out of that face. There were tear-dimmed eyes, now, and trembling, full lips, and white teeth biting them to keep back a sob.

"I didn't mean you ever to see me, here!" said the choked voice.

"No matter what you meant," said I. "Here you are, Alicia, and what the devil do you mean by it?"

CHAPTER XIV

THE MOMENT I abused her a little, she seemed to feel a lot better. Women are that way.

She wiped her eyes dry, and there were no more tears left to fill 'em! She eased herself onto the top of a big box, and there she swung her heels and grinned at me.

"Well, Joe," said she, "the old man opened up his shop again. And I couldn't stand it."

"Why not?" said I, scowling at her as black as I could.

"There was still—something on the floor," says she.

I felt that remark pretty deep.

"So you beat it?"

"Yeah. I beat it," says she. "Any way was a good way for me. So I just drifted up this direction. I wanted to have a look at you, but, when I arrived, you were too busy getting yourself arrested for me to see you. You certainly know how to raise a crowd, Joe!"

I paid no attention to this.

"You saw the funeral, down there in San Whiskey?" said I.

"So did the whole town," she answered. "Everybody turned out."

"Lew would have liked that," I meditated, aloud.

"Of course he would," said she. "There was a ton of flowers. There were speeches, too. There were songs."

"Did you sing?"

"Yeah. I sang, of course. I didn't know what to sing, but I sang something."

"I'm glad it was a good party," said I. "Now what are you going to do with yourself?"

"See the world," says she.

"In those clothes?"

Because she was dressed like a boy, of course; and I must say that, with her hair clipped short, she looked like a boy, too. She looked as fresh and mean as anything in trousers.

"Why not?" says she. "Skirts are always in the way."

"Look here," says I. "You've got to get out of here."

"You don't want me around?"

"No."

"What's the big play, Joe?" she asks me.

"It's up my sleeve," said I.

"If it was up your sleeve," says the kid, "you wouldn't be so worried."

"Well, you leave Kearneyville," said I.

"Why not let me stay and help?"

"How could you help?" I asked her.

"I can scratch," grins she. "And I've got good eyes and ears."

"Humph," said I.

But I couldn't help grinning back.

"I want you out of the way, Al," says I.

"Which way?"

"My way."

So she considered this, with her perky head tipped to the side. I have to admit that she had all the ways of a boy about her. A bright boy, all full of himself.

"When do I go?" she asked at length.

"Now, if you ask me," said I.

"It's a dark night," said she.

"You've got cat's eyes, anyway," I told her.

She began to nod.

"I'll go along, then," she yawned.

"How are you heeled?" I asked her.

"I'm heeled plenty," said she.

"Where did you pick up that lingo?"

"Off the street, where it was lying," says she, as pert as mustard. "Why? Don't you like it?"

"You're sure you don't need any money?"

"Not a bean."

"Then start, will you?"

"Yeah, I'll start. So long, Joe."

"I'll help you saddle. You've got a horse, I suppose."

"Suppose again," says she. "I've got what's called a horse. I've got a fifteen dollar cartoon. That's what I've got. But it has four legs, and what more can a man ask?"

I unlocked the door, saying:

"Where do you go from here, Al?"

"Away," says she.

I let it go at that. I was worried about her, but what could I do, with a kid like that hanging around? I had enough to fill my hands.

We walked out from the harness room together. The outside was a solid wall of black velvet, after even the dimness of the lantern inside, but Alicia says suddenly, gasping: "Down!" and kicks my legs from under me.

I don't know how she managed it, because I'm pretty steady and heavy on my pins, but down I went, slam, barely with sense enough to pull a gun as I flopped. I felt her falling beside me, and right before us, two revolvers were blaring in the darkness.

I was lying stretched out, my gun steadied by holding my right wrist in my left hand. And I shot in under the flash of the first gun. And it was sweet music to me to hear a man groan, and cut off his own groan with a click of the teeth.

Both the guns stopped firing. I heard two men running away, and tried two snapshots in the direction of the noise, but I was still only half seeing.

The back door of the hotel opened. There was Guernsey, bawling out:

"What's this? A damn rifle range? Get out of here, you worthless bums!"

There was something so funny about that—as though he were swearing at stray dogs—that I doubled up, and nearly choked trying to keep from laughing out loud. But I didn't want to be connected with any gun play in the mind of Kearneyville, just then.

I suppose that I might have sprinted after the pair of runaways, but chasing armed men in the dark is not a joke. Not the kind that I appreciate, anyway.

Guernsey went inside, slamming the door dark. I stood up and dusted myself. Al was doing the same.

"How can I be of use?" says she, mocking.

"That was the quickest turn that I ever saw," I had to confess to her. "The first slug knocked my hat off. It would have knocked my head off, if you hadn't tripped me. Where's that hat?"

"Here," says she.

"I knew you had cat's eyes," said I.

"You better train to get 'em, too," said she. "It looks to me as though your office hours are gunna be day *and* night, here in Kearneyville."

"Well, let's go and get that horse of yours together," said I.

"No," she argued. "I like Kearneyville better and better. I'll stay around for a while, thanks!"

"You'll get out, and get now," I told her.

She hooked her arm through mine.

"Say, Joe," said she, "what's the matter? I won't be sitting on your shoulders; you won't have to carry me."

"I don't want you around," said I.

"I won't catch any stray bullets, if that's what you mean," said she.

That was exactly what I did mean. I told her so, and then I told her besides that I didn't want to be bothered. I had my hands full already.

"Tonight," says the fresh kid, "you almost had your head full—of lead!"

"You pulled a good play," I admitted. "But now you're done. I don't want you around. I don't want a kid like you on my mind."

"Listen, Joe," said she, "are you afraid that you'll get sentimental about me?"

"What?" I barked at her.

"Because you wouldn't," said she. "A fellow like you, with so much experience, and old enough to be my father, you wouldn't get sentimental."

"Of course I wouldn't," said I.

"Of course not," said she. "How old *are* you, Slow?"

Somehow, I didn't like the way she put it. I didn't like to have to answer, either.

"I'm old enough to tell you that you don't belong with me in Kearneyville," said I. "You trot, Al."

"Are you twenty-five, Joe?" said she.

"The farther you get from Kearneyville, the better for all concerned," said I.

"Twenty-four?" says she.

"It's a jay town and a mean town, and it's no place at all for you," says I.

"Twenty-three?" says she.

"Damn it, Al," said I. "Don't be so like a fly, always lighting on the same spot."

"Does it tickle you?" she asked me.

"Aw, shut up," said I.

"About twenty-two is the trick, I guess," said Al. "I know how it is. When a man gets along to an age like that, he's got his mind full of things. Business, and all sorts of things. He gets mighty tired in the head. He can't be bothered with having children like me around. I just wanted to tell you, Slow, that there wouldn't be any danger of sentiment, though. I ain't that kind."

"I know you're all elbows," I told her. "I only wish that you'd shut up and get out."

"Well," said she, "I won't."

"You what!"

"I won't budge from Kearneyville without knowing what it's all about."

"You want me to confess, do you? You want to get all

stuck up in the same mess, do you? Well, you won't," I said. "If this has to be the last I see of you, good-by, Al. You're a good girl, you're a grand girl, and I hope you have a swell trip. Powder the end of the nose and you won't get it sunburned."

"All right," says she. "I stay on here. I knew I liked Kearneyville when I landed here, and it wasn't all on account of you."

"You don't mean that you'll stick?"

"Sure I do," said she.

I made a pass at her. I grabbed the air. She was an eel!

"Give me a job, boss," said she. "Even if it's only licking stamps. Give me a job! Let me help."

I was so mad that I could hardly see straight.

"Sure," said I. "There's two fellows here named Whitey Peyton and Frank Gregor. In Kearneyville or near it. Find enough stuff on 'em to hang the pair. Report here in the morning. That's all for your first assignment."

"Thanks, boss," said she. "I can't take more'n half pay for roustabouting like that!"

I said:

"Listen to me, Al; forget that. I want to tell you that if you don't leave Kearneyville you'll—"

By thunder, she was nowhere around. She'd faded out like a ghost, with never a sound!

CHAPTER XV

WHEN a man has himself well on his mind, it's easy to get other things off, even a girl like Al Doloroso.

I felt, somehow, that she could take care of herself, the four-footed little hell-raiser! So I went up the hotel back stairs to my room, locked the door, shot the bolt, looked under the bed, with a gun to feel and light the way, as it were, and pushed the same gun into the bathroom, behind the bathtub, and into the empty clothes closet.

I didn't have any apparent guests.

I like fresh air, but I pulled down the windows and locked them. Then I put a chair, legs up, under each window. It's astonishing how a chair in that position makes trouble for a man crawling in and dropping for an honest bit of level floor! Then I drew the curtains and felt a little better, except that my eyes kept trying to see over both my shoulders at the same time. I felt that I would never be cross-eyed, after tonight, if I lived to be a hundred, and studied the end of my nose all the time.

Then I put my hat on the table and admired, for a while, the two pretty half-inch holes that were clipped through both sides of the crown.

After that I undressed, took another bath, a rub down, good and hard, and went to bed. I needed that bed like an old friend and a bank account. The minute I hit it, it hit me. I slept like a dead man until the glow of the day worked its way through the window curtains.

Then I sat up, and saw Al Doloroso sound asleep on the other bed!

It was a funny thing. Before I wondered at seeing her there, I took in the way she was lying—just the way I went to sleep—spreadeagling the arms, the only way to rest.

I picked up a pillow, when I remembered to think of another thing. I heaved it at her. When it slogged her, she just says: "Coming!" And never a move!

"Hey, Al!" says I.

"Down!" says she.

And then up she sits and blinks at me.

"Why, hullo, Slow," says she. "What's all the racket about? Somebody trying to get in?"

"How did *you* get in?" says I.

"What's the matter with the door?" says she.

I look at the door. It's just the way I left it, bolted and everything.

"You didn't come through the door," says I.

"Didn't I?" says she.

She leans herself on one elbow and grins at me, sleepy, but comfortable with herself.

"You did, you Indian, you," says I. "And how did you do it, you pick-lock!"

"If you could pick locks as good as I can," says she, "you wouldn't have to ride so far between banks, Slow."

So she knew that I was a safe-man, did she? What *didn't* she know?

"Where did you pick up the art?" says I.

"When I was a boy," says she, wrinkling up her forehead to think, "my father apprenticed me to a wise old German locksmith. He was a hard taskmaster, but I stayed with him for seven years in his shop, and after that he sent me out on the road. I used to carry some black bread and a hunk of cheese in my knapsack—"

"Yeah, it sounds like a hunk of cheese," says I.

"And for five more years I went from town to town, undoing what the other locksmiths had done wrong. Then I went to college, and I spent eight years under the best instruction, and at the end of that time, I got my degree as a Lock Doctor, or Doctor of Locks. D.L. After that—"

"You slid that bolt and didn't wake me up?" says I.

"Nobody could of waked you up, Slow," says she. "All I was afraid of was when I opened the door and let out the roar of your snoring, all the people in the hotel would wake up and think that the big wind had hit the town. You were shakin' the whole place right down to the roots."

"Yeah?" says I.

I don't know why it is. I'm sensitive about snoring. Besides, I don't half believe that I do it. Other fellows have told me, but I never heard myself.

"Yeah?" says she, sticking out her jaw and twisting it a little crooked to mock me.

"Maybe that's all right," says I. "But how late did you stay out?"

"Me?" says she, very careless. "Oh, I was in about two or three, or something like that. I didn't notice, particular."

"You picked up a lot of night air, I guess," said I.

"Yeah, I picked up a lot of that, too," said she.

"Meaning that you picked up something else?"

"Not much. Just a little."

"All about Frank Gregor and Whitey Peyton, I suppose?" says I, sneering a little.

"Not all about 'em, but enough," says she.

"Enough for what?"

"Oh, to send them up the river for fifteen years, maybe."

I nearly jumped out of bed, till I remembered that I wasn't more than ten per cent dressed.

"Come out with it," said I. "You never could have got next to 'em!"

"I didn't," said she. "There was a whole window ledge and five or six feet of thin air between me and them."

I saw that she meant what she had said.

"Al," said I, "I don't think that you lie except on special occasions. Is this a special occasion?"

"Not more'n usual," says she.

"Then you give me the low down and the straight dope, will you?"

"I'm giving it to you, if you'll pull the wool out of your ears," says Al.

"It's out," says I, too excited to be mad at her. "How did you happen to get that close to the pair of them?"

"Nothing strange about it," says she. "It just happens to be that Frank Gregor is an uncle of mine."

"He's a *what* of yours?" I shouted at her.

"An uncle," says she. "Last night, it seems that he was an uncle of mine. I get into a saloon, and all at once it comes over me that he's an uncle of mine. It sort of breaks me all down, to think of me having a long lost uncle, like that. I just have to sit in a corner with one foot on top of the other, and I cry and cry."

"The devil you do," says I. "Nothing but salt in your eyes could make you cry."

"I tell you I was crying my heart out," says the brat, "until pretty soon a kind gentleman, he takes pity on the poor little kid in the corner that's crying his eyes out, and he comes over, and that barkeep says—"

"What barkeep?" says I.

"Fatty Carson," says she.

"Kind? The hobnailed heel of a boot, he's kind," says I.

"He wanted to know what was the matter, and I told him that I'd been looking all day for my uncle, Frank Gregor, and I didn't know what to do about it."

"Yeah?" says I, popping my eyes at her. I could see that she was full of ideas. So full that it sort of scared me.

"So then, Fatty got real mad, and he said that my uncle was a worthless sot, and I got to crying again, at that, and I said that I loved Uncle Frank with all my might, if only I could find him, because my mother, his sister, was pretty sick, and—

"Well, Fatty got hotter than ever, and he said he'd bring Frank down to me by the ear, but I said please I wouldn't disturb him, if only he'd show me the room. So he did, and it was right upstairs over his saloon, and I whispered to him to go down the hall so's I could pop in and surprise dear Uncle Frank.

" 'Dear Uncle Foot!' snorts Fatty, but he goes off down the hall, and all I had to do was to pick the lock of the next door, and get through, and slide around onto the window sill, and there's a fellow who looks like a breed, and another mug with a puffed upper lip—"

"That's the pair," says I. "Al, you're a wonder, and no mistake. What were they saying?"

"How much they liked you was all that they talked about for quite a while. Whitey allowed that you were on their trails and knew their names, and Gregor said that he had a saddle frame all ready for the stretching of your hide. You *have* a nice, thick skin, Slow."

I didn't talk back. I just listened and prodded her along.

"Go on, Al," says I.

"There wasn't much after that. Only the pair of them are going to hop out of the country, tomorrow or next day at the latest. Tomorrow morning, close to noon, Whitey is going over to see a blonde sweetie called Ruth Edgar, and try to persuade her to go along with him on the trip. He wants to marry her, and he says since Lew Ellis dropped out of the running, maybe he could make some headway with her. She's looking for the long chance, it seems. And then, after he's had a powwow with her, he and Frank Gregor are going to unload their stuff on a fence—"

"I don't follow that drift, honey," said I.

"You haven't lived close to the border all your life, Slow," said she. "That pair has been paid off for something—"

"I know what," said I.

"And it seems that what they're paid off with has the look of stolen goods. So they've invited a fence to come over and put a price on the lot. The fence is coming in on the three o'clock freight, and he's dropping off the train at the big grade, below town about two mile, just before the train crosses a trestle over a little creek. And in the creekbed, that pair of beauties are going to be waiting for him. I thought maybe you'd like to see them lay out their stock, Slow."

I licked my lips.

"It sounds good to me," said I. "Then what?"

"They broke up. I couldn't get back through the next window, so I turned myself into a fly and walked down the face of the wall into a back yard. And a dog came for me, and I had to kick him in the nose, and while he was sneezing, I hopped over a coupla fences, and came back home, and found in what you put your trust."

"In what?" said I.

"In locks," said the girl, and grinned at me again.

"I put my trust in you, ma'am," said I. "Now slide out of here so's I can get up and dress. I'll eat breakfast with you in the dining room pretty pronto. Order me a couple of steaks, and all the eggs they've got on hand."

CHAPTER XVI

IT DIDN'T take me long to get into my clothes and reach the dining room.

"Al," said I, "when are you starting for the skyline?"

"When you're out of trouble," said she, "and I guess that'll be when you're ready to leave Kearneyville, too."

"You're going to stay?" said I, gloomily, for I began to see that I couldn't *force* the brat to do anything.

"Yeah," she said. "You're liable to need a chief mourner, pretty soon. All those boys over in the corner are getting their heads together and looking at you like bad news."

We hadn't finished breakfast when who should come in but Tom Fellows. I was gladder to see him than Sunday, when you've worked all week. He gave me a look and said:

"Was it a long night, Slow?"

"Pretty long," said I. "This is Al Doloroso, from San Whiskey. Though you don't need to shout the last part of it."

"Friend of yours from San Whiskey?" says Fellows. "How are you, Doloroso!"

And he gave Al a good handshake and one of those straight, friendly, understanding glances of his. One look from Fellows was better than a year's acquaintance with most other men. He warmed you down to the tips of your fingers.

Tom sat down and had a cup of coffee with us, and Al sat still, and hardly ate, and watched the big, handsome face of my friend. I told Tom straight off everything that had happened, and above all, about the plant which Al had discovered.

"Al is a mighty useful friend," said Tom, with a smile for the kid, and Al blushed a little, and looked down.

Then he asked me if I thought that Whitey and Frank Gregor were the pair who had taken the potshots at me in the dark, the night before. But I pointed out that I certainly had nicked one of that couple of thugs, and when Al saw them, both Whitey and Frank were without a scratch. Then he suggested that he and I should go out and lay up for the two before the three o'clock freight laid up.

I had been thinking that over. I wanted Tom, and wanted him badly, but I said:

"Let me tell you, Tom. Two people make twice as many tracks as one, and Whitey and Gregor have their eyes open. The main thing is to have a look at their stuff, not to start in shooting. And one man ought to have a better chance at looking than two. I mean to go out there alone. We're only laying the road, Tom. We're not ready to drive over it, as yet!"

He finally agreed with me, though it was plain that he was itching to go. Finally he reached over and laid a hand on my arm.

"You know, Slow," said he, "that I ought to be in on the game. It's more my game than yours, really. And still you keep backing me out to the margin and the still water of the creek. Let me in pretty soon, will you?"

"Oh, I'll bump my head against a stone wall, pretty soon," said I. "And then you'll hear me hollering."

He got up and left us, and he shook hands with both of us before he went. No one had a hand-grip like Fellows' —so firm, so full of strength, but such a gentle touch.

Well, I settled down after he left, and saw the nigger waiter gaping at me. He came up and "sirred" me, and wanted to know would I like some more coffee, and nearly broke his back kowtowing. I knew what that meant. Because Tom Fellows had actually sat down and talked with me, the rest of the town would be willing to forget what it knew about me. Tom had given me a fresh start, and I was glad of that.

The girl tumbled to him at once.

"He's got all the aces, around this place," said she. "Is that right?"

"He has," said I. "He's the whitest man in the world, and don't you mistake it! Did he look through you, kid?"

"No," said she. "And you wouldn't, either, except that you knew my mug, beforehand."

She sighed, and began to dream out the window.

"Kind of hard hit by Fellows?" I asked her.

"Sure," says she.

"That's all right," says I. "It won't do you any harm. All the girls are kind of crazy about him. But he doesn't waste time that way."

"He's growed up, anyway," says Al. "Besides, I hate to get crushed in a mob. When do we start for the creek-bottom to wait for the train?"

I told her in strong words of one syllable that she would not be in on that party, and after a time, she seemed to feel that I meant what I said.

Shortly after breakfast she disappeared; I didn't know where. I only wished that she would fade right out of Kearneyville and trouble, but I couldn't really expect her to do that.

About noontime, I got some crackers and cheese from the grocery store and saddled Brindle, and slid out of town, heading north on the road to the Fellows ranch; but when I was half a mile out, and Kearneyville behind me half lost in the shimmer and dance of the heat waves, I cut across the fields and headed around the town in a big loop.

It might be that I was not followed, but I argued that the chances were ten to one that Whitey and Gregor, or their friends, would be trying to keep an eye on my movements.

When I got close to the railroad, I pushed on until I came to the creek with the trestle over it. Then I tied old Brindle on a long lead in the center of a group of poplars, where he could get pretty fair grazing. He was a great eater, but what he ate all seemed to stay in his stomach. There was never any flesh on his back or ribs or hips; but, when he fed well, he developed the biggest pot-belly in the world. I slapped him on the hip, and dodged. He might be tired from overwork, but his footwork was as fast as ever. He barely missed my head with a hard kick.

That cheered me up a good deal, somehow. I took it as an omen, and worked down into the stream bed.

It was hot as all thunder, down there, for the sun seemed to be gathered from the sides of the ravine and poured through a funnel into the middle of the hollow. Nothing was there but the heat. There was no stir of air. The brush stood still, and the dust lay untroubled, whitening the leaves.

I got back among some rocks, at a point from which I could see the railroad track, and most of the hollow stream bed. From this place, I ought to be able to spot my men, if they came up to keep the appointment of which they had spoken.

It was hotter than ever, among the rocks. I hardly knew that it *could* be so scorching in the world! But, after a while, I got used to it. I settled down, cocked my sombrero at the most convenient angle to turn the rays of the sun, and began to wait.

After a time, I began to notice that everything was not so dead about me. True, the bed of the stream was dry, and the rocks polished and glittering, and the bushes untroubled by any wind, but there were insects about, big flies that looked like bees, and real bees, and then one of the whackingest wasps, or hornets, that I ever had seen. It flew down, and lighted, and began to walk hurried around through the sand and the pebbles, with a sort of high-stilted, clumsy gait. Pretty soon it reached a little hole in the ground. Out popped the furry horror of a tarantula. When it saw what its caller was, the big spider, I thought, would jump on the wasp. Instead, it tried to get back down the hole. But the wasp grabbed it—by one furry claw, I suppose—and, with a yank, out popped that big murderous, bloated killer.

It was a sort of a grisly thing to watch. Murder killing said, but it was scared to death. It turned and made a bolt back for its silk-lined tunnel, but it was snagged again by the wasp. Then it turned about, and seemed desperate. It jumped on the wasp and they rolled over and over.

I looked to see the fight end pretty fast, and the spider settle down to chewing up its new meat. But by thunder, pretty soon they were standing up on their hind legs and I, leaning close, could see them struggle.

Suddenly the spider seemed to slip, and toppled backwards, with the wasp right on top, slipping its sting into the fangs of the nightmare! It made me sweat with interest, to watch that little affair! And then, zing! zing! into the breast of the spider goes the sting of the big wasp, and the killer is dead, or seems dead.

Off hops the wasp, cleans the dust off its wings, prunes itself until it's once more just like a semi-translucent condensation of the sunshine, and, laying hold of the spider, it drags the brute off.

It was a sort of a grisly thing to watch. Murder killing murder. Or justice, perhaps, at work?

I wondered if justice would ever jump me, like that? For suddenly it seemed to me that I was like the spider, lurking in a hole, covering myself with secrecy and intrigues, and always ready to pop out and to commit crimes upon the unsuspecting.

It wasn't a pleasant way to look at myself. It was about the worst way in the world, in fact. I damned that wasp for putting my case up to me so clearly.

And, just then, I heard the moan and thunder of the locomotive in the distance. No matter what danger was now right before me, I was more than half glad to get away from those thoughts about myself.

CHAPTER XVII

SOME people love the sea, and ships, and their ways. And some love to watch birds soaring. But for my kick, give me the sight of a pair of railroad tracks, streaking it across a thousand miles of dust and nothing, pulled into a single bright silver point on one horizon, and to another on the opposite side. Because it makes me think what a walloper this world is; and how doggone smart and strong men are, because they can jump around it, today, as quick as a flea over the floor of a room.

Now I saw the black smoke column of the train tumbling down the edge of the sky, and now the front of the engine, and the roar from the tracks became greater. I thought that I could see the trestle trembling, but I suppose that that was only the tremor of the heat-waves.

And, finally, there was the engine rocking and rolling along in the finest style, until it hit the up grade from the bottom of the next shallow valley. It was a sort of a quick pitch from there into Kearneyville, and it seemed as though the engineers had not wasted any time zigzagging. They simply wanted to jump home and get that mean little stop over with!

Up the slope that engine panted fast, and seemed to stagger and stand, every now and then, but it kept right on coming; and then, just before it hit the trestle, as I peeled my eyes to spot anyone who might drop down beside the tracks, I saw a slim kid riding the blind baggage, between the tender and the first box car. This kid leaned out. The sun winked on his red hair like fire. With his hand he made a beating movement, down, and then swung his arm hard, up and down.

I thought that he must be giving some sort of an order to the engineer. But then I saw that the engineer was squatted at his window, looking straight ahead.

It's a hard job that an engineer has, when you come to think about it. Look at the responsibility! He takes an engine that has been all washed by the washers, and oiled by the oilers, and wiped by the wipers, and all new filled with coal in the tender, and water filled up, and the thing inspected by inspectors. And then he has to take that terrible responsibility over, and run it along for five or six hours, maybe, or maybe ten.

And if he's early, he says: "Who cares?" And if he's late, he just says: "Damn you, kid,"—to the fireman—"was you born asleep? Don't you see that I ain't got no steam?"

Yes, it's a mighty hard life that an engineer leads there in his cab, with a good, cool wind blowing through the window onto his face. All he's got to sit on is a stool with a soft leather back on it. It's pretty cruel that he can't have a chair with a back to it, I suppose. And particular, when you think that the day before he's probably been out on a bat, I say that it's pretty hard, the sort of a life that the engineers have, and a doggone sight they're underpaid for their labors.

Well, this engineer, as I was saying, was sitting there on his stool, trying to look intelligent at the miles of track ahead of him, and trying to seem interested in Kearneyville, and he wasn't paying any attention to the signals that the red-head was making from the blind baggage.

Then an idea busted and elbowed its way into my brain and left my mouth ajar behind it.

That was Al Doloroso riding that blind baggage. It was the red-head from San Whiskey. What was she signaling? Why, something to me, of course, because she knew that I'd be there waiting in the hollow of the dead stream, where the two thugs were to meet their fence.

That down-beat of her hand certainly meant to lie low. That side scoop certainly was intended to tell me to clear out of the place. And you can bet your boots that the minute I savvied, I wanted to run for it. My knees turned to water, remembering how far away I had left Brindle. For I knew that Al was no fool. The slick kid had found out something that showed her the hollow was a sick place for me to be, and she was handing me the warning.

She didn't know on which side of the trestle I'd be, so she went to the other side of the blind baggage, and I could see her repeating her signals over there.

You can bet that I was fond of Al, just then. You can also bet that I wished that I were on that train with her.

But the engine was across the trestle, now, and the train was starting to gather speed when I saw a pair of hoboes drop off, just before the trestle, and from about the mid-section of the freight. They were the "fence," perhaps.

I narrowed my eyes at them.

I've seen fences, in my time. In fact, I've used them more than once. I've seen 'em big and small, fat and lean, Jew and Christian—by rearing, not practice. But mostly the fences I've known have been pretty well along. It takes time and years and brains to learn to be a good fence. You've got to have more information in your little finger than a regular pawnbroker has in his whole system. You've got to understand all about jewels, and price them at a glance, for flawlessness and weight and color. You have to know the market on those things. And you have to know all about bonds—the dead ones, and the negotiable kind. You have to know about market prices of stocks; and nearly everything in the world that can be priced and carried as hand-luggage comes within the studies of a fence.

So, as I was saying, most fences are pretty well along in years. You can't short-hand that sort of a course of education. But the pair of fellows who dropped off the train looked, as I said, like hoboes. And young ones.

Not common hoboes, but tramp-royals, who fly without baggage, fast and far. They're the kings of the tramp world. They're as far above the ordinary bindle-stiffs as dukes and princes are above commoners.

This pair walked right away from the train as though they knew where they were going; they soaked in behind a nest of rocks—and they didn't come out on the farther side.

I rubbed my eyes and looked hard, but they didn't appear again.

Now I began to think pretty hard. It seemed to me like a plant, and Al had discovered it and had wigwagged the warning to me. But how could they have known that I was to wait out there in the hollow—Whitey and Gregor? Perhaps the whole thing had been a sham, with Fatty Carson —the dog!—in on the scheme. Perhaps the pair of them had known that the young kid was stretched out there on the window ledge, and they had fed her boloney.

That seemed the best idea to me. That pair from the train were not Whitey or Gregor. They were another set of thugs, and I was the game they were after! That was what I made up my mind to, and I started drifting down the valley toward Brindle.

You can bet that I didn't go openly, or in a straight line. Instead, I took every bit of cover that I could find, and before I left one patch of cover, I peered all around me to make out what was what. But I could hear or see nothing.

Then I saw a big man walk out from among the shrubbery; and from the opposite rocks came one of the hoboes that had left the train. They shook hands. They sat down there together, in the full glare of the sun. I saw Frank take out a big wallet, and open it out—

But now I was sure!

The plant was clear enough, now that the kid had tipped me off. I was to be drawn in by this show. I was to be drawn in to sneak up closer to the pair of them, and when I made my sneak, Whitey and the fourth of the set would jump me. Perhaps there were more in the outfit. Apparently Whitey and Gregor had all of the backing that they needed to ask for.

I was about a hundred yards from Brindle, now. I figured that this made about twelve seconds, and that it might be worth making a straight bolt for the horse. But in twelve seconds about sixty bullets can be pumped at you by one man, with one set of fast-shooting guns. And here there were four!

So I chucked the idea of bolting, and just then, into the middle of my thinking, comes a soft voice on the far side of the rock where I was waiting.

"He went up higher," says the voice, panting. "You head up there, kid. I'll take the other way—"

There was a murmur. The voices ended. And then, just to my right, I saw a shadow slipping around the edge of the rock. I pressed close in to the ragged face of the stone. It was a big young kid. I could tell how young he was by the soft look and the smoothness of the back of his neck. He was carrying a shotgun, and he slipped along without a sound, like a real deer hunter. He was lost at once among the boulders and the brush.

However, I had only half an eye for him. The rest of my attention was lodged with what might come around the other corner of the rock—the fellow who intended to take the other way!

It was lucky for me that I had been training myself, lately, to look two ways at once, for, with no forward striking shadow to show that he was coming, around the corner of the big stone stepped my old friend, Whitey Peyton. He walked right into the muzzle of my Colt, and looked down at it, and dropped his nice new Winchester to the rocks, with a rattle, and pushed his hands up, above his head.

"Hullo, Whitey," says I.

"Why, hullo, old son," says Whitey, as cool as you please. "What's brought you out here?"

"What's brought you?" says I.

"Hunting for deer," says he. "I haven't had my teeth into a venison steak for months."

"I'm hunting for skunks," said I. "I haven't seen a good skunk skin for months. But it looks as though I'm going to get one now!"

He nodded, and narrowed his eyes, and waited. His arms bent just a little at the elbows.

"Don't do it, Whitey," says I. "The fact is, old son, that I'm aching to shove a dose of this lead through your insides. Don't you go and give me any good excuse. Your hands can't travel two feet faster than my finger moves a quarter of an inch on a hair-trigger."

"Is it a hair-trigger?" says he, mildly interested.

"I filed it down myself," says I.

"All right," says Whitey. "That changes things a good deal, I guess. Well, old boy, it's a hot day, for deer stalking."

"And for skunk shooting," said I, "but it looks as though I'm the only one who's going to have the luck."

"Don't be so sure," said he. "I'm not the only one in the party. You know that!"

"I know that," said I.

"What tipped you off to us?" he broke out, suddenly chucking pretense away.

"Never mind what. I'm a mind-reader, son," said I. "But now, about your own bacon. You can save it, Whitey, if we take up our last conversation just where we broke off. I mean: What's the name of the big boy behind you and Frank Peyton?"

CHAPTER XVIII

YOU never would have thought that I simply had addressed a few words of a question to Whitey. It was rather as though I'd stuck a knife in him and twisted the blade around between his ribs.

Finally he pulled his face out of its pucker and said:

"You'll never rest until you've got it between the eyes for you and me both, will you?"

"I'm full of curiosity, son," says I. "Now, I'll tell you

what, you pull the name out, and we'll give it the air, and maybe it won't roar so loud, after all."

"It'll roar plenty," says he. "And here it is. Take it and be damned. You've asked for it, and now you get it. Lefty Townsend!"

He gasped out the words, and then stuck out his jaw, grimly, as though he were waiting for me to fall.

I have to admit that it pretty well winded me, just the hearing of the name. Fellows and I had guessed at it, all right. But sometimes a shock is all the greater just because you expect it. I saw, between me and Whitey's mug, the mean, twisted, hairy face of Lefty Townsend. I don't suppose that there ever was in the world a man more hated than Lefty. Even the yeggs who worked for him hated his heart. But he kept them in good money; and, once in, they were usually afraid to quit, or, after working for him a few months, they were generally wanted for so many murders that they were scared to move around except with his orders and his protection.

Men who worked for Lefty never had a chance, if they were known to belong to his gang and they were caught by the law. There was no jail in the southwest strong enough to hold them. A crowd would gather from a hundred miles around, in twenty-four hours, and that jail was blasted open, and Lefty's agent was taken out and strung up. That had happened three or four times—enough to make a precedent, as one might say.

But still his power remained—even grew. He hung up there in his hole-in-the-wall country; and, though the posses and even the militia combed the mountains for him, they rarely had much luck. They got one or two of his men, from time to time, but they paid for what they got. Lefty's crew, when cornered, fought like rats, until they died. And men in that desperate frame of mind will generally give three for one. His power grew, I say, and it was known that he had his eye and his ears in most of the big towns within a radius of two hundred miles.

I thought of this, of all of it, as Whitey told me the name of the power behind his gun and that of Frank Gregor. It explained everything. It was no wonder that Whitey and

Frank had been picked. It made no difference to Lefty that they belonged to opposite cow camps. As long as they were hitched to him, he could do what he wanted with them. It explained the numbers of men, too, who were thrown into the field against me, at an instant's notice. I felt sick, all right. And Whitey leered at me, with a savage triumph.

Well, the first thing was to get myself out of that cursed, sun-baked valley.

"How many are up here with you, Whitey?" I asked him.

"Three," said he.

I believed that. Gregor and the two who had climbed down from the train.

"All right," said I. "You're coming along with me."

"You dirty crook," said Whitey, "it's a bargain that I made with you the other night. I tell you the name, and you turn me loose! Now you're double crossing me! You'll never get the two of us in alive. That's all that I tell you!"

"I'm going to turn you loose," I said. "But I need you for a while. Let's see how many new guns you've saved up?"

I searched him. He had, besides the rifle, one good Colt, and a bowie knife, the same that I had taken from him once before.

"You and your stuff, we're getting to be old friends," I told Whitey. "Give me your left hand!"

He gave it to me, doubting me with his eyes all the while. I took it in my left and with his right in my right, I turned my back on him. I kept a good grip on those hands of his. My own were now empty of weapons. But, if he tried to jerk away, before he could hit me, or grab me, I was reasonably sure to have a knife in him, or a bullet through his head.

My plan was to walk straight down the valley with Peyton behind me, that way. He would be a screen, not thick enough to keep a rifle bullet from driving through us both, of course, but his friends were behind us, as far as I knew, and they were not likely to open fire on us so long as they had to kill Whitey to get at me.

It was sort of funny, as we walked out from behind that rock and headed down the hollow, stepping fast. It was sort of like one of those vaudeville skits, where a couple of dancing-singers come waddling out from the wings, doing the lock-step. Except that the only singing we did came from Whitey.

He kept time to every step, cursing. I'd heard some pretty talented teamsters, a mechanic or two who could even move brass and steel with their language, but Whitey was in a class by himself. He damned me, my ancestors, my ideas, my friends, the ground I walked on, and everything that I ever had done.

But he kept in step behind me, though I was walking fast. He cursed, but he walked, and that was all that I wanted.

Now and then I glanced behind me, and finally I saw what was happening.

I saw a tall fellow that I took to be the kid who had been in the rocks with Whitey. He was running between two patches of brush on the hillside behind me. The others were probably doing the same thing, on one side or the other. But they didn't dare to take to the open for fear that I would turn about and, still using my living screen, open fire on them.

In the meantime, I was streaking for the mustang and making good time.

I dropped my despair behind me. It seemed a pretty fair bet that I'd be able to make the mustang, and, once on the back of Brindle, I would stack the footwork of that old goat, among rocks, against anything else that ever wore a saddle.

I got about twenty yards from the poplars. There was just one fear—that one or two of them might be waiting there, with a gun drilled on me. Five or six more steps, straining my eyes at them, and I could squint through the leaves and make out fairly well that there was no likelihood of anyone being there. But I could see the legs of old Brindle.

So could Whitey.

"Damn my heart!" says he. "Why didn't we think of *this* spot?"

"Hard luck, Whitey," says I.

Just then, I heard hoof beats, echoing hollowly up the valley, and over my shoulder and Peyton's I saw two riders coming fast, stretched out along the necks of their horses, taking their chance, I suppose, that my gunfire would go wild, or that the bobbing heads of the mustangs would shelter them.

Well, they didn't know how close I was to some four-legged help, myself.

I had one thing left to do, before I started moving fast. It was the second time that I had had Whitey in my hands. I almost felt that I had used up my luck with him, and I must say that it was a temptation to turn and sink a knife in that murdering cur. However, I couldn't very well do that. After all, there *was* a sort of a bargain between us. I just jerked myself clear of him, saying: "So long, Whitey, here's a souvenir!"

And then I slammed him with all my might on the edge of his jaw. He was so solid and strong that he didn't fall. He just started staggering backward, trying to regain his balance, and just failing, his mouth ajar, the wits numbed in him so that his eyes were blank, like a drunkard's.

That made a pretty picture, of my own painting. So I spun on my heel and lit out for the poplars.

Old Brindle looked to me better than any angel out of heaven. He lifted up his head and tossed it at me, crooking his ewe-neck, and dropping his ears. But I slashed the lead rope, jumped into the saddle, and broke him out of those trees on a dead run through the brush beyond.

I could hear Whitey Peyton, behind me, screaming that I had a horse and for the others to ride like the devil.

When I got well out into the valley; ahead of the riders, I had a glimpse of them, and knew Brindle could hold them. He was streaking it, side-stepping the boulders like a football player running for a touchdown; but those stones were pretty heavily on the minds of the others. They couldn't quite let their nags out.

Whitey seemed to guess that I was going to make my getaway. I couldn't hear him, but, even in the distance, I could see the contortions of his face. He leaped up and down. He threw his arms into the air, and finally he cast himself down upon the ground, and beat it with his fists. It wasn't the prettiest thing in the world to watch, but it was kind of a comfort to me.

Well, old Brindle switched me through rocks like nothing at all, and pretty soon I had a glimpse of the pair far behind me, pulling up. Then I rode out of the draw and headed straight back for town.

There was no use trying to disguise my direction. They would guess it, anyway. All I had to do was to make good time to Tom Fellows. And, on the way, I wondered whether I ought to be mad or glad about this day's work. I had learned from Whitey the man behind the guns. From his account, he and I would both be dead before twenty-four hours was out. Perhaps that was why he threw himself down on the ground so furiously when he saw that I was due to get clear. It was not only that he hated my heart, but it was even more because he was afraid that, once clear of him, I would start my talking, and that the word would get rapidly back to Townsend.

That was not what was in my mind, however. I had to tell Tom Fellows, of course, but I couldn't see any need of telling another soul in the world. Then why should the news be spread?

As for Whitey's ideas, he was a bit hysterical. Anybody who drinks as much as Whitey did, is likely to get a little woozy in the head, as time goes on.

So I burned up the pike back to Kearneyville, and when I came to the first narrow cross lane, I branched off and hit the road to the Tom Fellows place.

It looked mighty good to me, I can tell you, when I rode into view, and saw the trees drawing back, and the house standing out more clearly. Somehow, it seemed to me like a sort of haven. Heaven, I might almost have said. Every other spot in the world was a place of danger, but in the house of Tom Fellows, at least, I could be safe.

When I threw my reins in front of his place, I heaved a sigh that came right up from the bottom of my heart, and it was all clear relief.

CHAPTER XIX

THERE was not a sound in the house. Tom had no guests on this day, I gathered, and I was glad of it. I walked straight through to the patio, knowing that he would be there, if anywhere; and there he was.

It was much earlier than the time in the other day when I had stopped there. The sun was only half down from the zenith, or less. The patio bricks were so hot that you could feel them right through the thin soles of riding boots. But in the shadow it was cooler, and the noise of the fountain made it seem still cooler than it was.

Tom was seated in front of a table sipping orange juice. He had a frosted pitcher of the juice beside him. I must say I thought it was sort of a weakness in Tom that he should always be favoring his belly with something or other. But it was about the only weakness he had, and a man has to have *some* fault.

On a little table in front of him some papers were spread. He was studying them with a frown that hardly wore off when I came in. He got up and shook hands with me, still half frowning. He was worn. It was plain that some care was eating at him. I forgot my own message.

"What's the matter, Tom?" I asked him. "You look half sick!"

"I'm worried as can be," he said, frankly. It takes a big man to speak as openly as he usually did. "I'm beginning to wish that there were no such thing as money in the world. I have the full news here about that estate. It's no wonder that they murdered Lew Ellis. It's no wonder that they can afford to hire gunmen right and left.

They'll get me, too, in the end, unless I'm the luckiest man in the world."

"What is it?" I asked. "What's the figure, Tom?"

"More than a million and a quarter," said he.

He sat down, suddenly, his head bowed. I sat down, too, as though somebody had rapped me behind the knees. He might as well have pointed a whole flock of guns at my head.

A million dollars—and then some!

In those days every bush didn't sprout millionaires, as they do now. A millionaire is so doggone common, now, that you practically can't get any elbow room in the world. Common people, like me, I mean. But at that time, a hundred thousand dollars was a large fortune. Thirty bucks a month was good pay for a he-man, working fifteen hours a day. So imagine what it meant to me when Tom Fellows said a million and a quarter.

I had to speak out my first thought.

"Tom," I said, "it's too big! They'll get you. You'd better run for it!"

"Where?" said he.

His eyes were sunken a little under his brow. No wonder! He looked straight at me, and I tried to think—South Sea Islands—the higher mountains in Peru—Africa—No, it didn't make any difference. The rats who were after him would spend half their coin to make sure of the other half. And no man could stand out, it seemed, against such a weight of treasure. I felt as though we were being stifled with gold!

He went on, when he saw that he had made his point:

"It appears that everything is in order. The name of the old boy was neither Fellows nor Ellis—think of that!"

I nodded, mute and unhappy.

"It was Shaw. Irish-Scotch. I don't know just where the line crosses the Ellis-Fellows outfit. Somebody's grandfather married somebody's aunt. And there you are! Not American money, either. This Shaw goes to Wales and uncovers a lot of coal, and spends fifty years digging the stuff out and saving the dollars that he makes. And so, when he dies, we have to sweat for it—away out here in the West. Something ironical about that!"

I kicked against the pricks, so to speak.

"Tom," I cried out, steaming myself up. "You can beat 'em, anyway. If they're willing to spend money—*you* can spend money, too. If they hire gunmen, *you* can hire 'em, too!"

"What gunmen do I know, Slow?" says he. "And what gunmen do I want to know?"

That rather staggered me.

"No," he said. "I've kept my hands reasonably clean, so far in my life, and I hope to keep them clean to the end."

He said it very quietly, and softly. But I felt like a dog. I wanted to slink out of sight.

However, I came back at him a little.

"You've got to manage it, some way. You're fighting for a ton of money!"

"What more do I want than what I have?" asked Tom.

He made a gesture. He kept his calm, but his heart was in his voice.

"I have a house that's big enough and pleasant enough for me. My land gives me good horses, and money enough to go on hunting trips, or for excursions to the cities, now and then. I'm a quiet man, and I like a quiet life. But this hellishness is being forced on me!"

"Write to New York," said I. "Call the deal off. Sign over your share to charity!"

He smiled at me, a little sadly.

"You're a good fellow, Slow," said he. "You're a friend, too. But whatever happens in this matter will be over and done with inside of a week, I dare say. I'll be living—or dead—at the end of that time. And it would take three times as long to get the curse of the stuff off my hands!"

He took out a handkerchief and rubbed his fingers. I think it was an entirely unconscious gesture, but it was as though he felt the stain eating into his flesh.

Then he urged me to sit down again, and be comfortable. And he asked my pardon for bringing up his own wretched affairs. Because, he said, I already had trouble enough on my hands. One thing I must do, at least, and that was to clear out of the business and leave the thing to him, entirely. In the natural course of affairs, he would certainly either die or see that the murderers of Ellis died.

I heard him out. Great Scott, how I admired that gentle-spoken, fair, square, honest man! How I despised my rotten self. Some of my admiration come out in a childish burst.

"Tom," I cried to him, "right now I make up my mind. I'm going to bury my old self. I'm going to make myself over. I'm going to wash my hands of crooks and crookedness. I'm going to—I'm going to be like you, if God will let me!"

Well, sir, I shook with the idea of it. I fairly shook. It enlarged my heart and my mind just to think forward to the task I had before me—always to be brave—always to be gentle—never to lose my temper—always to be true to friends, though that wasn't so hard—always to be fair to enemies, also. To open my hand and my heart to everyone I liked. To make my own self-respect a high and mighty judge over my actions!

It gave me a mighty thrill, a lifting of the heart, as I made the decision.

The next instant I knew that I was being a fool. A puppy may howl, but he can't be a dog. He needs to grow, and I'd finished my inches of body—my inches of mind, too, probably.

"Good old Slow," said the gentle voice of Tom Fellows. "You've put me up on a pedestal. Take me down, for God's sake. Look at the facts about a very selfish, egotistical man. But let's step outside of personalities. They're always poisonous, in the long run."

I was pretty much upset. I simply shrugged my shoulders and then nodded.

"Only this," I answered him. "I'll tell you what, Tom. I stay through to fight the thing out. I saw the bullets knock Lew Ellis down. I'll never be able to leave the trail. Besides, Werner sent me. It's my ticket of leave to work out this job. And today I took a long step forward."

He didn't try to argue me out of the thing. He gave me

one long, careful look, and then seemed to banish all idea of persuading me. He simply said:

"All right, partner. What did you uncover today?"

Lord, how I liked that word, "partner"! I could guess that Fellows had not used it to many other men in the course of his life. He wasn't proud, but he wasn't promiscuous, either.

"I'll cut the story short," I said. "The gang got wind of the fact that I was to be there in the hollow—"

"What?" said Fellows. "How could they get wind of that? You and I and the girl knew. No one else."

"I'll explain everything, in a moment," said I. "What we're up against is ears in the ground and eyes in the air. Our minds are being read for us, as a matter of fact!"

Then I told him the entire yarn, just as it happened, leaving nothing out—not even my feelings.

When I came to the place about the girl wigwagging from the blind baggage, even Fellows was excited.

"How could she have found out the plant?" he kept asking.

And when I had finished the yarn, he hardly commented even on the name of Lefty Townsend, even on the lucky escape I had made. His enthusiasm all poured out for Al Doloroso. He said that she was apparently one of those rare things, a woman with the nerve and the talents of a man.

He wanted to know all about her, and I told him that, too, though I was a little sore because she got all of the praise. I could have stood a few pleasant words from Fellows for my own part of the game.

"If she's Mexican," said Fellows, "that's not against her. The blood in her is Castilian. If her father went wrong, it's because the poor devil has been living below his caste. You ought to marry that girl. You ought to chuck everything and marry her."

"Sixteen?" said I.

"It makes no difference," said he. "They develop before the cold-blooded northerners. She loves you. And she's wonderful!"

I grinned at him.

"Let her hear *you* say that she's wonderful," said I, "and see how long she has even half an eye for me!"

He snapped his fingers.

When I left, he went out with me, his big, powerful arm linked around my shoulders.

"You're one of the men who underestimate themselves, Slow," said he. "I'm going to teach you self-esteem, believe me! You've done a grand day's work. You've done a day's work so big that, somehow, I feel you and I between us may be able to beat the game! Beat them all!"

I felt pretty warm and good, hearing him say that; but, as we went down the hall, we passed Zip. He was just about to step through a doorway, but when he saw us coming, he stepped back again, and bowed to us from among the shadows, and I saw the yellow glint of his slant eyes. That took half the bloom off the moment.

But still it remains, to this day, one of the great moments of all my life. Nothing that happened afterward could quite dim it or tarnish its significance.

CHAPTER XX

WHEN I got back to Kearneyville, I was half up, and half down. I knew that I was playing a desperate game, but I also knew that Tom Fellows had called me "partner." The two things about balanced, and left me happy, on the whole.

When I got to the hotel, I went up to my room, and there I found Al Doloroso curled up on one of the beds, where the broad, slant hand of the summer sun would beat on her, reading a magazine. That was the Mexican of it. No white girl could have endured that sun for five minutes. But she was just soaking it up like a good fellow!

I said: "Hullo, Al. Where you been, today?"

"Huh?" grunted she, and went on reading.

"Where you been?" I repeated.

"Oh, just around," said she.

"Sit up and talk, you!" said I.

She shoved the magazine away, turned on her elbow and yawned in my face, openly. She looked like a cat, as pretty, and as sassy. She showed me all her white teeth, and then settled herself for a minute sort of wriggling and stretching in the comfort of that blast of sunshine.

"Why, hullo, Slow," said she, as though she had heard me and seen me for the first time since I entered the room.

Well, she could kid me if she wanted to. She had the right. I went into the bathroom, shaved, washed a few layers of dust off, and came out again.

"You're a sensitive man, Slow," says the brat. "I see that you blush when you look at yourself in the mirror!"

That sort of irritated me. I hate shaving; my skin's tender to the razor's dragging and scraping.

But I held on and said nothing, just tried to grin. I had an idea that if I ever let the little hound know that she was really teasing me, she'd be worse than a stinging wasp.

"Set up and do yourself proud and talk a while," says I.

"About what?" says she.

"About the red-headed brat that gave me the high sign from the blind baggage," says I.

She nodded at me, tucked her hands behind her head, leaned back against a couple of pillows, and talked. She could talk, when she wanted to.

"If you were so doggone interested in Kearneyville, Slow," says she, "I thought that Kearneyville might be pretty interested in you. So interested that some of the boys might drop around just to see the place where the great man was looking. That gave me an idea, so I slid across the street and got up to the top of that building."

She hooked her thumb across to indicate.

"I could lie out there behind the little parapet and look right through the windows into your joint, here," she continued. "I lay there for quite a spell. It got hot, but I like heat."

"You're a regular lizard," said I.

"After a time, in came a couple of flies for the lizard. A couple of boys that looked like thugs. You saw the pair that got off the freight coming up?"

"Yeah. I saw. Did they get into my room?"

"Sure they did. I saw them looking around through your luggage, so I went down to the street and waited till they came out.

"When they came out, I followed them to the railroad station, bought a ticket to the same place they were going to—it was only a little ways down the line—and then hopped aboard the next train with 'em. I took the seat behind theirs, and went plumb asleep. They kind of wondered why I should have had to pick the seat right behind theirs, when there was nobody else in the car, but when they saw how fast I was asleep, they didn't mind so much. They sat where they were—the fools!—and I listened in on their yarning. It appears that you're pretty popular with the boys, Slow. They like you so well that just the outside of you won't do for 'em. They want to get acquainted with your insides, too. In fact, they'd like to take you apart. Those two bucks expected to get a fine piece of money if they managed to lay you cold. They knew all about you going down the line to the creekbed, though where they collected the idea, I don't know."

"It was all a plant, kid," I told her. "When you listened in on the talk between Whitey and Gregor, it was all a plant. They knew you were there. They said what they did just to bring you on."

"White blackbirds!" said Al.

"It's a fact," said I. "The only way they could have figured to draw me, that way."

"Have it your own way," said she. "Anyway, they knew, and I thought that you'd be interested, too. *I* hadn't known what sort of a fool play you had in mind, either."

"Why was it a fool play?" I asked her, scowling.

"You against at least three men?" said Al. "Are you the champeen gun-thrower of this neck of the woods? The trouble with you, Slow, is that you always rate yourself about six feet six, whereas you'd really drown a foot shorter.

But anyway, when that pair got off one side of the train, I got off the other side, and sneaked around until I saw them meet up with a reverend old Jewish gentleman. He looked like a rabbi. He had a beard two feet long and horn-rimmed spectacles. He was real cute. I knew he was the fence they'd talked about on the way down.

"I laid out until the freight came that way. I didn't watch for the two bucks to hop it. I suppose they'd warned off the fence, and told him there'd be more lead than jewels to see, that day. But I hooked on the freight from the station side, because I reckoned that the other two would use the blind side of the train. I must have been right. I snuggled down behind the tender and nobody bothered me, and when I came to the trestle, I high-signed on both sides of the train. That's all I know about it, till you came back here and waked me up from a mighty good yarn. Goldilocks was just putting on her hat, and the duke had ordered his coach and *six*. Then you blow in and bring me back to Kearneyville. Say, Slow, what's the whole idea, anyway? Will you tell me that?"

"Suppose I tell you everything," said I, "will you blow right out of the picture?"

She hesitated.

"Everything?" said she. "Will you tell me everything?"

I said I would, and, after a minute, she nodded. She promised that she would keep her mouth shut, and that she'd haul train when I finished. Then she sat up straight and listened, while I gave her everything from the start. She blinked a little when I fitted into the picture the names she knew—Werner, Ellis, Whitey Peyton, Frank Gregor. When I finished, I was sweating a little. I mean, it sounded so black for me! For Fellows, too. It looked as though we had a great machine against us.

The kid said nothing, for a while. She just pressed her lips together and stared at me. All at once, she seemed older and wiser. After a while, she got up, shook hands, and went to the door.

"You want me to go, Slow?" said she.

"Yeah. I want you to go. You've got yourself into this too deep, already. They're the kind that wouldn't hesitate to wring your neck for you. So long, Al. You've been the best partner in the world."

"Bar one," says she.

"Yeah. Bar one," says I.

"All right," says she. "I'm going. I pull out. God help you, Slow. You're in for an awful trimming. So long, and good luck."

Just like that, she stepped out through the door, and I heard her heels tapping down the stairs, a moment later.

I can't tell you how lonely I felt, but I didn't have a chance to feel lonely long. The frame-up for me was not that way in Kearneyville. Everybody seemed glad to fill my time up for me. In about fifteen minutes, there comes a rap on the door, and there's a bare-legged kid with a letter for me that I open. He comes in and waits for an answer.

The letter says in a fine big, walloping, broad-hand scrawl:

"Dear Slow Joe,

"When you saw me that first day, you got the wrong idea about me. I want to talk to you again. I want to talk to you about Lew.

"You know, Joe, that you felt pretty hard toward me, and I'm sorry that I lost my temper, that way, but I was raised on the end of a stick, so to speak.

"Please tell me that you'll drop around and see me. For me, there's no better time than tonight. And I'll be home, here, at nine o'clock. Will you send back a reply by the boy?

Yours hopefully,
Ruth Edgar."

"You're in the piece again, are you?" says I to myself.

Then I sat down and wrote:

"Dear Ruth,

"Of course I'll come over. I thought that that first chat couldn't be all that we had to say to one another. I sort of knew that we'd meet again, and I'm glad that tonight is the time. At nine o'clock sharp I'll ring your front door bell.

Sincerely yours,
Joe Hyde."

I sealed that letter, gave the kid a quarter and watched him go through the doorway as though he were afraid that I'd change my mind.

Then I went downstairs, and found big Sam Guernsey in the hall. He was chewing tobacco, which was what he always did when he was excited. I tried to talk to him, but all that he did was to walk up and down, with his hands clasped behind his back; and once every round, as he turned past a big-mouthed spittoon in a corner, he let fly at it. Mostly he hit it, because he was a good shot. But sometimes he missed, and he didn't seem to care. I went right on talking, because it pleased me, somehow, to see him getting madder and madder. Finally he stopped right in front of me, and glared.

"Deputy marshal!" he snarls.

I nodded.

"Look!" said I, and held out the shield. "Pretty, ain't it?"

"Pretty be damned, and you be damned along with it!" said he. "You're a disgrace to the town. Doggone me, if you ain't a disgrace to the hotel that's over your head. After what you've done in the world—now you sneak around and get behind the fence. I hope that they tear the fence down and break the boards over your head. You're a sneak, Joe Hyde!"

I half expected him to go on and turn me out of the room I had in his place, but he didn't go that far. He talked himself out. He wound up, sort of sadly: "You used to be a good boy, Joe!"

I saw that he meant in the time when I had been busting noses in Kearneyville, or safes outside of it. Well, every man has a different standard, and so has every section of the country. In that neck of the woods, I knew that my name was now mud. But I didn't care so much, because I had Tom Fellows before me. And I swore that I'd keep on stretching my legs to try to go where he was walking before me down the road of honor and rightness.

CHAPTER XXI

I HAD supper. At a quarter of eight, I looked through a front window, and there, off to a corner of the veranda, I saw a couple of men sitting and yarning, and smoking cigarettes. It was a funny time for them to be there. The saloons soaked up most of the loose population about this time of the night.

Then I went to the back of the hotel, and from a blank window there I studied the yard. It was solid black. I was about to use the back door, when I saw a little spot of red, such as a cigarette makes, when the ashes have been newly dusted off, and somebody takes a whiff.

That made me a little impatient. So I went to a side window, worked it up by silent inches, slid through—and dropped into a pile of stickly brush underneath.

It's a mighty mean thing to have that sort of a break, when you can't even swear at it. I had to pick myself out of the stickers in silence, just grinding my teeth. The palm of one hand was torn. I licked it, spat out the blood, and damned sweetly and softly some more. I wished that I'd gone out the front door and let the two thugs take their crack at me—if that was why they were there! It would have been a pleasure, I felt now, to crack back.

However, there was Ruthie Edgar ahead of me!

I got down the driveway and to her house almost exactly at eight o'clock, a good hour before she had asked me to call. That was what I wanted. The front of the house was black. I looked through a lighted sitting room window on the side of the building, and saw Pa Edgar with his feet shoved into slippers, sitting back in a leather armchair, letting his belly expand after dinner and nodding a lot of wisecracks at the newspaper he was reading. He had white whiskers and a red, swelling face. He looked like an old stuff.

In the back of the house I had a squint through the kitchen window. It was a little steamy, but I could see Ma Edgar and my Ruthie. Ma was washing, and Ruthie was wiping dishes. She finished them. Ma pointed to a pile of pans, but Ruth told her where to get off. It was grand to hear her voice rise and swell in honest indignation. She wouldn't spoil her hands, she said. She wasn't a Chinaman or a nigger slavey. She had to write some letters, and she was going up to her own room.

Out she went and slammed the door, and Ma didn't follow. She made a step or two. She even set her fighting jaw and grabbed a broom, but she changed her mind. She'd been through it before, I decided.

From around in front of the house, I saw lamplight jump, tremble, and steady in a window just above the middle of the veranda. That made it easy. All I had to do was to pull off my boots, shinny up a wooden column not half so hard as a lot of snaky tree trunks I had navigated as a kid, and there I was on a little balcony. You might have guessed that Ruthie would have the best room in the house for herself.

She was inside of her room, but she wasn't writing letters. She was making a saddle pack. She'd already thrown off her gingham kitchen dress and stepped into riding skirts, and now she was making her pack. I had picked on her as a lazy girl, but I was wrong. She moved her hands fast, and every lick counted.

When she stepped into a closet, deep and dark, I stepped through the window, lighted a cigarette from the top of the lamp chimney, and was sitting down in the corner by the window when she came back.

She was quick, all right. At the sight of me, she let the clothes she was carrying drop; but she caught them again out of the air.

"Hello, Ruthie," says I.

When she straightened from catching the clothes, she

was no longer popping her eyes; she had control of her face, and smiled at me.

"Hello, Joe," says she.

She comes right across and gives me a good, hearty handshake, and looks me slam in the eyes.

"Afraid of the dogs, Joe?" says she. "Or just keeping your hand in with a little second-story work?"

"Why, Ruth," says I, very innocent, "I'm just on time. It's exactly eight. There goes the bell."

"I said nine, in the letter," says she.

"The deuce you did! I got it mixed."

I saw a shadow flicker across her eyes. She didn't believe me. But she tried to cover up the shadow at once. She smiled, and her eyes crinkled at me. By thunder, I began to be afraid of that girl. When they're bad and ugly, they're likely to be sort of sporting, anyway. When they're bad and pretty, they're just plain devils. I rated her in that class.

"It's all right, Joe," said she. "Feet won't get cold without boots?"

"No. I've got a good circulation in my feet," said I. "Taking a little trip, Ruthie?"

Her patience frayed in the center and popped.

"I wish you wouldn't call me that," said she. "Just because that big, red-necked ham of a—oh, well," she caught herself up, "it doesn't matter. I'm getting some things together," she went on, to answer my question.

She sat down on the arm of a deep easy chair, and swung one foot, jaunty and at ease. She was a slick one!

"I had to talk to you some more about Lew," she said. "You got me wrong, Joe. You thought I was hard. I'm not. I've led a dog's life, but I'm not hard. I loved Lew. God knows that I loved him, and I think he cared a little about me."

She lifted her eyes and turned her head a little away from me. She had real tears brimming—real ones. But I knew that she wasn't pitying Lew. She was pitying herself.

"Yeah, he cared about you, all right," said I. "He cared six thousand dollars and a pair of golden spurs about you as he died, that was all."

She jerked her head around and stared at me.

"And you gave six thousand to Mr. Way!" she snapped. "You—"

The veins stood out in her forehead. But suddenly she swallowed even that fit of temper. I never saw such a woman. She had more self-control than a State senator running for reëlection. By thunder, she was smiling again, right away!

"But you thought of a better way to have Lew remembered, Joe. And so why should I care? Six thousand dollars is a lot of money. But it would have saddened me to have what Lew had slaved for—what he had meant for our house and home together—"

She made her voice tremble away to nothing. It was a good piece of work.

I leaned forward.

"Ruth," I said, "you're wonderful!"

She flicked her eyes across my face. It was quicker than a whip stroke, but I caught it, and the keen interest behind it.

"I'm not wonderful, Joe," said she. "I'm just a mighty sad girl, now."

"You're wonderful," I insisted. "I never saw anybody like you. It does me good to sit here. I could feast my eyes on you. Yes, partly because you're so doggone pretty, Ruth. But because you have brains, too. Brains don't go so often with a fine, classic front like yours. And *what* brains! You knock me right off. I'm crazy about you! I've been thinking a lot about you ever since I saw you easing into that hammock under the apple trees. And now I see that everything I've thought is true. You're all by yourself. You beat the world. You're out six thousand dollars, just now, but you'll have it back again, before long!"

She raised her head. The coyness went out of her eyes. They were as steady and as mean as the eyes of any man. She said nothing, like a wise young fox. She wanted to wait me out, but I put the next one right over the middle of the pan.

"They must have offered you two or three thousand, at least, for tonight's job, didn't they?"

It got her off the arm of the chair, at least. But still she didn't speak. Only, she threw a quick glance toward the window at my side.

"Fellows like Whitey and Gregor wouldn't be go-betweens for pin money. They must have offered you something worth while. What was it, Ruthie?"

That name made her grit her teeth. She saw, of course, that she had lost her play—lost it from the first. I suppose she hated to think of the energy and the acting that she had been wasting on me, all of this time.

Then she pointed to the window.

"You can go out the way you came in, I guess?" says she.

"Sure I can, but I'm not ready to go, yet. I want to know some facts, first."

I got up and faced her. I stuck out my jaw. I wished that I were three inches taller, for the hundredth or thousandth time in my life, so that I could stare down at her, which is a great advantage that tall people have. I made up as well as I could by being mean.

"You can go straight to the devil," said she, not loudly.

"You'll come straight to jail," I bluffed.

"On what charge?" said she.

"Misprision, attempt to kill, manslaughter, larceny, and conspiracy," said I, putting together, real fast, about all the words that I could think of. I added: "I'm a Federal officer, sworn to do my duty. This will mean only about eight years out of your life, Ruthie."

She was swamped. She was a hardy sort of a girl, and she would be tool-proof steel, with a little more experience, but she lacked the experience, just then, and the bluff worked. She backed up till she hit the wall, and put her hands down against it to steady herself.

"Now come clean," said I. "What was the money offer?"

She gagged a couple of times.

"One thousand even," says she.

"The dirty cheap skates," says I, beginning to sweat. "And who were you to take the trip with? Whitey?"

She nodded, white—green-white, which isn't pretty.

"Marriage?"

She nodded again.

"Who was coming tonight, with Whitey, to get me?"
"Gregor!" she whispered.
"Where were they going to wait for me?"
"Down in the summer house—the little shack in the front garden."
I went to the door, locked it, and took the key.
"I'll see you later, honey," said I, and climbed through the window and skinned down the balcony pillar up which I had come. I felt that I had one section of the game in my hands, but when I looked up from the ground at her window, I saw that I'd slipped and simply made a fool of myself. She was moving a lamp in a circle in front of the window. I knew, then, that the birds would have the message that everything was off, and I'd have no chance to get at the two thugs that night and take *them* by surprise.

CHAPTER XXII

WHAT that girl had done to me, I can't say. But that white, sick face of hers stuck in my mind. It made *me* feel sick, too. I mean, a woman ought not to be that way. Old hags, yes; but not a young girl full of the beauty and the whole juice of life. I almost wished that I hadn't interrupted. I wished that she had gone off and married Whitey. They would have been good antidotes, one for the other.
I went back to the hotel. By this time, I figured that they would have missed me in the Guernsey House and would be scattering around to search, because it was a quarter to nine. So I marched right into the stable as big as life, and I was right. At least, I saw nothing, except the moldy old stable hand. He came and pointed out the bad

points of Brindle to me while I was saddling the pony, and he told me that a horse like that was more like a broken down barge than a real animal that can move out of its own tracks.

I let him talk. I knew that Brindle might not have clipper lines, but on the other hand, I knew that he would sail forever, almost, through any kind of weather. Just now, I merely wanted to get out of town with him and into the open, where a wind could blow in my face.

I didn't need to do much thinking. It was as clear as day that my friends were doing everything they could to wipe me off the slate. Now they'd got down to the woman dodge, which is about the lowest trick known to the game. If they would try that, they would try anything, all the way to poison. And I couldn't help remembering how Tom Fellows himself had urged me to leave the game. When I remembered that, I suddenly decided that he was right. This work was too stiff for me. I had hung onto life several times, now, by the grip of my finger nails. It was time to simply go to Tom and tell him that I was too weak for the work. I resigned.

So I tickled Brindle in the ribs and woke him up to a grunt and a trot, the water jouncing in his belly. But at the same time, I heard the soft chiming of the golden bells at my heels, and I reined in the mustang with a jerk and took another road out of town. For the thing came over me again, mysteriously and strangely, that somehow I was riding trail for the poor kid who was dead, and that the golden spurs of Lew Ellis would one day drive me to the end of that trail and give his ghost peace in whatever hell or heaven he had found. It was a queer thought and a foolish one; I don't like to talk about it. But the thing was with me, pushing me, from the moment when I buckled those spurs on my heels in Fatty Carson's barroom.

Well, I cruised out under the broad, bright face of the night. I passed a ploughed field that belonged to Doc Wallis. He was about the only real farmer in the county. Beyond that was summer-fallow, with an acrid scent of tarweed coming off the face of it. But I paid little attention to the ground. I had my head back like a moonsick kid, breathing deep and hard, and wondering why my heart ached so, and felt so lonely.

It was because I was beat. I had tackled a good many hard jobs and brought them off, in my time, even though my time hadn't been so long, as that brat Al had pointed out. But now I was beaten, and I knew it, and the knowledge was bad for my knees and bad for my heart. I weakened all over!

I got up to the forking of the Davis-Bridgetown road. One branch went on to Bridgetown. The other went towards the ratty little village of Davis, away off yonder in the mountains which were nudging the stars out of place along the northwestern horizon. As I came there, I pulled up, wondering which road I'd take, or if I should turn back to the dark, quiet hell of Kearneyville, behind me. I pulled up, and as the little shiver of the spur-bells died away, I heard the pound of galloping horses coming up the Bridgetown road.

I listened for a time, wondering. To me the gallop of a horse is like the pulse of the heart; one can tell what's happening by the sound of the hoofs. And these were lunging, beating a little unevenly, like a horse played out, but still driven hard.

I just pulled old Brindle back beside the brush, so that I wouldn't stand as an outline against the sky. And I waited to see how near my guess might have come to the truth.

Very soon, behind the leading horse, I could hear the rumble and roar of many more to the rear, and after that, I saw the dull silhouette of a rider with a saddled horse led beside his mount.

This fellow came to the crossroad and flopped from the saddle. The nag he dismounted was so beat that it staggered under him. And the man staggered, too, and groaned as he staggered.

He put his foot into the stirrup, but he couldn't drag himself up the side of the nag. I heard him cursing, not out loud, but half whispering, as though he didn't want to spend unnecessary strength in that manner.

And behind him, the roar of the hoofs was growing up.

I went out on Brindle; he jerked around and threw a gun on me.

"Steady, boy," said I. "I'm a friend. Here's a hand."

I reached down and gave him a strong pull, so that he made it into the saddle, but he swayed as he hit the saddle. He was all in. I could see him pitching to the road before he had gone another three miles.

"Ride straight into the brush," I ordered him. "I'll take the boys for a spin up the road, and come back. I know how to shake them."

For I thought I did. I knew that country, of course, like the lines in the palm of my hand.

I saw him drift his horse for the shrubbery. Over to my right I could see the heads and shoulders of the posse coming—if posse it were. I had waited long enough. Now I gave Brindle the golden spurs, and we scooted up the road. I didn't let him sprint, because he couldn't sprint. That pace just killed him in half a mile. But he could hit a brisk gallop and keep going like a rocking-horse. I rated him just inside his best pace, and looked back. That was enough. His gait was good enough to hold them hard. Then I laughed, because the game seemed so easy.

I went as far as the bridge on the road to Davis. Beyond the bridge the road dips into a lot of sharp curves that run for a matter of three or four miles. I had been going fast, increasing the lead. On the far side of the bridge, I ducked to the side, down the bank of the grade, and through the brush beyond. Then I pulled Brindle up and waited. My head was just level with the tops of the shrubbery. If they saw me, they'd salt me, but I swore that they couldn't see me, and I was right.

They went by with a roar of hoofs, horses snorting, saddle leather creaking. Nobody was speaking. Those fellows meant business, and there were a dozen of them. I ticked off the heads as they passed.

I was pleased. I wanted to laugh, somehow. That was my right place, I felt—on the other side of the fence, away from the law, fooling the wise ones, taking my chances, rolling the dice for the big stakes. Well, that was the way I felt about it, at least. Just then, I had forgotten about trying to shine like Tom Fellows. Then I jogged Brindle back toward the brush where I had left the hunted man, feeling pretty secure that the posse would go humming on down the windings of that road until it came out beyond the trees, and had a glimpse of the emptiness of everything ahead. Fooled like that, it would probably have a consultation, and then begin to circle and cut for sign. Or, perhaps, it would come straight back to the crossroad. But I doubted that! Altogether, I felt pretty secure.

When I got back to the crossroad, I found my man at once. He was sitting on the ground, with his coat off, and he was trying to work a bandage around his body. When I came out, I sang out to him, softly, and told him I was his friend. He only grunted.

Then I told him to light a match and I would do the bandaging. He scratched the match and I saw the hole—low down, through the soft flesh just above the right hip, a bad wound. I looked close. There didn't appear to be any shreds of cloth in the wound, and that was encouraging. But the Lord alone could tell what a probe would bring out of that hole! At any rate, the only thing now was to get the bandage on, because he was bleeding bad.

I got a handful of soft, thin dust out of the nearest rut in the road and I plastered that over the wound and held my hand firm, so that the blood would have a chance to soak into the dust and make a thick clot. There was nothing else to do, so far as I knew. Some people say that cobwebs are better, but I never found them so.

The fellow said:

"That's the stuff, partner."

His teeth were chattering, and not with cold, or with fear. Nerves were going, I suspected.

He was young. Younger than me. But he had a good beard on his chin, worn to a point, so that his face had a sort of distinguished, old-fashioned look. He had a deep brow, slanting back rather. There were strong, bony knobs at the corners of his forehead. They didn't disfigure him; they simply made his face look stronger.

When the dust was clotted, as it seemed to me, with

the blood that had soaked through, I took my hand away. A lump of mud stuck to his side.

That was promising. So the bandaging started, and I tied him up tight enough to make him damn once or twice as the cloth gripped him.

"You've been here before, brother," he said.

"Yeah. I've been there before," was all I said.

There was no use talking too much.

When the bandaging was over and he had his shirt on again, I told him to stand up. He asked for a hand, but I told him to manage it by himself. He did. It took him some time, but his weak knees managed to shove himself up straight.

"Well?" he said.

"I wanted to see how much you had left in you," said I. "Not much. You're about all in. Any little pin-points of red before your eyes?"

"No. Just darkness—moving a little."

"That's not so bad, then," said I. "You've got to get out of here, a ways, though. Ride up the Davis road."

"Great God, man," said he, "that's the way they went after me!"

"That's why you ought to take that way," said I. "They won't be looking for you behind them. By this time, they're probably scattering all over creation to pick up the trail of you. Climb onto your horse."

He muttered something which I failed to catch. So I helped him onto his horse, and I even rode a part of the distance with him. As I went I asked if he knew the country well, around here, and he said that he didn't. Only had a passing acquaintance with it. So I pointed out the landmarks, told him where the creeks were, and the fordable and unfordable stretches of the water. A man needs to know such things when he's being chased.

He kept grunting in response, and finally, a good distance up the road, I asked him how far he had to go before he reached friends.

"Only a little spell," said he.

"So long, then," said I.

"So long, old boy," he muttered.

I turned back, but after I'd ridden a few paces, I looked around. There was his horse, walking away, but there was nobody in the saddle!

CHAPTER XXIII

THAT was a stiff jolt, and don't you mistake!

When I got back, there was the kid stretched on the ground. He'd fainted out of the saddle, about as soon as I left him. Perhaps that was why he didn't waste any breath in thanking me.

First I caught the horse, which was too tired to run from Brindle. Then I came back and gave the kid a slug of whiskey out of my flask. That's the sort of a time that whiskey is needed—to give a fellow a hand up when he's in the gutter.

This fellow coughed, and then sat up.

"You can hang me and be damned to you!" says he.

Of course he hadn't recognized me.

"They haven't got you yet," I told him. "But you're a fool not to of told me how near you were to all in. You've got to get into this saddle again. But I'll take care of you, tonight. I won't leave you."

I held out my hand to help him to his feet. He just sat tight, and cocked his head back to gape at me.

"I'm Slip Garvey," said he.

"All right, old boy," said I, "you nearly slipped tonight, and no mistake."

"You fool," he said thickly, "I'm one of Townsend's."

Ay! But that was a shot in the pit of the stomach! That nearly doubled me up and took my wind. Perhaps this was one of the thugs who had been trying for me in Kearneyville?

"Been in Kearneyville, Slip?" said I.

"No. Bridgetown. They pinched me busting into the Elmer Brothers store, last night. They got a crowd together to lynch me tonight. I busted out of jail. They blocked the street. I killed one of 'em, I think, and I got this in the side. They know I belong to Townsend. If they catch you with me, they'll hang you, too. They're like mad dogs. They're crazy for blood!"

It was pretty clean. It was the cleanest that I ever have seen. He was all in, but, since I'd given him a hand, he wouldn't load me down without telling me the straight story. So that fixed him with me. The name of Townsend was a knife between my ribs, of course; and I could suppose that this kid had piled up his list of crooked jobs—killings, maybe. But still, in this pinch he was white, and my heart went out to him. I've been sick with wounds myself, and it's not so sweet!

I got him onto a horse again, and rode along beside him. He grabbed the pommel of his saddle with both hands. His head sunk between his shoulders, but his chin never fell. It just thrust out straight before, and the silhouette of the beard on the end of that chin made him look foolish, like a goaty old man. His back was curved into a bow, he was so weak.

Well, he didn't have to go far. There was a wooded hollow less than a mile from where he had flopped, and there I took him, wanting to hurry the horses, but not daring to take him along faster than a walk. In the hollow, I bedded him in all the saddle blankets we had. He took another shot of the whiskey, and settled down with a groan of comfort.

"Long ride!" he said to me, and went sound asleep.

That was the best thing for him, of course. But he would have to have food, before long, and this was the time to rustle it for him. A glimmer of yellow starlight on the side of the next hill told me the shortest way toward provisions.

When I got there, and had tethered Brindle, I decided that it would be better not to ask for grub—a lot safer to borrow it, unannounced. Because anyone who came to buy food at that time of night was pretty sure to rouse suspicions. And that infernal posse would be spreading all over the map, like oil on water, by the next morning.

So I left Brindle at a little distance and went exploring. The light in the house went out before I got to the yard, and I was glad of that. I wished the people in that house a quick and a deep slumber.

When I stepped into the yard, though, it was as though I had punched an alarm bell, for a dog got up from nowhere, a dog as big as the house, and let out a howl, and started straight for me. There was nothing to do except try for him with a kick. I felt the toe of my boot miss him, but the high heel lodged against his nose so hard that it almost broke my ankle.

It nearly broke the dog's head, too. He flopped on his back and lay stunned, while a window screeched up.

"It ain't anything, Jerry," says a woman's voice. "I told you that big overgrown fool of a dog would never do anything but eat himself to death. I told you so when you brought him home the first day!"

The window groaned down again. Voices murmured and were still. The dog got up, and ran with a whimper.

After a moment I tried the door. It was locked, but, though I wasn't as slick as that little devil, Al of San Whiskey, I could read the mind of that country lock. And in two minutes more the pantry was hiding nothing from me.

I saw half of a big loganberry pie, a big heel of a loaf of white bread that made my mouth water, some butter that smelled fresh, the breast and wings of a roasted chicken, and a pitcher of milk. I drank the milk and took the other things. Then in another cupboard, I found some bacon, a can of coffee, some eggs. I took those things, too. Of the bacon, I mean, I took the heel, that had the string hitched onto it. There was a sharp butcher's knife on the table to do the carving. Then I borrowed a coffee pot, too, an iron fork, and some salt. With these things I could make out.

On the table, I left behind me a five dollar gold piece. It paid for everything twice over, and I figured that a woman who could cook that well would have a good heart.

If she got her pay, she wouldn't be apt to talk too much, even if a posse came around that neck of the woods asking a flock of questions.

On the way back, the dog didn't bother me. I managed to get on Brindle even with my arms full, and, as I rode back to the woods, I ate that pie. It was prime. It was about the best pie I ever ate since I was a boy.

Slip Garvey was asleep and snoring. I hugged myself for warmth and propped my back against a tree trunk, and woke up a minute later to find the gray dawn in the sky, myself about two thirds frozen, and Slip still snoring, with his mouth open. He didn't look so pretty. There was a smear of blood over one side of his face that I hadn't noticed by match light the evening before.

I made a fire as small as possible, but without much real fear of detection, because there was a streaking of morning mist silver through the woods and beyond the trees I could see it in bright pools filling the hollows. That would cover the smoke of the fire.

So I started a second fire. Two small fires do almost twice the work of one big one, for cookery, and make a quarter of the smoke. On one fire, I started the coffee pot, filling it with water from a runlet that was talking about itself while it ran down the hillside. Over the other fire, I toasted bacon on the end of the iron fork. I sliced the white bread, and set it on sidewise near the flames to toast also. The eggs I buried in hot ashes and let them roast. And by the time Slip woke up, everything was ready, everything except the last of the bacon, I mean.

That boy seemed to have nothing the matter with him except a hollow leg. I never saw anybody eat so. I've told you what I brought, and now I tell you that Slip ate every scrap of it! I had a sip or two of coffee, but he fed his face with everything else, and then made a cigarette and settled down to the smoking of a cigarette, his eyes closed.

He hadn't said any more than a wild wolf would have done under similar circumstances, but when the cigarette was about finished, he opened his eyes suddenly and said:

"What did *you* eat?"

"Fresh air," I told him.

"Go on!" said he.

"Yeah," said I. "I got indigestion. I only eat on Fridays and Sundays, and mighty sparing on those days, at that!"

He grinned a little at me, but wiped the grin out to say he was sorry he had been such a pig. He didn't need to apologize and I told him so. My main job was to get strength back into the long, loose hulk of him. Then he could go ahead and finish off his own ride by himself.

He wanted to start at once. He felt full of ginger and said that he had eaten enough to put back all of the blood that he had lost. That was nearly true. I felt his forehead. It was cool, and his pulse was fairly strong and very steady, only a little slow. However, I made him stay flat until noon. That meal would have to digest before it would do him any real good.

About noon, however, I brought up some water, sat him up and let him wash his face, which is a great bracer when you're down and out. He had slept the entire morning away, so that it was plain he lacked rest as much as he lacked the blood he had lost.

By this time, he seemed in very fair shape. Of course he had an inflamed side, and it pinched him a good deal when he got to his feet, but with my help he got into the saddle, and we rode off together.

I kept to the woods, all the time, until it occurred to me that posses would be looking for one man, not for two together. So then we went into the open, and took obscure trails. If we were seen from a distance, it didn't so much matter. We'd be spotted as volunteer hunters for the escaped criminal.

There were plenty of them around. I think we saw forty or fifty horsemen, from time to time, every one with a rifle balanced across the pommel of the saddle. No doubt there was a reward out for the apprehension of Slip Garvey.

But nobody came near enough to draw any sparks from us, and by the middle of the afternoon, we were climbing through the higher foothills, and making tracks for the upper mountains.

This was a region where Slip seemed pretty much at home, and I asked him if he felt well enough to go on by himself. He said that he did. He said that he never felt better in his life, really, except for the pinch in his side, now and then, but when I looked under the shadow of his sombrero, I saw that his face was gaunt and white. He was one of the game kind who take their poison and don't cry for help. I liked that kid better and better. I liked him all the more because he wasn't running over with gratitude, all of the time.

When I saw that he was so far gone, I decided that I'd have to go on with him a little distance, at least, and come within hail of one of the Townsend places. The kid said that there were several small ranches which Townsend subsidized and where he'd be perfectly safe and well taken care of.

So we aimed for the first of these, and made it. It was a good thing for me, when I saw that shack, and when I got the kid to it, because he was wobbling in the saddle, already.

I dismounted and was helping Slip down from the saddle, when the door of the shack opened, and out came three men. I only saw the first one and he was enough. It was Lefty Townsend himself.

CHAPTER XXIV

You know how a terrier looks, one of the woolly kind, with nose and jaw sticking out, and not much forehead, and the eyes shining through a shag of hair? That was Townsend. I thought that I could never forget just what he was like, but I had forgotten. It jarred me plenty to see him now. The two fellows with him looked like red-faced cowpokes; I knew that they were something more than cowpokes, though, or they would not have been with Townsend so far in the mountains.

Lefty was cheerful and almost friendly. He shook hands with me and said he was glad to see me that far up; which set me wondering. A rope could hoist me higher, of course!

Then he introduced me to the other pair, as we all got Slip Garvey into the house. One was Bud Chalmers, and the other Henry Parker. They both knew Slip, and they handled him kindly, which I was glad to see.

Slip was about all in. At the doorway, he put a hand on the shoulder of Townsend and said:

"Joe Hyde got me out of the teeth of the posse from Bridgetown. He bandaged me up. Stuck with me all night. Fed me in the morning on grub he swiped for me. And then he brought me clean up here."

Townsend said:

"Oh, that's nothing. Slow Joe can do more than that, can't you, Slow?" and he laughed a little.

I didn't like that laughter. I reached into his words and didn't like any of the meanings that I could attach to them.

We got poor Slip into a bedroom upstairs, and a big, broad-faced, red-skinned woman came in and took charge of him as though she knew what she was about. She was Mrs. Townsend!

That was the queer thing about that crook. He had a wife, and he had a family of boys, too. And he raised those kids as ranchers, keeping their noses to the grindstone. Not one of them was allowed to use anything but a shotgun, people said, and they were as straight as a string, the whole bunch of them. The money that bought their lands and their cattle for them—well, that was another matter, but the kids themselves were said to be as honest as the next man.

In that ranch house, none of the sons were about. It seemed to have been taken over as temporary headquarters by Townsend, and I discovered, before long, why he and Chalmers and Henry Parker were so much at ease. From the top of the house one of the band was keeping a lookout, and on the heights all around the place there were other watchers, ready to signal, by night or by day, if suspicious characters came that way in numbers worth attention. They had let two riders through, as a matter of course. Three they probably would have stopped at once.

When we had Slip stowed in the bed, he gave me a faint grin and a weaker handshake. That was his way of thanking me. I went down with Townsend to the dining room of the house. He sent the other two away, and, without asking if I was hungry, he yelled for the cook. A nigger stuck his head through a door.

"Get some steaks in here, pronto, you son of a tar barrel!" says Townsend.

I smoked a cigarette while the cookery was hissing and rattling away in the kitchen, and I chatted with Townsend, all the while estimating chances, if it came to a showdown. But I saw that the chances were a long distance away from any escape. Suppose that I should pot Townsend, in a row, there were still his men scattered all around the house, and on every commanding point of land. And I would have to shoot my way through them.

Well, I knew my limitations. Every fellow in the Townsend gang was apt to be as good a shot as I. A lot of them would be a pile better. Townsend himself was greased lightning. And so, what was the good of making a break?

No, I was pretty well inside of a net, but I didn't dare even to sweat. I had to seem at my ease, and take things as they came; because, although I felt that I was at the end of my rope, there is always some hope tucked away in the breast of a man.

Townsend talked for a while about all sorts of things —the weather, the run on the Tolliver Bank in Springfield, where he said he was banking some money—the liar!— and a lot of other things.

He got around to my work, after a time, and said that the Tolosa deal was one of the slickest jobs he had ever heard of. I looked down at the emerald on my finger and said nothing. I only grunted, because I remembered what Marshal Werner had said and how he had spotted that stone of that ring.

I asked him, naturally, how business was. He said that he was getting tired of the game. I'll try to reproduce some of his way of talk, because it was rare. He laid back in his chair and chewed on a ragged old cigar that had been frayed in a pocket for days, it seemed. It was only a weed, but he had stuck brown cigarette papers on it, to hold the leaves together. Still they were crumbling away, and getting in his mouth, and he was always spitting them out, or taking them out of his beard with his fingers. He had on a greasy vest and an old blue cotton shirt. The elbows were out of it and showed the red flannel of his underwear, and that same suit had been worn so long that at the elbows the red was turning black, and slick. He had on plain jeans, very wrinkled about the knees. The only thing decent about him was a pair of fine riding boots, the best shop-made stuff, supple and easy, and a pair of beautiful spoon-handled spurs on the heels of them.

There was no reason why he should have dressed like the commonest kind of a tramp, except that he was so plain ornery, and mean, and lazy, and dirty by nature. Besides, I think that he liked to pull a big roll of bills out of his vest pocket, and play the tramp millionaire.

I must say that I hated the sight of him, and yet he interested me, the way strange animals interest you in the zoo. But there, you have 'em behind bars.

Townsend said:

"No, things ain't going so well. The trouble with my business, Slow, I don't mind tellin' you. I'm over-extended. I've reached out too far. I've got my fingers in too many pies. That's what the trouble. I've built up too much overhead. And by God, I'm gunna cut it down!"

You'd think that he was running an honest, legitimate business, to hear him talk. He got all heated and excited about it, that man-eater. Just then Mrs. Townsend came in, and she heard the last sentence.

She said:

"Ain't I been telling you for years that you been running too big a show? Didn't I tell you so?"

"Shut up," said Townsend. "How's the kid?"

"Sound asleep," said she. "And I come down to pour coffee for the boy."

She give me what was meant for a kindly smile, but it was only wrinkles on that hard pan of hers.

"And don't you start tryin' to shut me up, young feller," says she to her husband. "You can talk big other places, but you pipe down, when you're around me."

He laid his hands behind his matted head of hair, and clasped his soiled fingers, and looked at her, and turned the cigar in his mouth with a sound like the rustling of dead leaves, it was so frayed. It seemed from the blank look of his eyes that he was wondering whether he ought to cut her throat, or not. It made me cold to see the way that his eyes turned hard and flat as he watched her. But she didn't care. She breezed right along. She sat down and banged on the table.

"You said you're gunna cut down, and you are!" says she. "I told you before that you was gunna cut down, and now the time has come! Overhead. That's what's eatin' our hearts out! Look at the balance last month, when we're all in the red, an—"

"You keep your face closed!" says he.

She banged on the table again.

The nigger poked a scared head through the door.

"Callin' me, Ma'am?" says he.

"Yeah. I'm callin' you," says she. "Rustle up that food, you good for nothin' black lump of coal dust. The next time I catch that stove without a fire inside of it, I'll feed *you* into the fire box!"

The nigger had disappeared before she finished speaking. He was so scared that he was gray, as though ashes had been dusted over the ebony.

"What we want," says the woman, "is more boys that are worth their feed. Am I right, Pa?"

"You're absolutely right, Ma," says he.

He didn't seem to mind the way she horned into the business.

"We want," says she, "boys that can go out and take care of themselves, not soft lumps like that kid upstairs that has to ask for help along the road, even when he's coming back with empty hands. Am I right, Pa?"

"You're absolutely right, Ma," says he.

"What we want," says she, "is more boys like you, Slow Joe!"

That paralyzed all my nerve centers at one jab, just as the wasp had done to the tarantula. Luckily, whatever was in my face was covered up by the nigger. He kicked the door open, just then, and came in piled up to the chin with food.

He dealt it out to me, and it was a good hand. They certainly ate, in the Townsend camps. There were a couple of steaks that made even me feel like letting out my belt right at the start, and there was fried hominy, and molasses, and roasted potatoes, black on the outside and mighty fine inside. Then there was side dishes of chopped up meats, and, just to make me feel at home, a stack of the best tortillas a foot high, and a gallon of coffee that smelled as sweet as heaven and as bitter as hell, if you know what I mean. I surveyed that stack of chuck, and then I couldn't help grinning till my ears budged.

"You feed, up here," said I.

"Yeah," said Mrs. Townsend. "I feed my boys, no matter what else is said. I feed 'em, and I hate to throw away man-feed on young soft pups that ain't worth their salt. Am I wrong, Pa?"

"You're absolutely right, Ma," says he.

"That being the way of it," says Ma Townsend, "you lay yourself right out and tear into that chuck, because it's for the likes of you that the steers is rustled, and slaughtered, and the meat hung till it's prime. It's for you that I roast them coffee beans with my own hands, and grind it, too. Am I wrong, Pa?"

"You're absolutely right, Ma," says he.

I took a big swaller of coffee. It eased me a little—the lump that was gathering hard in my throat, I mean.

But thinking I couldn't do. It upset all of my ideas. There wasn't any doubt that the Townsends could lie, if they wanted to; but just now it certainly looked as though they would be mighty glad to add me to their list of riders, long and short.

It beat me. Fair and square, it beat me.

"Have some more of these here tortillas," says Ma Townsend. "I patted them out with my own hands."

It gagged me a little. Her hands weren't so white, at that. But I kept on eating. I've eaten tortillas in Old Mexico, too!

CHAPTER XXV

WELL, they chatted along while they watched me eat. Ma Townsend did most of the talking, as she had from the first. She painted a pretty rosy picture of the way that things could be for her "boys," as she called them.

"You can have a straight salary, or a regular commission—a split," said she.

I nodded.

"Well," said I, "how does it work out?"

"Commission basis is the only one for a self-respecting man," said Ma Townsend. "I don't cotton to the boys that work on a salary. We've had 'em with us up as high as two hundred dollars a week!"

"That's a lot of money," said I.

"Yeah. You bet it's a lot of money to get—and to pay! Am I right, Pa?"

"You're absolutely right, Ma," says he.

"And look at what becomes of the fellows that go on salary! Look at it!" says she. "There was Sam Keeper, for instance. He got a hundred and fifty bucks a week, winter and summer, rain or shine. Maybe you knew Sam?"

"I've heard about him," said I. "Sam was the fellow that killed the two Wells Fargo guards, and shot Silent Winchell in El Paso, and blew the First National safe in Stockton, wasn't he?"

"Yeah," said Ma Townsend. "There was a time when he was a handy man with a gun. He could do some nice tricks, too. But all those big jobs were before he joined us. He just sat around and pulled down his salary, and seemed to think that he'd retired from business, or something. That come from working on the salary basis. It sort of took all of the ambition out of him."

"Like a dog that's got its toes frost bitten," says Pa Townsend.

"Yeah, just the same," says she. "Takin' a salary ruined him. He run down so far that you know what become of him?"

"No, I never heard tell of that," said I. "He just sort of dropped out of sight."

"That's what he done, all right," said Mrs. Townsend, bitterly. "He just ups and drops out of sight. I'll tell you how he finished. Him, the man that he was, he got down so low that one day along comes an ornery, yaller-fever half breed of a Mexican greaser, and passes words to Sam Keeper, and beats him to the draw, and lays him out cold. It made me so mad, when I heard about that, that I wouldn't hardly let Pa go and have that greaser killed. Am I wrong, Pa?"

"You're absolutely right," said Pa Townsend. "That was a good greaser. He fought like hell, he did!"

He wagged his head. His matted, greasy hair swung about behind his ears. He wasn't pretty.

"He was a dead loss to us, that Sam Keeper," said she, "account of him laying up and losing his ambition. He didn't bring in hardly a thousand dollars cash, all the six months he was with us!"

"Eleven hundred and forty-two dollars, and some small change," said Pa Townsend, looking thoughtful at the ceiling.

"Pa's got the head for figgers," said his wife, admiringly. "He can add like chain lightning, and the sums he never forgets. Am I right, Pa?"

"You're absolutely right, Ma," said he.

"But commission is the right way," says she, full of enthusiasm. "Look what it does. It keeps a man on the go, on his toes, tryin' to get ahead, savin' his money, buildin' up a reputation for himself. There was Dogface Murphy. Dogface wasn't much to look at, but he was a man. The stage business was what he mostly understood. He stuck up some of the fattest stages in the West. It was good business for him, and good for us. Am I right, Pa?"

"You're absolutely right, Ma," said Pa Townsend.

"Dogface," says Ma Townsend, "laid up something over forty thousand dollars in two years!"

"Forty-nine thousand, eight hundred and eighty-six dollars, just even," said Pa Townsend.

"You beat me, Pa, you got such a wonderful memory," said Ma Townsend.

"What became of Dogface?" said I.

"He was gunna retire to California, one day," said Ma. "He was always talking about the Piedmont hills, which they're off of a town called Oakland, in California. A kind of a funny name for a town, ain't it?"

"You're absolutely right, Ma," said Pa, unasked, this time.

Ma's expression changed. She shook her head with a sad sigh.

"Buckshot was what done the trick," she said. "Rifles and revolvers, they never bothered him none. But buckshot was what tagged him out. He just managed to drag himself home. It was a sad day for us. We ain't had many money makers that was better than Dogface."

"He wasn't no hog," put in Pa Townsend, with a sober enthusiasm and approval. "He didn't lie around waiting for a million dollar haul. But he kept busy. Fifty dollars here, five hundred there, he didn't mind. He picked up what he could get. He kept busy all the time."

Ma banged on the table. All the dishes jumped and rattled.

"Because he loved his work! He was an artist. That's what he was," she declared. "When he was around camp, he was always mopin' and broodin' on the ground, or on the stars. Sometimes in the middle of a meal, he'd just stop eatin' and stare right in front of him. I never bothered him. I knew he was thinkin' about his work. I've seen him set like that, silent as a trance, as much as fifteen minutes.

And when he was ready to eat again, I'd give him a fresh piece of steak. He didn't care much what you put before him. Coffee might be cold or it might be hot. He didn't know the difference. He was kind of a visionary, always lookin' ahead, always seein' into the future. And that same day, sooner or later, he'd melt out of camp. I'd look in the letter box and find a letter addressed to me. Always to me. Am I right, Pa?"

"You're absolutely right, Ma," said Pa Townsend.

"He'd just say short and plain: 'Have two men and four horses waitin' for me at the crossroads eight miles east of Hackville, at three-thirty a.m. Tuesday. (signed) Dogface.' That was all. He knew that we'd never fail him. Others made smarter and bigger hauls, but we always sent Dogface our best hosses and our best men. It was a sad day for us when he faded out!"

"It was," said Pa Townsend.

"So he missed his home in Piedmont?" said I.

"Yeah. He missed it. But that money wasn't wasted. We took out a ten per cent commission, and we sent every penny of the rest of the coin to a young half brother of his."

"It's good business, to be square," remarked Pa, in explanation. "When you're doin' business on our scale, what I mean."

"That money didn't do the kid no good," said Ma. "We kept track of him. We sort of thought that he might fit into the place of Dogface, one day. But he goes and blows most of his dough on the ponies, and then one night he goes out with some friends in a sailboat in San Francisco bay, and the boat turns over, and the funny thing is that the kid is the only one that don't make it back to land."

Pa Townsend shook his head.

"Yeah. There's some dirty tricks played in this little old world of ours!" said he. Then he turned his head brightly toward me.

"Made up your mind what your lay will be, son?" says he, very kindly. "Commission or salary?"

"Aw, I can answer that for him," says Mrs. Townsend. "Commission is the only thing that'll attract a fellow like him!"

"Listen, Townsend," said I. "A couple of your men have been to me before. They've sort of suggested that you and I might get together. I know there are advantages. You can take care of your men. You can give a fellow a hand when he needs it. You can show him to a lot of plants. But the fact is that the only way I'm at home is playing by myself! I'm sorry, but I'm made that way."

The two Townsends stared at one another. They said nothing, for a moment.

"Is that right, Slow Joe?" said Ma, at last.

"That's where I stand," said I. "The only reason I'm up here is because that kid couldn't make it all by himself. So I helped him all the way. I didn't want to pry into your secrets. I brought the kid this far because I had to."

The Townsends looked at one another again.

"You're absolutely right, Ma," said Pa, though she had made no new remark.

At that, she got up, glared at me, and walked out of the room.

"Do some fast thinking, Slow," said Townsend. "You've seen us both, now. You've looked over my plant, in part. You've spotted some of my best men. What sort of a boss would I be if I let you come and go, with all that information on you? Besides, you're an officer of the law, now!"

I was amazed that the information should have come this far.

And still I couldn't quite fit my ideas together and explain this deal. If the Townsend gang was behind the murder of Lew Ellis, why should it be willing to take me in, unless Townsend himself really trusted implicitly to the gang oath, and the well known fact that nobody had tried to quit the gang and lived long to tell the tale?

I was rather dizzy. I was badly scared, too. I gripped the edge of the table and tried to pull myself together. It was no time to weaken.

"I see how you feel, Townsend," said I. "But you see how I feel, too. As for squealing on your crowd, you know that I wouldn't do that, because I have a pretty fair reputation for playing the game on the up and up! Isn't that so?"

Townsend rolled the crackling cigar clear across his mouth.

"You're a good boy, Slow," said he. "And I'm mighty obliged for bringing back Slip Garvey to us. Not that he's much use now, but he's the kind that will grow into something, maybe! You're honest, too. I know that. But every man has got a price. And the price that some folks would pay for what you know about the outfit up here is too much for you. I couldn't trust you away from camp, son, unless I've got you salted down with the oath that we read out of the book. Everybody in this old world is for me or agin me. Which are you?"

"Are you fixed on that, Townsend?" said I.

"Yeah. Fixed."

"Then it's me or you!" I said through my teeth, and got my hand on my gun.

Townsend merely smiled at me.

"Is that the way you feel, son?" said he. "I didn't reckon you to be such a fool, Slow. Well, boys, come on in!"

Two doors opened. I didn't look around, but I heard the floor squeaking under the tread of men. I knew that my goose was cooked.

CHAPTER XXVI

THERE wasn't any argument. But Townsend made a speech. He pointed out to his men that from his way of thinking, the only safe thing was to have me bumped off right away. I'd been in the camp and seen too much, and heard too much. But there were two things against that. In the first place, I'd been a white man in bringing up the kid. In the second place, perhaps I'd change my mind. The second thing was what he counted on, and he was willing to give me three days. After that, he would see!

Well, I knew by the way he said that he would see, that at the end of three days I would get mine, quick and sure.

His boys searched me and took away every solitary thing that I had on me—guns, knife, a couple of battered old letters, everything except that cursed steel shield, which had the name of Marshal Werner scratched on the back. Just to make me solid with the boys, old Townsend passed the shield around. They cursed it and me. Chalmers urged Townsend to finish me off right now, and not run any risks of my getting away. But Townsend laughed at him.

"Where I put him, there won't be any risks," said he. "But a couple of you boys will have to be on duty, all the time."

They marched me up to the top of the house and down a long hall. At the end of the hall, they opened the door into a vacant room. I say it was a vacant room, but, as a matter of fact, there was a pallet of straw lying on the floor. That was all the furniture. There was a window about eighteen inches square. I shoved my head out of this, and looked down five hundred feet into the bottom of a creek, where the white water was foaming. When I came up to the place, I had heard a roaring like distant wind, but it hadn't occurred to me that the house was backed up against the creek so closely.

Then old Townsend fitted some irons on me, and he did a good job of it. He had quite a collection. He said—I think he lied—that those were irons which the law had affixed to his own arms and legs, from time to time. At any rate, they fitted me pretty close. And they were the best make. Even if I had had a picklock, I could have worried for a year before I undid those locks.

Townsend kept grunting, panting, rolling the crackling cigar around in his mouth while he fixed me up with those shackles. And he talked. He said:

"You see how it is, kid. It ain't for myself. Lord, man, I'd as soon trust you with an arm or a leg of my own. But it's the principle of the thing. It's the folks that I represent. What would the boys think if they knew that I turned you loose, knowin' what you know? Tell me that? They'd lose all their respect for me. I'm only sort of a president of the company," went on the old liar, "and I gotta take care whether I please the rest of the stockholders, or not. You can stay here and have a good rest. It'll do you a lot of good. When a man is restin', he thinks a lot better, you know."

He was still working away on me when Ma Townsend bellowed up from downstairs that there was a visitor to see him.

"Who is it? Let him wait a minute!" says Townsend.

"Aw, he's all right," says Ma.

And steps came lightly and rapidly up. I turned around. In the door of my room was standing Zip! Yes, sir, the long, lean, dark-skinned rascal was standing there smiling a little with his eyes. He looked at my shackles, and then he bowed and called me "sir" and hoped that I was well, and that I would enjoy a good rest in the mountain air.

Townsend broke into a great laughter.

"Ain't Zip a card?" said he. "Ain't he a regular card? Oh, he's a rare one. There ain't many that knows the ins and the outs of that lad. But I know 'em. He's a jim-dandy! Come along, Zip. Let's have a drink together!"

I turned a little sick. I mean, it was the thought of Tom Fellows living in his house with a creature like that around him, trusted, confided in. Like a snake living with an honest man. Yes, it sickened me. I couldn't speak, and they went out together.

Chalmers and another fellow I hadn't seen, a little, active-looking, black-moustached man, were left behind.

"Now, you damned turncoat," said Chalmers, "you deputy marshal, you, you've got that room, and nothing else. If you try to get through that door and make any funny plays, we ain't going to ask for explanations. We're just going to sock a slug through the crooked head of you. That's all."

And he slammed the door on me.

He left me alone, and I was so weak in the knees, that I sank down on the straw pallet. It didn't crackle under me. It was too soggy with mold. I sat there until the day turned dark, and the rats began to come out and whisk and scamper from corner to corner, getting used to the fact that I couldn't heave anything at 'em.

While I sat there, I did some thinking—as much as I could. But all that really mattered to me seemed to center down on one face. I suppose that this sounds pretty foolish, but it's the fact. I saw the face of big Tom Fellows, honest, kind, gentle, strong, fearless Tom Fellows.

Tears came stinging into my eyes. And then I remembered, when I was a kid in Kearneyville, a tall old boy with a black frock coat on him, and a high hat, and the look of a cadaver had stopped me when I was crossing the street once. And he put his cold, bony fingers under my chin, and he said:

"My son, when you go to bed at night, after you've undressed and put on your little nightgown, do you turn down the wick of the lamp, and get down on your knees beside your bed, and pray to your Maker?"

I was so rattled that I only said:

"Pray to my which, ma'am?"

"Your Maker—your Father in Heaven," says he.

I admitted that I didn't.

Then he says:

"Make Him your friend, my child. The world comes and the world goes, but God will stand by your right hand forever! He sees the evil that you do. But He can forgive. He sees the good of your deeds and of your thoughts. He understands!"

Now, I don't suppose that I had thought of that meeting for fifteen years. But now it jumped back into the middle of my brain with a splash. And I told myself, like a sentimental fool, that I was trying to do the right thing and the white thing. That I had rather die than join the gang of old Townsend. And that, after all, there was some power in the universe which knew what I was doing, and *why* I was doing it. And yet I think I would have preferred to have Tom Fellows know. He seemed just a shade bigger and finer than God Almighty, to me!

Well, along came dark, and I was hungry. From dreaming daydreams, and pitying myself, I suppose. Then, when the night was solid through the room, there comes a step and a voice says:

"I promised you three days. You'll get the three days!"

The step went away. It was the voice of old Townsend.

And while I sat there, fumbling at his meaning, I heard Chalmers, in the hallway, asking briskly, why they didn't knock me over the head, right then, and what was the good of wasting the time of two capable men to watch over a crook who was bound to pass in his checks on the third day?

Then I understood. Old man Townsend had changed his mind. It was too late for me to turn over, now. I couldn't join him if I wanted to. He had promised me a three-day wait. That was his way of discharging the Slip Garvey obligation to me. At the end of that time, I was to be put out like a light!

Good-by all of my fine ideals! I would have beaten on the door and begged, but I knew, with a cold and falling heart, that old Townsend would never be changed.

So I sat still. I fell asleep, and all of that night I saw the face of Tom Fellows through my dreams, and he seemed to be coming like a thunderbolt, breaking and smashing his way to me, and drowning that cursed house with blood, until he struck the shackles away from me, and made me a free man.

I wakened in the dawn. I was hungry and thirsty. I was shivering with the cold of the mountain air, too, and the soggy, moldy pallet had soaked me through to the skin on my right side. I wasn't wet. I was just damp, and sick.

That was the beginning.

I knocked on the door, and after a while the voice of the black-moustached fellow asked what the devil I wanted. I said that I wanted breakfast.

He laughed—like a fool—or a devil—or both. Then he said:

"Well, wait a while."

I waited till noon. There was no breakfast. Then I beat on the door again, and told the voice that answered that I knew I was not to be starved to death.

"How do you know that, you stool pigeon?" asked Chalmers.

That froze me, you can bet.

"Chalmers," I said, "if that's the way of it, I'll do with water, thanks."

"You'll do without it, damn you," said Chalmers. "If I had my way with you, I'd roasted you an inch a day. You stool pigeon!" he repeated.

There was loathing in his voice. I understood, because I had felt the same way, in my time, about fellows who turned to the shady side of the law, and made a living by the information they gave about their old pals. That was what they thought about me.

But as I sat down on the pallet again, I was not thinking so much about the death which was to end the three days. I was thinking about the days themselves, the starvation, the frightful agony of thirst!

And those three days went by. I was able to sleep, or doze, a good deal. I could feel my belly shrink and my body wither. My eyes burned, night and day, and, toward the end, my tongue began to swell badly. For the days were hot, and I was under the roof, high up.

Then, on the last morning—that evening there would be an end of my three days' imprisonment—a driving thunder shower beat in at my window.

I stood there with my shackled hands cupped. I lapped up the drops that fell on my hands, dirty as they were. My sleeves were soaking and I bit and chewed and sucked the moisture out of them. That shower lasted forty-five minutes, or so. It about saved my life. It removed the red hot band from around my forehead. It gave me back strength, and let my senses clear, so much that, that same afternoon, I could overhear the talk in the hall, between Chalmers and Ma and Pa Townsend.

CHAPTER XXVII

THEY were talking about when and how I should be done away with. They talked loudly. Of course, it didn't matter if I overheard them. Ma says:

"His time's up. Get him out and finish him. Dump him into the creek. It'll bury him for you."

She laughed. I've known a lot of bad women, but Ma Townsend was the hardest of the lot. She was the only thing in skirts that I would have killed as I'd kill a wild beast.

Pa Townsend said:

"Look here, Ma. He oughta be made an example of."

"Yeah, maybe he should," said she. "And if you're going to make an example of him, you ought to have some of the boys around, to see. Am I right?"

"You're absolutely right," said Pa.

"Tell me just what he done?" asked Chalmers.

"Son," said Ma Townsend, "it ain't hardly fitting that anybody should know what a skunk that feller is. It really ain't. It would make a fine, upstandin', self-respectin' fellow like you feel kind of ashamed of just bein' a man, I tell you."

"Stool pigeon, ain't he?" asked Chalmers.

"Stool pigeon?" said Ma Townsend. "He's a dirty, sneakin', poisonin', rotten spy, is what he is. Am I right, Pa?"

"You're absolutely right, Ma," said Townsend.

"Then call some of the boys together, and take him out now," said Ma.

"Wait a minute," said Townsend.

His step came rather shuffling to my door. He calls:

"Hey, there—Slow Joe."

I had an inspiration. I bent my head far back, opened my mouth wide, and uttered a sort of dry, whistling moan, that had some semblance of syllabification in it.

The devil on the other side of the door laughed.

"Listen to that!" said he. "That's what he's getting. Hell! What's fire, compared to this? No, no, Ma! Let him enjoy a few more hours of that. Then we'll take him out, tonight. We want to get some of the boys together, to let 'em see what we do to a spy and a traitor, in this gang!"

"Well," said Ma Townsend, "it'll look better at night, too. You can have some torches, and a bonfire to light things up. I wish he wasn't such a runt. He don't look like nobody at all!"

"He's got a pretty good name, though," argued Townsend. "He ain't any world-beater, but he's pretty well known. Yeah, it'll mean a good deal to the boys to see Slow Joe popped off."

"It's the first time that a killing like this was ever made a real ceremony," said Ma. "It'll be good for some of the younger kids to see what happens to the backsliders, won't it?"

"You're absolutely right," said he.

I heard them talk some more to Chalmers. The three of them were all of accord, finally, that the job should be done shortly after dark.

And I started walking up and down my room, not really because I was so very nervous, as because I wanted the movement and the clanking of the irons to hypnotize me, and keep me from thinking. That, I knew, was what would do me in.

My room looked north, but, when the sunset came, I saw that even the northern horizon was flooded with rosy light, and the mountains looked as big as half the world and as blue as heaven. I had been through those very mountains, and cursed the cold and the wind of them!

The day darkened; the color went out. I listened to the pounding of hoofs up and down the road, and there were always footfalls thundering and creaking on the stairs. The twilight came on.

And it was through the twilight that I heard the song come. I must say that that stopped my heart, with horror. They could make a ceremony out of my murder. They could make me an object lesson, and all that, and I thought that I could try to stand up in front of them and take my final dose of medicine. But singing? Why, it sounded as though they were making a regular festival out of my finish!

I listened to the song. It ended. It was in Spanish, and I was too horrified and dull-witted to make much out of it, except the high sweet thrill of the singer's voice, like the voice of a girl, or a young boy. Afterward, I heard a patter of handclapping, and then some shouts. This was the first number, I guessed. I was to come on as the main attraction!

Apparently an encore was wanted, and the voice started again, in Spanish still. I followed the drift of the song, this time. It was one of those long-drawn-out, wailing love songs that Mexicans love. It told about a pair of lovers who were separated, and the girl was shut up by her cruel father. You know that kind of a thing. They're all the same. And then the man is talking, and he's saying to the girl that no matter where she is, he'll come to her, he'll come to her, with the darkness he'll come to her!

And so that song goes along, and there's a thrill and a rise in the voice of the singer that stops me, a little. And then, suddenly, it snatches me back to Doloroso's room in San Whiskey.

That's the place—and that's the voice—and it's Al Doloroso, Al of San Whiskey, who's out there somewhere near the house, and singing to me that she'll come to me, with the dark! By thunder, it made all the blood shoot to my brain and explode there, like flashes of lightning.

Well, she would be too late, of course. There was no way she could reach my room, and, even if she got there, there was no way she could help me out of the house, even if her magic touch managed to undo the locks of my shackles.

She didn't know, poor kid, that I was bound to step West when the darkness was fully settled! And there she was, out in the front of the house, singing her way into the good-nature of those wolves!

They called for another song, and another. But, somehow, they were always love songs, and somehow they always swore that the singer would come for the beloved—

Well, I knew that I was not the "beloved," but it was just a poetic way of naming her partner for the moment, and of telling me that, somehow or other, she would try to manage to break through to me, as soon as she got a chance to break away from the others.

Then, looking out the window, I saw a steady, bright eye looking in upon me. It was one of the stars of the Great Dipper, and I knew that the complete night had begun. A little more, and they would come tramping up the stairs, and more loudly down the hallway. They would tear my door open, and call for me, and drag me out—

I got that far in my thinking, each time, and then something went wrong with me each time, so that I had to go back to the beginning and start all over again.

But reality blots out all the thinking in the world, unless it's some early Christian martyr who's doing the thinking; and I'm not in that class, quite.

Up the stairs comes the very tread that I've been waiting for, and down the hall it marches, and I hear a couple of the boys sing out that they want me.

"Well," says the voice of Chalmers, "he can hear you saying it, I guess. Unless he's nutty, by now. The last sound out of him was pretty thick. Maybe the old man has gone and pulled this too fine, and Slow Joe won't know what's happening to him when the time comes to bump him off."

A big, coarse, brawling laughter answered that.

"The way he's gunna be bumped off will bring him to."

"How's he gunna be bumped off?" says Chalmers.

"Like this," says the other.

His voice lowered. I strained my ears, but I could only make out one word—"fire—"

It was enough.

Even Chalmers busts out:

"My God, are they gunna do that?"

"Why not?" roars the fellow with the big voice. "Don't he deserve it, the sneak?"

"Yeah—maybe—" says Chalmers. "Sure he deserves it! And be damned to him! Only, it kind of made my flesh creep, for a minute."

"You're young, kid," says the other. "You'll get used to worse than that before you're through with your stay with Townsend."

Outside I heard a faint scratching sound—just outside my window, and then the red-head of Al of San Whiskey showed above the sill. I gave her my hands to pull her in. Then I stopped myself.

"You God blessed brick-top," I whispered to her, "it's almost worth dying to see that thatch of yours, all on fire. But you're too late, kid. They've come for me now. Go back. If they caught you here with me, they'd fix you the way they're going to fix me—or worse!"

"Shut up!" says Al, and wriggles through the window like a snake. Behind her, she pulls in a length of thin twine, and gives it a tie around her arm.

Then she starts working on the manacles that weight down my wrists. She's whispering something. I won't repeat what. It was in Spanish, anyway, so I only partly got the drift of it, but it made me feel mighty queer.

The wrist shackles suddenly came away into her hands. Those on my ankles are still holding when a hand bangs on my door.

"Well?" I call.

"Are you well?" says Chalmers, outside of the door. "You won't be so well, pretty soon. We're ready for you, Slow Joe. Are you ready for us?"

"About half ready," says I, as the girl shoves a big, man-sized Colt into my hand.

"Well," says Chalmers, "if you're so ready for us, wait a while at the station, will you?"

And they roar, all of them that are in the hallway.

A moment later Al Doloroso, at my feet, brings the ankle irons softly away.

I faced the door, while she hauled up on the length of twine, giving a harder and harder pull. And while I faced that door a very odd thing happened to me. I felt cool, and light, and calm as a bird in the air that can fly out of range of the hunter and watch him, and laugh at him. Only, I began to hope and pray that Chalmers or one of the others would push the door open, so that I could turn loose with that Colt.

It was a beauty, fixed the way I liked a gun, in those days—a hair-trigger with the hammer resting on an empty chamber. But there were five shots left, and I swore that I would shoot carefully, and make every bullet mean a life. I thought there were four men in that hall. I promised myself all of them. I prayed to get them all!

Then I saw Al pulling in the end of a rope.

CHAPTER XXVIII

THE end of that rope she tied about the middle of the pallet. And she motioned me out the window. I waved her ahead, to go first, and when she danced up and down, silent, shaking her head, I just grabbed her and shoved her through, feet foremost.

"Hurry after, Slow!" she whispers, and down the rope she goes.

I waited until there was slack on the end of the rope, and the pallet no longer hugged the window so hard, bulging through in the center. Then it was my turn, and a mighty hard fit I had of it, getting through the opening.

I was still there with my legs spraddling into the outside air, and my shoulders stuck, when the steps come down the hall again, and there was a hand banging on the door.

I said nothing, in answer, but squeezed my shoulders through.

"Hey, Slow Joe!" called the voice.

I wound my legs and arms into the rope and started to go down, easing myself, because I knew that I had a long journey, and it would be easy to burn the flesh off my hands to the bone. So down I went, and as I passed, I heard the hand bang on the door again.

Well, it was a matter of mere seconds, now, before I would be on the ground. Not out of danger, God knows, but with a half of a tenth of a fighting chance to get away —once I could put horse flesh between my knees.

God bless the darkness. They had wanted it to make their show better, and now it might be the saving of my hide!

I struck the first knot, the second, the third, where lariat after lariat had been tied together, and then a yank came above me, and another yank, making the rope swing.

They had come into the room and found me gone!

I doubled my speed downward, then, you had better believe. And then—zing! I dropped like a rocket. They had cut the rope away!

I told myself that it would be the hard bottom of the creek that would get me, after all. And then my feet hit firm ground, my knees buckled till I was squatting, pitching slowly backward into nothing.

The hands of Al grabbed me and hauled me back to the ledge that ran between the house and the wall of the ravine. Up above us, we could hear curses streaming like smoke.

"This way—fast!" says Al, and streaks before me like a rabbit.

I went after her. I remember that I couldn't run, really. I could only gallop, my leg muscles were so done up with the weakness of starvation, and the lack of any exercise for the three days.

Down through the house, I could hear the shouting run, as the alarm was spreading, and the thunder of the feet racing to get to the ground level.

Then I saw Al before me, again, and two horses held

on lead-ropes. One was a long-legged speedster. One was old Brindle. I knew his pot-bellied outline mighty well, let me tell you. And it never looked so good to me as right then! For he was your horse for darkness, and rough trails.

"Let's go, Al!" I gasped, as I tumbled, winded, into the saddle.

"Not yet. The other nags—we've got to turn 'em loose!" says Al.

And she leads the way at a gallop, on her horse, around the side of the barn. There was the corral, filled with the shadows of twenty or thirty horses. The Townsend men, as they came in, had naturally put up their nags. And a fine lot they were, grazing there in the big corral-pasture.

We could hear voices roaring outside of the house, and lights began to swing and dance, as we reached the far side of the corral and began to let down bars.

I heard one voice above the rest.

"Mind the hosses! Get to the barn, some of you blind rats!'

That was Townsend, putting his finger at once on the sore spot, as you might say. But Al and I were on our horses again, and rounding in behind the bunch of nags in that corral. Those horses didn't have to be coaxed. They smelled the freedom of the open range, and they exploded toward it like nitroglycerine. There was one outbreak of squealing, one rush of thundering hoofs, and out they spilled through the night and toward the open beyond. Those unfenced fields, they would be sweeping over them like water running down hill. And how long would it take men on foot to recapture them?

I blessed Al again, in my heart, as I never had blessed any human being, not even my own mother. She'd given me my second life, and she secured it by this forethoughtedness in routing the horses before we slid back toward the lowlands.

And that was where we started. She had to pull her arms out, keeping her horse back to old Brindle, as we galloped and put five hard miles behind us.

By that time, we were through the dark headlands where

the outposts of the Townsend gang might be waiting, on the outlook.

After that, I shouted, and we came back to a moderate gait. We had plenty more mileage to put behind us, after all, and there was no sense in burning our horses to a crisp before we got home.

Home?

Well, home was the lesser hell of Kearneyville—only lesser when compared with Townsend's place.

Now that we were dog-trotting, the horses at ease, I started to talk to the girl.

"Where'd you get the idea, Al?" I said.

"Me? Oh, nowhere," said she. And she yawned. "I'm mighty sleepy," she said.

"You been going ever since you left Kearneyville, you worthless little liar, you," says I.

"Yeah. All the time," says she.

"You didn't leave at all?" says I.

"I thought I'd get a slow start to make a fast finish," says she.

I wished, mightily, that I could see her sassy face through the darkness. There was no hope of that. I just rode along and sort of ate up the idea of her.

"Go on, Al," says I. "After this, I stop giving orders. You can be the boss."

"When you didn't show up at the hotel that night," says she, "I picked up the trail of your horse—"

"Trail of old Brindle? How could you do that?"

"Aw, you know that he steps short with his right hind foot, now and then, and digs the toe into the ground?"

"No, I never knew that," I confessed.

"Well, he does. And I just happened to notice it. I followed him out to the forking of the roads, where you'd been, and then up the Davis road, and alongside of it, coming back. I found the blood on the ground. That was where the man from Bridgetown had been, I guess?"

"Yeah. That was the place," said I.

"Well, I went on. I ranged the country. I found where you'd bedded down in the woods. I found your trail streaking up this way. After you got into the open, it was pretty easy. Uphill, old Brindle sticks his right hind foot in pretty frequent, you know!"

I said that I knew, all right, since she told me, but I bet my socks that nobody else in the world would ever have spotted the trail. She merely said:

"So I came along here, and turned myself into a greaser minstrel, as you'd call it."

Suddenly, my mind jumped all that had passed between. She didn't need to explain any further, about how she'd pulled the wool over the eyes of the Townsend tribe, or how she had spotted the exact room in which I was lodged. If she could follow me that far, of course she could find just where I was holing up.

I said: "Al, I won't thank you."

"Don't you do it," says she. "I couldn't hardly stand that."

"But tell me," says I, "where your old man got the red hair?"

"There's red-headed greasers, you know," says she. "I've seen plenty of 'em."

"I've only seen a couple," says I. "Where'd he get it from?"

"I dunno. From his Scotch dad, I guess," says she.

"Was his father Scotch?" I shouted, with the dawn of a new idea breaking in my mind.

She pulled up her horse, short.

"Does that make a lot of difference to you?" says she.

"All the difference in the world!" says I.

"I wouldn't hardly be good enough to ride alongside of you, if I was straight greaser, would I?" said she.

"Don't put it that way," says I.

"What way you want me to put it?" fires up Al. "You make me tired. You make me sick! I ain't a human being, hardly, so long as I'm a Mexican, but once you find that I'm crossed with the holy Scotch strain, it makes a lot of difference. It pretty near makes me able to get into the same church with you. I'm pretty near good enough to dust your boots, ain't I? Well, your boots can be damned, and you inside of them!"

"Hold on, Al," says I. I reached out and caught her arm. "I didn't mean it that way," I told her.

"I don't care what you meant!" says Al. "I'm sick of you. I wished that the night would never end, if it'd mean that I'd never seen your crooked face again, you yegg! You cheap skate! You leather-skinned, stupid four-flusher! How did I ever get tied to *you,* anyway?"

"You never got tied to me," says I, pretty sober, now, so sober that I clean forgot to be happy for what I had escaped from, that night. "You're as free as the air to beat it away from me. Only, Al, I wish that you'd listen to me. Because I owe you—"

"You don't owe me nothing!" breaks out Al. "It's me that owes everything to you. Except for you, I'd still be back there in that hell-hole of a San Whiskey, and well I know it. You gave me the taste of something else. I never would have known the low heart that was in my father, except for you. You rooted me out. I know that—but I hate your heart, Slow Joe. That's what I do! I hate your poison heart—you gringo!"

It made me pretty hot. It made me so hot that I saw red, and was blind. I was about to say something mean. I was picking around in my mind for something hard to say, when I heard her bust into a sob.

There she was, doubled up in the saddle, sobbing fit to kill.

I didn't know what to say. I remembered somebody had once said to me:

"Never argue with a woman."

So, finally, I just gathered in the reins of her high-stepper, and I led that horse along, and we walked down through the black of the lower foothills, never speaking a word.

CHAPTER XXIX

THROUGH the night and into the dawn we rode with hardly three words from Al. Five times I stopped at water and drank, each time a little more. But the thirst that was built up in me was so great that I never dared to let myself loose and take as much as I wanted. However, by the time I got near to Fellows' house, it was not thirst but hunger that I was thinking of. It was funny to see how I had wasted. I had no stomach at all. My belt was in the last notch, and flopping loose. I could feel the pinch of my cheeks against my back teeth; my mouth was all puckered up. By dawn light I saw myself in the last pool of clear water that I drank from, and I looked like an old man.

Al was asleep most of the way. She was so used to the saddle that she had an instinctive sense of balance. She would reel just so far to one side or the other and then wake up, and begin to nod all over again. If I had tried it, I would have fallen on my head.

When the sun was almost up, she gave herself one shake, and the sleep was out of her. So were all bad memories of the night, it appeared. Suddenly she was as fresh as a daisy.

"Where are we driving, Slow?" said she.

It was pretty good to have her with me, again.

"Fellows," said I.

"Why Fellows?" said she.

I looked hard at her.

"Why God, then?" said I.

"Is he as much as all of that?" said she.

"He starts where the others stop," said I.

She looked doubtful, but after a moment she nodded at me.

"He's a big one," she admitted. "You think that he can mate Lefty?"

"Yeah. And checkmate him," said I. "His job was pretty hard when he and I were both in the dark, simply *guessing* that Lefty was behind the game, but not sure. Now that we know Lefty is the man—well, something is apt to happen to Townsend, one of these days."

Now I told her in detail all that had happened to me since I left Kearneyville. She had already guessed at a good part of it, through the accuracy of her trailing, but she seemed pleased to hear all the story. When I got through, however, she rather stumped me. She said:

"Look here, Slow."

"Well?" said I. "What's in the little old think-machine, now?"

"Dynamite," said she.

"Go on. Turn it loose."

"It'll blow you out of the saddle," said she.

"I'll risk it."

"Townsend's not the man behind the deal. He's not the fellow who sent Gregor and Peyton to San Whiskey after Ellis."

That was a sock, and a hard one, all right.

"Where do you get that idea?" said I.

"It's nursery stuff," she answered. "Townsend's a hog. A money hog, too. Do you think he would have hesitated, once he had his hands on you? D'you think he would have offered you a job? Not at all! If he's the fellow they've hired to bump off the heirs of the rich man, they're offering him a big slice of cash. He'd knock you over the head and rake you in, and the reward afterward. That's simple."

It seemed so, but I shook my head. I argued aloud, this way:

"You put it right when you said Townsend was a hog. He had me, and that meant the reward, but he figured that he might be able to collect some hing more, out of my natural talents as a crook." I grinned. "He didn't know that I'm going straight, from now on!"

"Are you?" said the kid, gaping at me.

"Leave that alone," said I, annoyed that I'd spoken my mind so far as that. "Anyway, Townsend thinks that he can join me to the gang, let me work for him a while, and then poke me over. He collects my earnings, as he calls 'em, and he also collects the reward. Besides, look at some of the other things. Townsend is big enough to make the whole Peyton and Willow outfits dance for him, let alone one from each bunch. He's a czar, so he shows his power by taking one of each for the job. Look at another thing. Gregor and Peyton are paid in stolen stuff. You know that. Who's so apt to pay with stolen stuff as Townsend? Why, Gregor and Peyton would have refused that sort of pay from anybody else, but from Townsend they take it because they half expect to get it just that way. Isn't that clear?"

She turned her bright, clear eye on me. There wasn't a line in her face to show that she'd been through almost as much hell as me. A kid can take a sock and recuperate pretty fast.

"Putting it that way, it sounds pretty clear," said she. "Now, where does Zip come into the picture? You saw him at Townsend's."

"That's what I'm going to find out," said I. "That's one reason that I'm streaking it for Fellows' house. Tom has to be warned. Everybody's known that Zip is a bad egg. Tom's too good-natured to believe it, but this time I have the proof. Zip is simply Townsend's spy in Fellows' house. That's all. At least, that's the beginning of him!"

"Well, you may be right," said the girl, "only—"

But she let her mind wander from what she was saying. She threw out her hand toward the countryside and began to sing a song about May mornings.

I must say that everything looked pretty slick, with the dew drenching the grass, and the leaves of the shrubs, and all the trees wearing a halo of rosy, reflected light. She shut down the piping when we got close to the Fellows place.

I didn't want to ride right in, because, of course, when

Zip saw me, he was pretty apt to run for it. So we left the horses at a distance and walked in.

When we got to the entrance of the patio, we heard the stamping of feet, and the clashing of steel. When we pushed the door open, we could hear panting breath drawn, and a scraping and sliding about as though men were having a desperate battle.

Still in the dark throat of the passage, we could look into the patio, at last, and there we saw a thing worth seeing, believe me. For there were Zip and Fellows stripped to the waist, bare-footed, and fighting like two devils with machetes.

You know that in Cuba and Mexico, particularly, they have a system of machete play almost as complicated and scientific as rapier fencing. And this pair seemed experts. They went at one another so savagely, in the rose of the morning light, that I was certain that they meant it, in the beginning.

Then I saw that most of their strokes were for the body, and, next, that the edges of the blades were rounded and dull. They were simply having a little practice set-to.

But it was a savage looking go. That Zip was a brown snake, darting here and there, sure-footed, flashing as fast as his swinging, leaping blade. He was all over the place at once, and the long, lean, twisting muscles in his right arm seemed tireless.

However, when you looked away from him to Fellows, you saw that he had met his master. I was telling you, before, that Fellows was big and famous all through our country for strength, but I never had seen him stripped as far as the waist before, and I was amazed. I thought I was prepared for anything, but not quite for this. Ordinarily, his face was a clear color, but rather pale. His body, on the other hand, was like bronze. It had been burned so deep that the color would never change, very much. People who spend a lot of time on the beaches get the same tint, all over! His color wasn't the most surprising part, though. He was as smooth as a stone, and, when he moved, ripples of light went over him. All his strength was under the skin. There was nothing standing out, nothing big and bulging. He was sleek, supple, and so fast that he made the other seem to be standing still. Yes, Zip seemed to be dancing up and down in one spot while a great brown panther glided in and out around him.

After a moment, it was plain that Fellows could have had Zip's head any time that he wanted it; but he didn't want it, of course. And, while Zip fought furiously, with a demoniacal look in his face, Fellows was perfectly at ease, smiling a little, only taking a great heaving breath, now and again. There was no mockery in his smile. It was just the look of a man having a good work-out, and without any malice behind his skill.

But what skill!

Al grabbed my arm and clung to me. Down through the dark of the passage I looked at her, and saw her eyes wide, and glowing with wonder. Well, she probably had seen machete play before, enough to appreciate this, and it was plain that she never had seen the parallel of this before.

She kept catching her breathing, until finally, by a maneuver so lightning fast that I couldn't begin to follow it, Fellows stepped in, whacked the machete out of the tiring hand of Zip, caught it by the blade as it whirled in the air, and handed it back to him, handle first. Zip, with a snarl, dashed the thing down on the bricks of the patio. But Fellows patted him on the shoulder.

"You press too hard, Zip," said he. "Take it more easily. Let the other fellow come into you. Try fewer leads and more counters. Then there's that undercut I was showing you. It's a beautiful stroke, and you didn't try it a single time, today. But you're coming on, Zip. The next time you need to use anything, from a machete to a cutlass, you'll carve the ears off the other fellow."

"Hai!" said Zip, with a look of joy. "D'you think that, d'you think that?"

"Theenk" was the way he pronounced it.

"Of course I think it," said Fellows. "When you cornered me, over there, you almost had me, but you were too eager. You slipped a little, and that spoiled the next stroke."

"Ay," said Zip. "But you—but you—"

He made a slow gesture, his hand going up, and out, and out. He seemed to be indicating a giant—and that, as matter of fact, was what Fellows seemed to me. He was big enough and strong enough to be formidable anyway; but, equipped with this uncanny speed, why, he was superhuman!

"We'll go down and take a plunge in the pool," said Fellows.

"Too cold!" said Zip, with a shudder. "I bring a bucket of hot water from the kitchen—"

"Stuff," said Fellows. "No water is very cold, once you've dived into it, like a man."

I believed it, looking at that sleek body of his. I remember seeing a fresh-caught mackerel, once, the most trim and lovely thing, for lines, that I ever have looked at. One felt that a single flip of its tail would shoot it fifty yards through the water. And Fellows, for all the size of him, looked just about as agile, and slippery, and swift.

But now I stepped out into the light of the patio, softly. I had a gun in my hand.

"Zip," said I, "you'd better wait a minute, before you take that plunge!"

CHAPTER XXX

THAT was a good moment, a fat moment for me. There was nobody else on the stage, except me. I was playing the main rôle, and, with Fellows there to watch, I must say that I liked the job. I tried to take it easy, look nonchalant, but I was fair quivering with excitement.

Fellows himself seemed half ready to drop. He actually gaped at me, steel nerved as he was.

"What the devil is the matter, man?" he said. "Don't point that gun at Zip! Are you mad, Slow? You're sick—you *look* sick!"

"How does Zip look?" I snapped back.

Green, that was how Mr. Zip appeared, just then. Kind of a dull green, the sort that gathers on old bronze, slowly. His thin upper lip was writhing. One could see his teeth to the pink of the gums. The sun was up. A bright rim of light appeared along the western top of the patio square. After a single look at Zip, Fellows said:

"What is it, Slow? God knows I'm glad to see you back. When you faded out—well, I thought for a time that it was the finish! What's happened?"

"Ask Zip," said I. "That trusty Zip of yours can tell you where I've been."

"Zip," said Fellows, "what's all this?"

Zip still stared at me, his mouth working. But he didn't answer.

"You must be wrong, Slow," protested Fellows. "I've had old Zip out everywhere. He's spent all of every day searching for you."

"Yes. I saw him three days ago," said I. "And he saw me!"

"Where, in heaven's name?" asked Fellows.

"At Townsend's place!" said I.

That was a ten-stroke! It fetched even Fellows, through all his calm and poise.

"Townsend's!" he muttered.

He looked from me to Zip as though still he expected the scoundrel to make an answer.

I went right on, planting my shots.

"Yes," said I, "we've all known—all the rest of your friends, Tom—that this one is a bad egg. We've always seen it in his face."

"Slow," said Fellows, "I've owed my life to Zip."

He said it solemnly. Well, it was a solemn thing to say!

"Sure," said I, quickly, "and you'll owe your death to him, too, one of these days. Damn it, Tom," I went on, seeing ahead of me with a flash of inspiration, "all that you are to him, you and your place here, is a blind, out of which he works at his real business, and that's Townsend's business, too. Through Zip, Townsend has you in the hollow of his hand. Townsend crooks his little finger, and the next day, the world walks in and sees Tom Fellows in his bed, his throat cut from ear to ear. And no Mr. Zip around! Tom, don't you see the play? Don't you see how simple and clear it all is?"

I never saw a sadder face than Fellows', as he turned to Zip. Once more he laid his hand on that brown shoulder.

"Zip," he said, "tell me that it's not true. You haven't been seen at Townsend's! You haven't seen Slow Joe Hyde there and failed to tell me?"

"Bah!" said Zip.

He said it for me. All his heart was in his voice. He could have cursed me for an hour solid and never said so much.

So I explained a little.

"I picked up, three or four nights ago, a poor poke who was down and out. Plugged in Bridgetown. He belonged to Townsend, and he was so all in that I had to take him up there. Townsend is our man, all right. He's behind the Ellis play. He's the one who'll get you, Tom, if he can. But he thought that I was such a fool that I'd work for him, too. I held out on that. I could have lied, and then run when I had rope enough. But the idea of taking the damned oath gagged me. I held out a little. Townsend slammed me into starvation confinement, and before I could holler for help, along comes Zip, gives me a smile, and apparently tells Townsend enough to settle me. Lefty gives me three days to starve and think things over. Then he's to have my head. I suppose Zip, here, had listened to you and me talking, so that he knew we suspected Townsend of the Ellis play. At any rate, I never got a chance to change my mind about joining the gang, and I should have been where the birds are singing, or where the worms are digging, by this time, Tom, if it hadn't been for Al, here!"

I nodded toward her. The instant that my head was turned a little I saw something flash into the hand of Zip. It was a knife—a throwing knife with a little weighted handle and a blade like the light that drips off an icicle.

He didn't have a chance to heave it into me, though.

The reason was that a walking beam smashed against the side of his head and lifted him off his feet and slammed him hard against the wall. It was a steel-headed walking beam, and I wondered that the head of Zip didn't cave in like an eggshell, because the beam was the fist of Tom Fellows, and the power came out of his mighty body, from the toes to the driving shoulder.

I never saw such a punch. I mean, it literally flung Zip against the side of the house!

There was no question of him getting up at once. But I went over to him to see if he had any more knives on him.

"The scoundrel!" said Fellows. "The black-hearted scoundrel, Slow! He would have knifed you!"

"No, he wouldn't," said Al Doloroso.

I glanced hastily back at her. She was just putting up a gun, a neat little thirty-two. She used to practice with that gun a lot, throwing apples in the air and cutting 'em in two before they dropped. You know, the chief advantage of a forty-five is that the weight of the slug drops a man, even if it doesn't kill him. But when you're as accurate as Al, a thirty-two is poison enough, believe me.

"I was waiting for the nigger to make that play," says she, as she gets the gun out of sight. "But I'm glad that you soaked him, Mr. Fellows! My, but that was a whang!"

It seemed curious to me that Fellows made no reply to this remark of hers, but he stood still and straight, with one hand lightly resting against the wall of the house, just as he had been when he was about to lean over Zip. And he looked at Al with a straight and a steady glance, full into her eyes.

And she looked back, without a waver. Something passed between them, then. To the end of my life I never will be able to tell exactly what. But I can guess.

I went on with the search of Zip. But that knife was the last thing in the way of a weapon that he had on him.

I told Tom that he would have to go to jail in Kearneyville. In the first place, he was too dangerous to be allowed loose. In the second place, it was possible that out of Zip we might pump enough to jail the entire Townsend bunch by opening up their tracks and their secret trails.

It gave me a glow when I thought of that possibility. If I could pull stuff as big as that, Kearneyville would stop damning me because I had turned over to the side of the law. It would be fame for me. It would be such a mountain of good reputation that my shady past would be buried under it.

And, once that happened, the road would be clearer. Tom Fellows, of course, would be almost out of my sight on the horizon, but still, the way to him would be straight. And as I stood there beside him, I felt pretty proud and happy, and the future was boiling in me like morning coffee in a pot.

Fellows agreed with me, as a matter of course. There was no doubt that the proper place for Zip was in the jail. But he said that he had a place where not even a snake could get away and he suggested that we lay Zip away there to ripen, while I had some food tucked under that loose belt of mine.

That was an idea that made a great hit with me. I was beginning to feel a little dizzy, after the excitement, on top of my three days of nothingness. And the pain in the middle of my stomach, of course, had never stopped gnawing away at me.

I tied the hands of Zip. Tom tied his feet together. He hadn't recovered consciousness. He was only beginning to groan and come to as we carried him down the cellar steps. We took him into a dim underground room. No, there was one peep-hole of a window that allowed a few rays of light to enter.

As we put him down there on the bare floor, he got back his wits, and sat up. He stopped groaning as consciousness completely returned.

Tom Fellows dropped on one knee beside him.

"Zip," he said, and his voice was gentle. It was a beautiful thing to hear him. "Zip, God knows that I'm sorry for this. I counted on you as I counted on myself, and now it seems that I was wrong. You're going to jail, Zip. You're going to be faced with one of the worst charges that one man can lay against another. I'm going to see that you have the finest lawyer money can hire for you—and then,

God help your unhappy soul if you're proved guilty. I only hope that the mob doesn't try to tear down the jail and murder you. I'll see if I can't protect you from them; and if they break in, they'll have to get me before they get you. That's all I can say now. I'm sorry I had to use my fist on you, but it was that or your knife in the heart of my friend Joe Hyde. Besides, Zip, the youngster had you covered. Her forefinger was just a quarter of an inch away from your life, when you started to flash that knife!"

Zip said nothing, which was what I expected of the poisonous snake.

Then we went back to the patio.

Fellows ordered breakfast from the cook, and went for his plunge while the meal cooked. I stayed in the patio and tried to talk to Al Doloroso, but she had struck on a silent spot, and wouldn't answer. She just strolled around and looked things over, and stood for a long time, admiring the way the head of the fountain shook in the morning light.

Tom came back, dressed. We had breakfast together, and the hardest part of my fasting was controlling my appetite. I could hardly have done it, but Tom was there watching, and my pride, under his eyes, was just enough to pull me through. I retold the story of the Townsend place for him, and, at the rescue part, he looked at Al and never took his eyes from her till the end. That was his compliment to her, and it was enough.

He didn't say much about his plans. The future of Zip seemed to be heavy on his mind, so after breakfast we went down into the cellar and opened the door to the room where we had left him.

We found the ropes on the floor. That was all that remained of Zip for us to find!

CHAPTER XXXI

FELLOWS and I looked at one another; Al looked at the lock of the door. She said: "If he was smart enough to get out of those ropes, he was smart enough to pick this lock."

"What with, in the name of heaven?" said Fellows.

"A toothpick, maybe," said Al. "That's about all he'd need. Any splinter. I never saw such a lock. It's only good to keep the wind from blowing the door open, and there's no wind down here!"

That was rather fresh, but Al seemed disgusted with us both. Fellows was in a fury, murmuring under his breath. When we came up into the patio, his face was set, and his jaws working a little. He gave me a glance and told me to get to bed, either in his house or at the hotel. For his part, he was going to comb the country for Zip.

I saw him start out with his rifle as Al and I left for town. And I pitied Mr. Zip, if ever he came within range of that gun.

Al was still gloomy, all the way to town. She said:

"That's a bad spill. Now everything is completely in Townsend's hands! He knows what he knows; and he knows everything that we know. You and Fellows made a mess of the whole play!"

"What could we have done?" said I, throwing up my hands.

"Keep that nigger under your eyes every second. You could have done that!" says she, sharp and snappy.

I gave her a mean look. She certainly could be the most irritating brat in the world.

"All right, Al," said I. "The next time there's a play, you can organize the whole deal, if you want to."

"I mean to," said she.

We rode on another while. It was no fun having that kid sulk, because usually she was on the crest of the wave.

"Break out of it, Al," said I. "What's the matter?"

"I'm thinking about you," said she, "and that's enough to give anybody cramps in the brain."

"Now, you lay off that lingo, will you?" said I. "It's no hair out of your head, anyway."

"No?" said she. "I'm in this play as far as any of you, pretty near, by this time. The nigger will tell Townsend who pried you loose from the house, up there. That will please Lefty a lot, the hairy-faced rat!"

"They'd never touch a girl," said I.

"He'd murder his mother for a nickel, and you know it," said she.

I *did* know it, as a matter of fact, and that shut me up pretty hard and tight.

"All right," said I. "You sulk. I'll sing."

I began to whistle.

"You're out of tune and off key," says she.

"Oh, shut up," says I.

"What's your plan now, Napoleon?" says she.

"Will you quit?" says I.

"What's your plan?" she insists. "What's your big inspiration now, Bonaparte?"

I glowered at her.

"I've got no plan, just now, if that's any help to you," I told her.

"I knew you didn't," said she.

We went on again. I kept looking across at her. She kept scowling at the dust of the road.

"Listen!" she said at last.

"I've been listening to nothing for a long ways," said I.

"You'd better get a real man up here—to help out," said the brat.

She sneered when she said it. I just about hated her, then.

"I know I'm only a roustabout," said I. "But what about Fellows? Isn't he big enough and real enough to suit you?"

"He's big enough and real enough and fool enough to trust Zip," said this acid kid.

"You been living on lemons too long," I told her. "Who'd be better, then? Who's the real man you've got in mind?"

"The boy that sicked you onto this trail," said she. "You better send for Marshal Werner."

"Humph!" said I. "And admit that I'm beaten?"

"Admit you're beaten before you admit you're dead," said she. "That's the best way, Napoleon."

I was getting madder and madder. But still, I could see that there was something in what she said. Just the thought of the calm, mist-gray eyes of Werner was a great comfort to me.

"Maybe you're right," said I.

"So long, then," said she.

She pulled up her horse.

"What's the matter?" said I.

"I'm sliding off. There's no reason why they should be allowed to bag the pair of us, at one scoop of the hand."

"Where you going?"

"You won't be weighted down by things that you don't know," said she, still as mean as a wildcat.

I wanted to slap her sassy face.

"Besides," she went on, "I borrowed this horse from Mr. Lefty Townsend, and it's good enough to attract a little attention. It might even come to the attention of the fellow that owned it before Townsend did *his* borrowing. I see a stylish brand on the shoulder. So I'll just take this beauty down the back way and leave it out of town, where it'll get plenty of air."

"I'll go along with you, then," says I.

"Why?"

"I don't want you wandering around alone, Al, with all this danger in the air."

"If you can take care of yourself, that's all the help that I want," says she. "That'll be a weight off of my hands. Don't you worry about me. I land on my feet from any heights they've got around here. So long, Napoleon!"

And down she goes, sashaying along a by-lane.

I was half of a mind to go after her, but her horse was

galloping so fast that Brindle could hardly have kept up, and something about the set of her shoulders told me that she wouldn't pull up and wait for me even if I sprinted the mustang and hollered to her.

So I gave a good look after her, damned a couple of times, and then rode on into town.

Mad as I was, I thought that I could recognize some good advice. I went straight to the telegraph office at the station and wrote out a wire:

"Marshal Werner,
El Paso,
Texas.

Have found the right house but need you to ring the bell. (Stop) Come hopping.

(Signed)
Joseph Hyde."

I shoved that under the nose of the telegraph operator. He was one of these tough boys.

"Is that code?" said he, out of the corner of his mouth.

"For you, boy," said I.

He looked as though he wanted to slam me. I was so nervous that I lost my temper. I stuck my face through the window and said:

"Whatcha want? A broken hand?"

He looked at my crooked jaw. Then he decided to say nothing. I paid him, and went off up the street feeling like a fool, and mighty ashamed of myself. Because, after all, there was nothing gained, and a lot lost, by that sort of foolishness.

And what would big Tom Fellows have done?

Well, he was a hard example for a fellow like me to follow. Besides, he never *had* to be nasty. He didn't even need his home town reputation. His big shoulders, and his wise, kind, steady eyes, were all the passports he needed to take him through the nations of the world, without a single voice being raised near him.

The next thing was to see the sheriff. I was lucky to find him in his office. He was whistling and seemed pretty gay. I found out later on in the day that he had just picked up a couple of yeggs down the railroad line, in a tramp jungle. That was why he felt so good.

He even kept on smiling a little when he saw me.

"You look a little worn, Mr. Deputy," says he. "Ain't the boys treating you right, here in Kearneyville?"

"Oh, the boys treat me as well as they know how," says I. "They got so few manners in Kearneyville, these days, that it don't need much of a run on the bank to clean them out. The boys don't bother me much, though. I just dropped in to give you some news."

"*You* have?" says he.

"Yeah," says I.

"About what?"

"Townsend," says I.

He brightened up a good deal, but gave his head a little shake, as though real news about Townsend would be too good to be true.

He had a big relief map of the county hanging on the wall. It was supposed to be regular stuff, truer than true, though it was all full of imaginings that never were true at all. However, it was clear enough for me to point out what I had to tell him. I showed him the trails up to the house where I had been three days with Townsend. I didn't tell him that I had been there. I simply said that that was the place where Townsend and his gang had all been the night before. No matter how careful they were, they must have left some outtrails behind them. Particularly because, the way those horses ran, it would be a few days before they were all rounded up again. I told the sheriff about the scattering of the horse herd, too, and suggested that he take along a memorandum of some of the brands of ranchers hereabouts.

Wallie Blue listened to me for a time, with his head canting downward and his eyes doubtful, but gradually that naked narrative of facts convinced him. He fired up, finally.

"Slow," he shouted at me, "you've been there yourself! You've seen it all."

"No," I said, "I just had a little dream about it. I was sort of sleep walking."

"I want you on that posse," says he. "This is nearer to something than anything we've ever had on Townsend before!"

"You won't have me on the posse," says I. "I've still got plenty of work down here in Kearneyville. Townsend," I lied, "is just a sort of a side-issue, with me."

Then I walked out on him, leaving Wallie pretty much flabbergasted. Because I suppose he thought that Townsend was about the most important figure in the whole Western world. That is, from a sheriff's point of view.

From my point of view he was, too, but I was too tired out to ride and fight again. I didn't really expect that Wallie Blue would accomplish much, but any stirring up of the hornet hive might divert attention from me. Just now, I was pretty sure to be coming in for a good piece of it up yonder, at the hands of Ma and Pa.

CHAPTER XXXII

WHEN I got down to the street, I went as far as the Haskell Lunch Counter. Then I turned in through the door and leaned over the counter and asked Haskell what he had to eat. He showed me. All the way from venison steak to trout. I told him that only half-wits and tenderfeet ever would eat at the Guernsey House, so long as there was chuck like this in town; and that warmed Haskell up more than the fire he was working over.

For an hour and a half by the clock, he cooked and I ate. I was all alone, in that place, because, though the morning was young, it was a late breakfast hour for cow-pokes used to breakfasting about dawn. I took a chance on half killing myself with food, but I figured that what I had

had at Tom's house would serve to break me in, and that now my stomach was ready for a real day's work.

Before I finished, even coffee could hardly keep me awake.

Then I paid my bill and went out onto the street, feeling a little dizzy in the head and puffed in the center section, but otherwise quite all right.

There was a change in the air of Kearneyville. That was plain. The moment that I got outside, I noticed people standing around in groups. You would have thought that presidential election returns were coming in, or that news was expected from a heavyweight championship fight. Yes, or even something more.

In front of the Running Iron Saloon, four or five fellows were so busy talking that they forgot to go inside for a drink. As I went by, they brought their heads up, and stared at me, and were quiet.

There were others sitting out before Guernsey's rival hotel, and they were talking, too; and they lifted their heads and stared at me, and stopped their noise, also, as I went by.

"This town hates me, and this town can go to the devil!" I said to myself.

There were groups standing around at every corner. Something was in the air like the noise of wasp wings.

I was a good deal too tired to be even very angry at the way I was being treated.

When I got to the Guernsey House, I turned in up the stairs, and Hooch Oliver, an old bunkie of mine, was sitting on the veranda next to the door. He was one of those who had been turning up his nose at me, lately, so I pretended I didn't see him and started by. Up gets Hooch and sticks out his hand.

"Say, boy, you ain't forgot Hooch, have you?" said he.

I was a good deal surprised. I shook his hand and said I was mighty glad to see him.

"If you're glad to see me come and drink it down, son," said Hooch, real cordial.

"I want to, and I'd like to, Hooch," said I. "But I can't. No, I've got to go upstairs."

"You're wanted with me in the Kicking Mule," insisted

Hooch. He grinned like a happy fool. "I wanta talk to you," he said to me.

"Aw, leave him alone, Hooch," said one of the boys in the tilted chairs, close by. "Can't you see he's all in?"

I was more amazed, still, for this was almost like sympathy and I wasn't used to that in Kearneyville. It almost turned my head. Hooch slapped my shoulder.

"Yeah," he said. "I guess you wanta turn in. I guess you're tired out, and who's got a better reason?"

That staggered me more than the rest. When I got inside, I was groggier than ever, with bewilderment. I walk up to the desk and big Guernsey rises up and plants his fists on the desk and leans toward me. I figure that I can understand what that means.

"I suppose that you've let my room to somebody else, Sam?" says I. "Well, put me in another. I don't care which!"

"Let your room to somebody else?" whoops Sam. "I'll see somebody else damned! Let *your* room to somebody else? Boy, that room is yours, rent free, so long as you wanta stay in it!"

I grabbed onto the back of a chair. It was all that held me up after this pop.

"Are you kidding me, Sam?" said I. "Or are you just a nacheral clown?"

He came out from around the desk, puffing. He put an arm around my shoulders. He was a whale of a big man.

"I had you wrong, son," said he. "Everybody here had you wrong. I thought you'd gone and turned yourself into a stool pigeon. How was we all to know that Townsend was the little playmate that you wanted to tag? How could we tell that you'd have the guts to go up there all by yourself and finger his beard for him? No wonder you look like hell, now! Because you *been* in hell. You're solid with Kearneyville. Nobody else ever showed that much nerve."

"Aw, quit it, old man," said I. "Who's been chattering?"

"Nobody but the sheriff, while he worked up his posse," said Guernsey. "He's the only one that talked. He said that he could hardly pry the yarn out of you."

"Listen, Sam," said I. "It was all a kind of an accident, and—"

"I know, I know!" said Sam, slamming me on the shoulder with his fat hand. "I know all about it. You don't have to toot your own horn. It ain't a whole brass band that Kearneyville likes to hear playin' in front of a gent, down the main street. You don't have to say anything. Sure it was an accident. It just happened. It don't mean anything, hardly. Now you're going up to bed. You look half dead. I reckon you are. And you'll sleep, boy, and you'll sleep safe. That's all I mean to say! I'll have your room watched. Nobody but your friends get to see you. And not none of them, either, for about twelve hours!"

He went up the stairs with me, while he talked.

I saw what that fool of a Wallie Blue had done. He'd embroidered considerable on what I'd told him. I suppose that the hollow look of me had excited his imagination, and he'd turned me right into a fairy story. It made me kind of sick. I wanted to explain that I wasn't any hero, at all, but I was honestly too tired to talk. I got into that room and just fell on the bed.

My eyes closed, pronto. I heard old Sam creaking about the room, clucking like an old hen while he pulled the window curtains. Then he drew a blanket up around my shoulders, and that was the last that I knew of anything.

I slept, and I slept, and I slept. I dropped into a deep, pitch dark well; and the world, it hung above me like a little yellow star that didn't amount to anything. But, after a time, I was back in the world again, riding trails, through heat and dust. Twilight came on, and the kind, soft night. Lights began to twinkle and dazzle. Then voices sounded, deep, and musical, and high and light. They spoke carefully.

I rushed from sleep to wakefulness, and the voices were still there. The room was pitch dark; it was night, but the curtains had been drawn to let in the cool of the night air. Outside, I could see the gleam of the lamps along the street. I could see stars, too, through the upper half of one of the windows.

It must have been a hot day, because my pillow was all damp, and my hair was wet at the back of my neck.

I listened to the voices, still only half awake, and then I made out that it was Tom and Alicia Doloroso. Well, I just sighed, and settled back again. If they were around, there was nothing to worry about.

They heard me sigh, and Al comes and stands by the bed.

"How is it, Slow?" she whispers.

"I'm awake," says I.

"When I heard what you'd eaten, I thought you were going to die, you old boa constrictor," says she.

"No," says Tom Fellows, "he just swallows an ox, now and then, and crawls off into a cave and sleeps a month or so. There's nothing that he can't sleep off, between you and me."

I pushed myself up on my elbows.

"What happened to Zip?" I asked.

"No luck," said Fellows. "I got the track of him, but he grabbed my bay mare. You know that one? She's a fast trick, and he rode her full speed, straight for the high ground. If we didn't kill *that* snake, at least we scotched it. He's gone home to his own kind. Before this, he's had a pretty little story to tell to his boss, Townsend."

It was a disappointment. I had rather expected more than this from Tom; but, after all, Zip was a slippery one. At a glance one could see that much!

I asked for a light. Al lit the lamp and put it on the corner table, so that too much wouldn't shine in my eyes. It takes a woman to think of little things like that.

Fellows says: "I've been having a talk with Al. I think that she ought to pull out and go East, to a school."

"She knows too much already," says I.

"Listen at him!" says Al.

"I've been getting very serious," says Fellows. "You ought to know what I've been saying to her, Slow."

"No, cut that out," says Al, sharp and brisk.

I looked at her; she was red as a beet, and tapping her toe on the floor.

"Go on, Tom," said I.

"I've been trying to tell Alicia," said he, smiling at the girl, "that if she can consider me, and if I can manage to pull through this Townsend business, I hope that one of these days we can marry. Mind you, I know she's a shade young. I thought she might want to travel, or go to school, or whatever she pleases, for a couple of years. What do you think of the idea?"

"Why," said I, "I'm so used to having her around, and her mean ways, and everything, that it makes me feel sort of hollow and empty to think of losing her. But what do I think? I think she's the luckiest girl in the world. That's what she thinks, too, Tom. Look at the red of her."

I laughed, not very heartily.

Al came over and stood by the bed. She scowled down at me.

"Don't you laugh at me, you crooked faced four-flusher!" said she, through her teeth.

That made me feel better.

I eased back into the pillow and grinned at her.

"I'm not laughing at you," said I.

"You are!' said she, stamping. "I know why. You're laughing to think that Tom Fellows would be serious about a worthless little greaser, like me! Be honest! Tell the truth, will you?"

"That's the way she is," I said to Tom. "There ain't much to her, but what there is, is mostly claws. You take her. Nobody but you could ever handle her, except in a cage!"

And just then, clang, bang, crash, goes a gun, three times, and Tom Fellows pitches out of his chair to the floor of the room!

CHAPTER XXXIII

Al dropped, about the same time; but, as she fell, she had her thirty-two, and it was streaking fire toward the window through which the first three shots had been poured.

I thought that Tom was dead, and the world stopped

for half a second, for me; but when I jumped from the bed, Tom was already leaping from the floor.

That fall of his had made the murderer think that his job was done, or else, it had thrown him off his aim, and the volley from Al had routed him.

He and I got to the window and jammed our heads through at the same time. I saw somebody drop to the ground just under the window and leap around the corner.

We plunged to the other window, but there was no one to be seen in the street, for the alley was not lighted, and the lamp inside the room, had dazzled us a little.

There was not much good running down to the street. Neither of us would have been able to recognize the assassin, even if we'd met him face to face, for all that we had an impression of was the shadow that had dropped to the street from the side of the hotel. Just a slimpsy shadow, and no more!

Besides, there was enough traffic coming up the stairs, just then, to have stopped the Mississippi river in full flood. Sam Guernsey was pretty old and fat, but he fairly won the sprint and was the first through the door. It seemed as though most of the rest of the town was behind his shoulders, and every hand was heavy with a gun. I met Guernsey and explained things. It was hard for him to understand. He wanted so bad to help that he kept glaring past me, looking for something to fight.

"In my house!" he was always repeating. "Right in my own house! By God, Slow, I'm gunna leave this rotten town. There ain't any good in it. Right in my own house, they try to slam Slow Joe Hyde—it's a damn disgrace, even for crooks!"

I told him for the thousandth time that it was not I. It was Tom Fellows they had tried to get. He had had three bullets whiz around his ears. Finally I got Guernsey turned around, and he waded down the stairs driving the rest of the boys in front of him.

A lot of them poured out into the street. We could hear them babbling for quite a while. The loudmouths were talking about lynching. I don't know what or who they wanted to lynch, but that word is apt to get into the air when a crowd meets and gets excited around Kearneyville.

However, I was almost glad of the hubbub. It kept on showing me that my unpopular days in Kearneyville were at an end, at least, for a time. Now they were making a hero out of me—for no real reason at all. I was half shamed, but I was more glad. It's mighty easy to accept praise and a good name even though I hadn't worked for it all my life, like Tom Fellows.

He was the coolest man I ever saw. Ten seconds after that try at his life, he was as easy as could be. I swear that his color hadn't altered, and when he rolled a cigarette, there was no tremor in his fingers. He tried to turn back to the subject of Alicia.

"In a way," says he, "I should have consulted you first, Slow, before I spoke to Alicia."

"Why?" I ask him.

"Because, in a way, you're her guardian while she's here in Kearneyville," says he, as sober as a judge.

"Guardian?" says I. "Don't make me laugh with cracks like that, Tom, or I'll do myself a real harm. I'll sprain a rib. Guardian? I'd rather take on the job of guardianing a wildcat. Guardian!"

I whooped.

"Don't be vulgar, Joe Hyde!" says the girl.

I popped my eyes at her. I hadn't expected to hear her speak like this. I never had heard her in that vein before.

"You *are* a shade inconsiderate, Slow," says Tom.

That got me off the bed. I grabbed Tom by one arm, and Al by the other.

"Listen, Tom—listen, Al," says I. "You know I haven't a very fast lingo. I can't talk a lot. All I got to say is this: You're the greatest girl I ever met, Al. You're the cleanest, the straightest, and the truest. I owe you my life. You can have it back any time you want, on a platter. Tom, you're the *only* real man that I ever knew. I can't say any more. I'm getting too excited. Only—you've got to let me string along with my cheap line of chatter. I don't know how to speak like a book. You do, Tom. You take Al. She's the finest thing out. I've seen her proved. She's the steel that bends but never breaks. She's got a cutting edge, too, take it from me. And you tell Tom that you'll follow him around the world, Al," says I. "Because he's king. The rest of us ain't any higher than his instep!"

I stamped to make my point. The little, thin noise of a golden bell answered me from my heel.

"Hush, Slow, hush!" says Tom Fellows. "Don't speak of me like that. And there's no need for you to make up your mind at once, Alicia, only—"

"Great Pete!" cried Alicia. "Let the old cat die, Tom, will you? I've been on the swing so long that I'm groggy. I wish I had a drink. Marriage? I'm mighty obliged. But I don't want to think about it. We're likely to have our three throats cut a long time before there's any marriage in the air."

I thought she was a wild young fool, to speak of Tom like that, and *to* him, like that. But there was no taming Al. I was a little relieved, also, to tell you the truth. I mean, she and I had been through such a lot of white water together; we were close, even while we were fighting.

"Who tried to slug you, Tom?" says Al, walking toward the window.

"Keep away from that!" I call to her.

"All right, Mother Hubbard," says she, and leans right out. "Look what they did," says she. "They used spiked boots, like the boys that climb the telephone poles."

"They?" said I.

"No, there was only one of them. I can see where the spikes went into the boards. Sort of risky, at that!"

"Townsend's men are willing to take risks, I guess," said I.

"No, it wasn't Townsend's men," said she.

I looked at Tom, expecting him to answer, but he was sitting in a chair in a corner, studying the floor with a frown. I imagined that his mind was still on the way that Al had talked to him. Well, I would lay my money that he would never talk to her again, seriously, about any subject—including himself. And there that girl had chucked away her chance at the finest man I ever had laid eyes on!

All right. You fellows who understand women, step up and talk. I've always been beat at the start!

Now he lifts his head.

"You don't think that one of Townsend's boys tried the trick, Al?" says he.

"I know it wasn't one of his outfit," says she. "Look here. You know there's nobody that ever rode for Townsend that would have three shots, point blank, like that, and miss his mark every time. No; it was either a woman who did that shooting or else a man so excited that his gun was shaking in his hand!"

She was so cocksure that it made a mighty impression on me. Even big Fellows began to nod, slowly.

"Not a woman," he said, however. "I don't know many women. And as for men—why, outside of Townsend's lot, I didn't know that I had any bitter enemies."

"You're bound to have," says Al. "A man like you is too big for the digestion and the pride of most ordinary people. You've run Kearneyville for a pretty long time—"

"No, no, Alicia," says he. "I never have been in politics!"

"Tut!" says she. "Are you such a big innocent that you don't know the boys fall down and kiss the ground when you've walked over it? But some of 'em must harbor grudges—the ones that didn't get your support for office. Wasn't it you who gave Wallie Blue one bright smile, and put him in office?"

"Wallie's a good lad and a friend of mine, I trust," says Fellows. "But I can't say that I had anything to do with—"

"Oh, all right, all right," says she. "You had nothing to do with it, then."

She was mighty impatient. Tom sat and took her impatience. He was quiet as an old horse.

Just then Guernsey came up and said Miss Edgar wanted to see me. I was about to tell him that Miss Edgar could waste the time of other people, but not mine; but then he said that she was downstairs, and that altered everything. I couldn't stay away from her, naturally, when I knew that she had bluff enough to come to the hotel, where she was sure to be a fish out of water.

So I told Fellows and Al that I would be gone for a few minutes. They said that they would wait a little while, and I went downstairs. Guernsey showed me into a little back sitting room, dark and dull, with a dingy lamp burning in a corner of it. As I went in, Ruth Edgar stood up and faced me.

She was more angry than shamed. Conscience was not a thing that troubled that beauty very much. She came right across and shook hands with me, giving me a good grip and a good pumping, up and down.

"I'm mighty glad to see you, Slow," said she.

I almost laughed. She had a few reasons for not being so very glad.

"You don't think I mean it," said she, "but I do. I'm glad, because I want to use you, and you can use me. I could go to the sheriff, I suppose, but I don't know just how I could put it to him."

"What's the matter?" said I.

"I'm tired of the little game," said she.

"What game?"

"Aw, you know, Slow," said she. "You don't have to pump me. I'll talk."

"You talk then, sister," said I.

"The dirty dogs, they've double-crossed me!" says this sweet young thing.

"How come that, Ruth?" says I.

"How come that? I'll show you how come that!" says she.

Then she took out a purse, and out of the purse she extracted a ring with a ruby in it.

It was a big baby. About two carats, I'd say, and worth a thousand dollars of anybody's money.

Then I looked closer, because it didn't seem to catch the light very well, or have the old fire condensed in the heart of it. All at once I understood. That ruby was not worth ten dollars, with its setting thrown in. It was a fake, and not a good fake, either!

CHAPTER XXXIV

RUTH EDGAR's indignation was wonderful to see. When I gave her back the ring, she bared her teeth at me.

"Think of that little mongrel trying to come the low-down on me?" said she. "That runt of a Whitey Peyton, and his talk about a trip to New York, and a trip to Paris, and the way we'd throw the money around. The dirty little faker—he tries to slip this across on me!"

She trembled, she was so angry; her voice was a snarl. Hate made her so ugly that I could see a picture of her as she would be ten years from that day. It wasn't a pretty picture, either.

"I never really intended to marry him, anyway," she said. "I was only kidding him, I guess. And then he tries to be smart with *me!* Whitey Peyton!"

She groaned. She was even more wounded than enraged.

"I'm going to sock him where the socking will do the most good!" she said. "I'm going to let you in on the ground floor, Slow!"

"Sit down, Ruth. Take your time," said I.

I backed her into a chair, and took one near by. I felt that I was about to get a break that might put the entire game into my hands, but I didn't want to seem too eager.

"I'll take my time. There's only one thing I'd hurry to do—and that's to poison that ham, that Whitey Peyton," said she.

"I don't like him myself," said I.

"You got no reason," she answered. "All he wants to do is to have your hide, and he'll get it if he can buy it or steal it, or shoot it. Besides, he hates you. I dunno why. The fellow you've wronged, you always hate the man that you've wronged."

I admitted that. I wanted to get quickly at the gist of what she had to say, but I thought it was better to let her do it her own way.

"How was he going to get to Paris, and all of that? Why on the price that's hanging on you, Slow!"

When I heard that, the gooseflesh formed all over me. It was winter for me, right then.

"What's the price, Ruth?" I asked her.

"Twenty—five—thousand—bucks!" said she, slowly, but running the words together so that they almost made one word.

I didn't make any remark on this. I couldn't. There was no breath in me. I suppose that I might have said that it was a compliment, such a high price, but I didn't feel that way at all, let me tell you.

I've known fellows who went around with a thousand, or a couple of thousand hanging on their heads, not very much worried. But when the price went up to five or ten thousand, they just chucked up the sponge and surrendered all hope. They knew that they couldn't last for long, when they were marked with such a tag. Somebody was pretty sure to come along and pluck the plum. And they were always right. When the price was scaled up like that, they got famous, but their fame didn't last more than a few months, before somebody dropped a slug of lead into the machine and it stopped ticking.

Five or ten thousand—that was enough to bury better men than me. But twenty-five thousand!

It didn't make much difference. I could wait to be scared to death and then murdered, or I could take it easier and go and jump off a cliff. Both ways would come to the end of the same road.

"I guess that puts me in the envelope, Ruth," said I. "I'm about ready to be stamped and posted."

She didn't deny it. She was a hard-boiled girl, if I ever saw one. She just said:

"That sews you up, I guess. But you oughta take a fal. out of a couple of 'em first. Five dollars worth of ruby!

You know, a girl has to take care of herself. I got that ruby this morning, and this afternoon, I just slanted down the street and had it priced. Old Rubens, he didn't even screw the glass into his eye. He just looked at it through his seventy-year old standing fog and said: 'No good!'

" 'Flawed, eh?' " says I.

" 'It's not good enough to have a flaw,' says he. 'That's a five dollar jewel, ma'am!'

"Five dollars—for me! Five dollars, from that undersized runt of a broken down cowpoke, that Whitey Peyton! I always guessed he was a cheap skate. I never knew how no good he was, before!"

"You've told me a lot, Ruth," says I. "I'm glad to hear it, too. But could you put me next to Whitey, some way?"

"Why did I come here?" says she. "For tea, or to put a hammer in your hand?"

"The hammer, I hope," says I.

"The hammer it is," says she. "The Edgars are a funny lot. We're like elephants. We never forget and we never forgive. The little tricks between you and me, they don't count. And we had about an even break, at that. A game is a game, but dirt is dirt, and that's what this blond boy is tryin' to work on me. I'm gunna give you a chance to wreck him."

"When?" says I.

"Tonight," says she.

"The sooner the better," says I. "Now tell me the lay of the plant."

She did.

"You know Garret's old mill?"

I knew it. I had been out there when I was a youngster. It was a favorite fishing place, up and down the creek, and we used to go swimming in the big, broad pool below the mill.

"I know it like the inside of my hand," said I.

"You may need to, before the night's over," said she. "At nine o'clock Whitey and Frank Gregor are going to be there to meet somebody—I don't know who. Somebody mighty important. And it's about you, and they're going to fix the plant that will seal you up for delivery, old son.

Afterward, Whitey is coming on down the road to meet me. Only, he won't find me waiting there!"

"You be there," said I. "Why get his suspicions all stirred up?"

"I couldn't see him without scratching his eyes out," said she.

"You want Whitey rolled," said I. "If the chance is good, I'm going to try to get him under the gun tonight. But the chance may not be good. I don't know. If the chance isn't right, I may have to meet up with him later on, and catch him just at the time that he and the rest of 'em are planning to catch me. This isn't as simple and easy as falling off a log, Ruth. This job may take some planning and some waiting around."

She agreed, finally, and she said that she would be on hand if Whitey got through me, and went down the road to meet her. But she was sour on that part of the job. She wanted Whitey out of the way. She wanted him killed because he'd given her that phoney ring. I never saw such a cold-hearted girl. It was the offense to her pride that upset her so much, I guess!

She wouldn't leave the matter in my hands. She gave me advice.

"Get some boys along that can shoot the bull in the eye," she urged me. "You're good, Slow. Everybody says that. But other fellows can slip a gun, too. Get some of 'em. What about Fellows? He's a champion. He's greased lightning, and they say that he's chumming around with you, now!"

"I see him now and then," said I, feeling proud of my reputation as Tom's friend.

"Then there's Wallie Blue. They say that you're working for Marshal Werner. But let Wallie have a slice of the pie. There'll be enough of it to go around. Whitey's a fighting fool, and that Frank Gregor is a devil, I know. He *looks* like one! Besides, they've got another man coming. Whitey wouldn't name him, but it's somebody mighty important. That third man may be the works. Maybe he's what you're after, at the bottom of everything."

This interested me. I hadn't spread the news around

that I was looking so far beneath the surface. I leaned forward and asked:

"Who am I after, sister?"

She shrugged her shoulder.

"I ain't a prophet," said Ruthie. "I don't know who you're after and I don't care—so long as you get Whitey Peyton—the short sport!" Then she added: "This meeting at the mill is for nine. You've got an hour, still. You'd better get along. Look here, Slow. We've buried the hatchet, haven't we?"

"Of course we have," said I, more heartily than frankly. For I was afraid of that vixen. As I said before, the bad ones with the pretty faces are the worst of all.

"Then everything's fixed," said she.

She shook hands, giving me a firm grip, and a straight, deep look into my eyes, as though she were trying to read my mind. Then she left the hotel.

I went up to my room pretty desperate, but determined. If they had hung that price on my head, I was a dead man before three days went by, and I knew it. It was only wonderful that I had managed to last as long as this. Now I could understand why Zip's visit to Townsend had probably made Lefty determined to polish me off instead of giving me a chance to join the gang. Even a fifty-fifty split on the twenty-five thousand would have been enough to make up Lefty's mind!

But at the same time that I had learned about the extent of the price, I had also learned of the lever by which I might topple down the power that was working against me. And, upstairs in my room, was the clever brain of Al, and the resistless hand of Tom Fellows!

So I hurried for them, pulled open the door of my room, and found it—empty!

But on the sill of the door, there was a slip of paper, which I picked up. It simply read:

Dear Slow,

Back again in an hour or so. Tom and I are stepping out.

Al.

That was all. And it was enough.

There I was stripped of the two on whom I'd counted most—one for advice and one for action! I walked up and down the room, rather dizzied. They were coming back in an "hour or so"; and the need I had of them was instant. In ten minutes, I would have to line out for Garret's mill! I damned my luck pretty hard and fast.

There was Wallie Blue, but he was gone, too. He was off chasing after Townsend, or Townsend's ghost. And outside of Wallie and the other two, who was there in town I could really trust?

They were all making a fuss over me, just now, but a fuss doesn't always come from the heart. And if I tried to pick up helpers, they were as likely as not to be on the other side of the fence and stab me through the back.

I was worth twenty-five thousand dollars to any man's knife or gun!

CHAPTER XXXV

BESIDES, I was annoyed with both of them. They might have known that I was called out of the room for something important. Otherwise, I wouldn't have left them. Yet they'd chosen to go off rambling. Down to the hash joint where they served the Spanish beans, perhaps! That would be just like Al. She was never happy unless she was feeding her face with hot, peppery stuff.

Well, I got so irritated that I gave the waste paper basket a good kick. It slammed against the wall, tumbled over on the floor, and chucked a ball of crumbled paper at my feet.

I picked that paper up because I had nothing better to

do, and spread it out. It was in Al's handwriting, and it was worth a look. This was the way it ran:

"How do things stand?

"All balled up!

"That Zip is a panther, all right, but he's not the brains behind this deal.

"Townsend may be the cute boy.

"Fellows is too good to be useful. This job needs somebody who's not afraid of dirty hands.

"Slow is earning his name. He'll go just far enough to fall down and break his neck.

"Me, I wish I was a man!"

Of course, that wasn't signed. She had simply been sitting down and talking to herself with a pencil and a piece of paper. I thought what she said about everybody else was pretty true, but I must say that it made me mad to read what she had written down about me.

I might be "Slow" in more ways than one, but it seemed to me that I had been doing pretty well in this business. If I hadn't uncovered the main crooks, at least I had been stirring matters up around Kearneyville, kicked Townsend in the face, got the town pretty solid behind me, listed up Wallie Blue to run Townsend some more, made myself strong with Tom Fellows, and wangled a lot of information out of Ruth Edgar.

I didn't really doubt that she had told me all of the truth that she knew. Still, I would have liked to get the advice of a keen head like Al, or Tom Fellows. It might be, still, that she was framing me again. She was smart enough to of play-acted all the emotion, and the hatred of Whitey.

However, my time was up. Garret's mill was my next stop. So I went downstairs. I simply stopped a minute at the desk to ask Guernsey when Fellows and the girl had gone out. I was surprised at the answer.

"Fellows went out right after you came downstairs," he said. "A minute later a gent I didn't know came in and ran up the stairs, whistling. I was about to ask who he was, but he seemed to know his way around, and some of these cowpokes don't like having the brakes put on them. So I let him go. I was right, because he came down again with that friend of yours, the ragged looking kid. They were sassing one another. What about it, Slow? Anything at all wrong?"

I must admit that it rather stopped me. I couldn't make head or tail of it at all. So I went out toward the stable, still turning the matter over in my head, and feeling more and more in a whirl. Things were happening too fast for me. I remembered what Al had jotted down: I was too "slow."

So I went into the stable and found the old boy in there chewing a straw and pouring crushed barley into the feed boxes. I stopped a minute and breathed the air. I like the smell of barley. It's sort of fresh and sweet.

When he saw me, he came over and watched me saddling Brindle—that old stager. And he says, very confiding:

"I'll bet that Wallie Blue'll come in with some news for you, Slow. That's what he will. Wallie's the boy to go and get 'em!"

I wished Wallie to the devil, just then. What I wanted, was somebody right on the spot to help me that night when I rode out to try my hand against three thugs, in the middle of the night. So I led out Brindle, forked him, and started off.

* * * * *

Here I've got to branch off on another trail that I learned about later. I would like to work it in right along with what happened to me, but the trail branches off so far that it has to be followed a ways by itself.

It's the trail of Al, and the whistling cowpoke who had gone out of the hotel with her.

It begins with the time when I left the room, and Fellows, all at once, starts up and says that he'll have to leave her for a moment. He'll be back in just a minute.

She sits down, after Fellows leaves, and catches up a piece of paper and scribbles down some of her thoughts. I've told you before what those thoughts were, and how I came out at the short end of the horn.

She's just finished when a knock comes at the door. She

crumbles the paper, chucks it into the waste paper basket, and turns around in her chair.

"Come in!" she sings out.

In steps a gent with a five gallon hat and a sort of peaked, brown face, and good-natured eyes, all wrinkled around the corners, as if from continual laughing. In fact, he was always laughing or whistling, or smiling, or doing something with his mouth.

She says: "Hello there, stranger. Did you miss your way?"

"You're Al, ain't you?" says he.

"Sure," says Al. "What of it?"

"Nothing much," says the stranger, grinning, and looking her over.

"Heavyweights don't do all the winning," says she, a little peeved.

"Slow is down the street. He wants you to step over," says the stranger.

"Slow wants me to? What for? What's the trouble?" she says.

"Trouble? I dunno anything about trouble," says he. "All I know is that Slow sends me for you."

"Why didn't he come himself?" asks Al. "And what's your name, partner?"

"Logan's my name," says he, pretty patient. "Slow couldn't come. He said to tell you that he was talking confidential to a lady, and that you would understand."

"Humph!" says Al.

But she thinks to herself that it's Ruth Edgar. Not likely to be anybody else. And perhaps she'd better go. Besides, she likes the laughing eyes of that hombre.

So she gets up and jams her hat on her red head, and goes down with Logan.

They step out onto the street, and, in a jiffy, he turns her down a dark alley.

"Dark as a wolf's throat down there," says Al.

"Follow me," says he. "I know the way and where to step."

It was raining, a thin, steady mist that turned the lighted windows into great stars. Here and there, in the alley, the water had collected in pools.

"All right," says Al. "You lead on, Logan. I'm right behind you."

They go on down to a dark doorway. The door seems open, but there's no light inside.

"Here's the place," says Logan, and, turning around, he chucks a sack over her head; and, at the same time, somebody that must have come out of the doorway grabs hold of her and swings her off her feet.

She's carried a bit, trying to squeal out, but only eating sackcloth every time she opens her mouth. Then a lamp is lighted, or a lantern. She sees the light filtering through the interstices of the sacking.

"Put your thumbs onto the holler of her throat," says Logan's voice, "and if she wriggles, or starts to yip, press down."

"I'll be damned if I will," says the other. "You've crooked me, Logan. It's a girl, you fool! It ain't no boy at all. It's a woman!"

There was such a lot of horror in his voice that Al felt a lot better. She thought that she might be going to get a break from that fellow who didn't like to see a girl manhandled.

But Logan says, calm and steady, like a man who knows his way around by night:

"What difference does it make? *I* didn't know it was a girl, neither. But Al is what we've got to snag, and here is Al. Listen, Al!"

Al manages to choke out: "I'm trying to, but I'm getting dust in my ears."

She hears Logan laugh, softly.

"She's a good kid," says Logan. "Listen, Al. We don't wanta be rough. You're all right if you play the game with us. We'll take that sacking off from over your head and put a little gag in its place that won't hurt you a bit, and let you breathe easy through the nose. D'you say yes?"

"Yeah. I say yes," says Al.

They took the sack right off of her, but Logan had his thumbs at the hollow of her throat. However, she could see that he kept right on smiling. She began to hate that smile with all her heart, you can bet! All she could see was the ceiling. It was cracked in a lot of places. There was an old chandelier hanging in metal rags. It looked like the wreck of an abandoned home. There were plenty of those in Kearneyville, of course. But she couldn't see anything by which she could identify it. She wasn't even sure how far she had walked down the dark alley. That was because of the puddles she'd been dodging, and the dark, and the mist of the falling rain that makes the distances always seem much greater.

The other fellow with Logan—the one who had been upset because it was a girl they were handling—was a glum-looking, sour-faced man, late in middle age. But, because of what he had said, and because of something baffled and not unkindly in his eyes, she took a fancy to him from the start.

He didn't argue any more, after the beginning.

They fitted a small gag into her mouth. It didn't choke her. It was an expert job. They tied her hands together, in front of her, lashed her feet, and passed a rope between the two bindings.

Then Logan said:

"Listen, kid, we know you're slick at getting through things and out of trouble, and we're watching you. The way to keep out of bad trouble is to lie still."

His voice was gentle, but she saw that he meant business.

Then the older man wrapped her up in a big piece of tarpaulin, and carried her into the darkness. She was laid in the bed of a wagon, and the wagon started off, jolting and sloshing through the wet of the night.

CHAPTER XXXVI

SHE started to work at the ropes. She was an expert at all sorts of bonds and bondages, but she decided that it would hardly be worth while to get her hands free. The lights of the town no longer flashed dimly across her eyes. They were spinning out through the country; and, while she was still in doubt about making a serious effort to free herself, the wagon stopped. She was picked up and placed on the driver's seat, between the two men. Then they drove on again.

The rain was easing up. The clouds blew across in patches, and the stars whirled between. Logan had begun to sing, and the horses clumped along steadily, with the wheels sloshing through ruts filled with water.

"Jerry," says Logan, "take the reins."

And he handed them across and began to fill a pipe, which he lighted with a shower of sparks blowing from the bowl over his shoulder.

"Now, kid," says he to Al, "we're going out into the country for a piece, and when we reach a shack that I know of, we're going to lay up, there. Nothing will happen to you, so long as you take things easy. You hear?"

"I hear, all right," says Al.

"And believe me, too," says Logan. "This is no deal of Jerry's and mine. I get my marching orders from higher up—a long ways higher up. Such a lot of distance higher, that we follow 'em to a letter. Our orders are this: to keep you living if we can, or to plant you dead if we have to. And that's the way that we mean to march. You savvy?"

Al said that she did. She was pretty much afraid of

Logan, because of his good humor, and the cheerful way he always acted. He had a smile for everything, but the smile didn't mean anything, she could see, when it came to action. When he spoke of killing, he meant just that. Jerry was a different cut, but Jerry would do what Logan told him to.

They went on for a few miles after this, and then Logan got out of the buckboard, freed Al from the foot rope, and tied the free end of the lashing about her wrists to his arm. He waved Jerry on, and hiked straight across country with Al.

It was a hilly lay of land, with a good deal of brush, sometimes growing so thick that they had to force through it, which drenched them with raindrops from the hips down. There were patches of trees, also, mostly scrubs, and in a considerable grove they found the shack.

It was hardly more than a lean-to—one room and a horse shed propped against the back of it. Inside of the shack, there was a lantern, a bunk built against the wall, a rickety stove with a worm-eaten tin chimney above it, and hardly anything else except a mackinaw that hung on a nail against the wall, rotting and green with mold.

It wasn't a very cheery place.

Logan tied Al to the foot of the stove! That shows his brains! If she tried to pull away, there would be a racket that could be heard for a mile.

Then he went out, and came back presently with some wood, with which he filled the stove, and lighted it. The stove smoked through a hundred cracks, and more smoke poured out through the holes in the chimney, but by degrees the draught began to pull, and the white cloud in the room rose gradually to the ceiling. They had warmth, then, and life didn't seem so bad. All this while—since leaving the buckboard—Logan had not said a word. He was simply smiling and humming to himself, and giving Al a greater chill, every minute.

When the fire was going pretty well, he untied her from the leg of the stove, led her to the bunk, and tied her to that, instead. Then he stood back by the fire, drying his trousers, spreading out his hands to the heat.

"How old are you?" says he.

"Seventeen next month," says she.

He nodded a while.

"You've started raising hell young," says he. "What hooked you up with Joe Hyde?"

"A long chance and a little luck," says she.

"Luck?" says Logan, and he laughed for a long moment, softly, to himself. He kept nodding. He seemed to be reaching a lot of conclusions.

"A lot of luck you had when you met up with Hyde," says Logan. "Where did you find him first?"

"San Whiskey."

"Long time ago?"

"I was only a kid," says she. "It was five years back, I guess."

"He was a kid, too," says Logan.

"He was never much of a kid," says Al. "He was always kind of grown up."

"That come from using a gun about as soon as he could use a knife and fork," said Logan. "But he ain't such a fast hand, at that."

"Yeah, but he's fast enough," says she.

She wanted to draw out Logan. She thought that the best way would be to get him angry.

"He's got all of your gang buffaloed," she went on.

"Buffaloed?" said Logan. "*He* has the gang buffaloed? What you talkin' about, Al?"

"He's making his play," she replied. "They've tried to stop him. Shot at him by day and by dark. But they never got him. You think they're fire. Well, he's handled that fire, and he ain't been even so much as singed. But he's kept the rest of your hopping."

Logan stared at her, gloomily.

"You'll learn better, before the finish," says he. "I'll tell you one thing. He's dead right now!"

"That's a lie," says Al, but she said afterward that her heart jumped pretty high. However, she kept a straight eye on him.

"It's God's truth," says he. "He's dead, or as good as dead. They've waited a long while and they've given him plenty of chances. But now he's gone too far. He's a dead one, I tell you. They've got the wheels moving that'll grind him to bits. You forget about him."

"He's nothing to me," says Al, "but the wheels they start will never grind on Slow Joe."

"Why not?" snaps Logan, interested, and curious.

"You guess," says the girl.

She closed her eyes and made herself smile, as though she were seeing pictures of what was to happen.

"You're bluffing," says Logan.

"Wait and see," says she. "Wait and you'll see what happens to your higher ups. Not you. You'll be safe enough, Logan. Slow Joe don't waste his time picking on the little fellers. He saves himself for the big ones."

"I'm a little feller, am I?" says Logan.

"Well, say," says she, "would they have given this job to a real man? No, they'd just use a roustabout to pick up a kid like me."

He glared at her, for a moment. Then he grunted.

"Yeah, they said that you had a tongue in your head, and a brain, too. I guess they're right. That's why they wanted you away from Hyde. They said that you'd saved his neck about three times running; and, without you, he'd just go and bump his head into the first wall they built across the trail."

It interested her to hear this, but just then she heard no more, for Jerry came in; and he brought with him a load of blankets, and a saddlebag filled with food. He had brought in two horses and put them in a shed. Perhaps they were the horses from the buckboard, which had been stowed at a distance.

A pot of coffee was put over the fire at once, but she said that she wasn't interested in coffee. She asked to have a blanket pulled over her, because she said that she wanted to sleep. Jerry spread the blanket, and she turned on her side, facing them, and closed her eyes, or seemed to.

But those eyes weren't really closed. She parted her lips a little and breathed regular, soft and deep, as though she were asleep, but all the while, through the thick, long fence of her lashes, she was studying the pair of them.

Logan began to talk. Jerry glanced at the girl and rumbled at Logan to shut up and let the poor kid rest. That was so much the better. Silence makes for drowsiness, and she hoped that Logan would finally begin to nod.

In the meantime, she was working at the rope on her wrists. I've seen her do the trick, turning her hands into collapsible snake-heads. In two minutes her hands were free, and she was waiting for a break.

They drank their coffee, the pair of them, and Jerry braced himself against the wall and began to snore. Logan, however, kept on sipping coffee, and every minute or two, he looked at the girl. Finally he turned around on the box where he was sitting and faced her. His eyes never left her for a moment, even when he was raising the tin of coffee to his mouth.

She was amazed. She saw, then, that Logan was no roustabout. They had told off one of their best men to catch her and this fellow would never close an eye while he was guarding her if it had to be for two or three days.

When she was sure of that she made her plan. I can see her lying there apparently sound asleep watching Logan through the droop of the lashes and figuring her chances.

Then she made her play. Moving her hand up stealthily, she worked a grip on the upper edge of the blanket. She measured the distance, charted her way to the door so that she would not waste a quarter of a second—and flung the blanket over Logan's head.

She was up with the same movement, and sprinting for the doorway. Oh, she could move. I've seen her go like a greyhound! But, fast as she was, Logan had knocked that blanket aside, and jerked a gun before she was out in the dark. He took a snapshot at her, but it was just as she dodged into the darkness, and the bullet only clipped through the side of her blouse.

Then she was away in the night!

Did she run straight ahead?

No, sir, that fox just turned the corner of the shack and stood still while Logan, silent, and Jerry, shouting, rushed out from the doorway into the trees.

"I seen her!" yells Jerry, running hard.

He takes the lead, and Logan after him, toward whatever Jerry thought he had seen in the dimness under the trees. And Al steps into the horse shed, unties one of the horses, hops on its back, and starts.

Cow ponies rein over the neck. This one had a few bucks in its system, but it soon straightened out, and Al dug her heels into its flanks, and drove it away for the road that would lead her back to Kearneyville.

She was needed, by that time, as you'll soon find out.

CHAPTER XXXVII

TO GET back to what was happening to me, which was plenty, I had rocked old Brindle along out the road to the Garret mill. I had on an old slicker, and the showers rattled off it, and Brindle was dashing up the muddy rain water from puddles in the road.

That was discouraging. I don't know of anything that lets a man down more than rainy weather. Wind or cold or heat, a fellow can stand. There's even something stimulating about setting your teeth to endure and to overcome odds, but the dreary monotony of rain is good for nothing except the mute growing things. A man would almost prefer to be a blade of grass, or a standing tree rather than a human, battered by a driving rain. Nothing that lives likes a steady rain. The birds get into shrubbery and shiver there miserably. The toughest range cows drift with their heads pointed away from trouble, and, when they reach a fence, they line up along it, unable to retreat any further, heads down, waiting for the end of the world. Even fish may like water, but I'll bet that they hate rain. I felt that way, on this night, and it seemed an unnecessary piling up of troubles. As if I didn't have enough on my hands already!

Then the wind changed. The clouds broke up, tumbling to the south. The rain only came in passing showers, and I could see the stars, and I was mighty glad to see them.

About this time, I got into sight of Garret's old mill. It looked different. I had not seen it since I was a youngster, and then it had seemed a great big rambling pile of buildings. Now it was as rambling and as rickety as ever, but it was a lot smaller to my eye. The tower at the farther end had fallen down. Perhaps that was one reason the whole thing looked so dwarfed. Then, all around it, a growth of shrubs had sprung up, dark and thick, gleaming faintly, under the starlight, with the rain water which had slicked the leaves or loaded down their hollows.

I went into the woods south of the mill and tethered Brindle on a long rope. I felt sorry for the old horse because he had to stand there under the drip from the trees. Then I went to look things over at close range.

I went up the bank picking my way through the shrubs getting pretty well drenched and cold on the way. Behind me I could hear the roar of the cataracts that thunder down White Horse Gulch, so called, I suppose, because the noise and the white leaping of the water looks like the galloping of wild horses. When we were youngsters we used to go and stand on the cliff above the gulch and watch the riot of the water for half a day at a time. Now and then we'd see a whole tree shoot into the froth and watch it dissolve to matchwood as the iron-hard long teeth of the cataracts chewed it to bits.

I saw the big pond expand before me. The same snag was sticking up in the center, the one we used to swim to, and then dive off again. It cheered me a good deal to see that snag, but on the whole Garret's mill was the darkest, dankest, most dripping and depressing place you'd want to see.

There was nothing worth noting to the south and the east. Nothing except a couple of panes of glass which miraculously still remained in their frames. I suppose that every boy in Kearneyville, sooner or later, heaved clods at the windows of the mill, but still a few targets remained.

I went up the western side. There was nothing there. I turned the far corner, and then, by thunder, I saw a gleam of light from the inside of the mill. I came closer, and heard the crackling of wood that was burning.

Hai! but that made me feel good! Half the crawling fear dropped out of me. The ghostly feeling disappeared, too. There were men ahead of me, and I had a couple of good Colts along, triggerless, hair-trigger affairs, with five shots waiting in each cylinder. Those ten slugs might take care of several crooks, I argued, before the night was ended!

I sneaked up on the window where the light showed through. It wasn't easy to come close, mind you, because there was a veranda running along the side of the place, and the wood of that veranda was so rotten that it threatened to break down with a creaking and a crashing as soon as weight was put upon it.

I heard a murmur of voices, and that made me wild to get within accurate earshot. So I hurried back to the far end of the building, and when I got there I found a door fallen in, and a clear passage down the inside hall. A flicker of light from ahead guided me, and I got quickly and noiselessly down to the room next to that in which the voices were sounding. Through the open door, I could see everything, and what I saw was enough to fill my eye, let me tell you.

Whitey and Frank Gregor were both there, and they had built a good, hot fire in the center of the floor. They had torn up enough planks so that the fire was burning on the ground; that kept the building from taking flame. And the wind was blowing through the ramshackle old place fast enough to carry away the smoke.

They were both pretty wet, and they were sunning themselves at the fire, drying off, and chatting together comfortably. Whitey, I remember, was talking about a poker game where he and Gregor had played crooked partners, being crooks themselves with the cards. Whitey was complaining bitterly.

"There was ten thousand bucks in that crowd, Frank. We could have salted it away. You went and played yourself like a fool! You let him run up the deck on you!"

"How was I to tell?" says Frank Gregor, very ugly and mean. "When he shoved the pack to me for a cut, I fingered down the edge of the cards, and found a crimp, and I knew enough to pass that up, so I reached a little deeper, and gave him the cut. What more could a man do?"

"You jackass!" says Whitey. "The first time that the sandy bird passed me the cards to cut, I found that he was running them up with two crimps. And after I cut—shallow—didn't I pass you the high sign?"

"What sign?"

"I put two fingers on the edge of the table, like I was resting my hand. What else did I mean?"

"I never heard of anybody that could run up a pack and put two crimps in it for cutting," says Frank Gregor.

I could sympathize with him on that. *I* never had, either.

"You never heard of a lot of things," says Whitey. "Pull the cotton stuffing out of your brain, and maybe you'll get some new ideas that would be worth something to you!"

Frank Gregor picked up his head and raised one finger at Whitey Peyton.

"You've been and said about enough!" says he.

"Have I?" says Whitey. "I ain't hardly begun. You beat us out of about ten thousand iron men. And I dropped six hundred, instead."

"Why should you cry?" says Gregor. "I chucked more'n a thousand."

"It don't matter about your money, so much," says Whitey. "If you didn't lose it one way, you would another."

"I've had enough yapping out of you," says Gregor. "Now shut your face, or I'll make you shut it!"

"No, you won't," says Whitey. "In the first place, I'll take you on any time you want trouble, you yaller faced Polack; and, in the second place, you ain't fool enough—not even you—to try a play on your own hook while you're working for *them!*"

He said that last word in a certain way that I'll never forget. Gregor glowered at him, but didn't argue the point.

I sat there and feasted my eyes, in a gloomy sort of way, on the faces of those two rascals. I never saw a meaner pair. And, as I watched them, I thought of two things—the way Lew Ellis had dropped out of his chair, with the slugs of lead still whacking into him, making his body quiver; and of the golden spurs I was wearing, with the little bells muffled with grass.

I sort of prayed, without words, that I might finish off Lew's long account with them, before that night was ended. I even pulled a gun. But I couldn't do that—shoot them down from the darkness, without a warning, while they stood out there bold and free in the light. Yet that was exactly what they had done for Lew Ellis!

The more I looked at Whitey, the more I knew it was a pity if he did not marry Ruth Edgar. They were meant for one another, that pair, to make life one long, sweet hell.

"He oughta be here, pretty soon," says Gregor, changing the subject, growling the words.

"He'll be here," says Whitey. "What's your hurry? When he comes, it means that we start work. The longer he stays away, the longer we got to dry ourselves."

"What'll it be?" asks Gregor.

"Hyde, of course," says Whitey.

"He won't give us that job again. We've fallen down on it too often," says Gregor.

"He'll give us that job," insists Whitey. "That's the great trick, right now. Hyde has to be bumped off. Then we sit pretty."

"Twelve thousand five hundred apiece," says Gregor, turning up his eyes while he does the piece of mental arithmetic.

"Yeah, and we'll double that, tonight," says Whitey.

"Double it?"

"Yeah, I'm gunna hold him up. Why not? Twenty-five thousand was enough when the whole town was agin him; but now Kearneyville wants to wrap him up in cotton batting, and the job's worth more. Besides, Hyde is lucky. Otherwise we would have got him long ago. Am I wrong?"

"You're right," says Gregor. "But will the chief stand for a hold-up now?"

"He's gotta," says Whitey. "And I need spare cash. I'm gunna be a married man, before long, Frank."

"You'll make a beauty," says Gregor. "You'll be a fine addition, as a married man. You crook!"

"Why, you thug," says Whitey, "I'll do as good as the next one. The girl I'm getting is the stuff. I tell you that!"

"Yeah, I've seen her, too," said Gregor. "You'll wake up with your throat cut, a coupla weeks after you've married her."

Whitey looked at him, and was about to answer, I think, when a light rap came at the window opposite the door through which I was watching and listening—the window that opened out over the veranda.

As I said before, *I* could never have crossed that veranda without making a noise like a stampeded cow through dry brush. But somebody else could. In through that window stepped a tall, light figure, and there was my old friend, Mr. Murderer Zip!

CHAPTER XXXVIII

IT FILLED out the picture pretty well, I must say, to have that long, dark-faced knife-thrower added to the others. He came in and gave them a nod, and they nodded back.

"What is it?" said Whitey. "A plant for Mr. Slow Joe, again?"

"Gentlemen," said Zip, "you have been hunting little antelope. Now you hunt the big moose."

"Slow Joe is little antelope, is he?" said Gregor.

"He's big enough to fill a hand, here and there," added Whitey.

I don't know why I didn't feel flattered by all of this talk, but I didn't. I was too interested and excited, and too much leaning into the future. I was a little dizzy with surprise, too, to find that I was out, for the moment, at least. Perhaps the bloodhounds would be turned on somebody else, for a minute.

"Who's the big moose?" said Whitey, point-blank.

"Fifty—thousand—dollar," says Zip.

I blinked. I couldn't help it. Suppose, in the old days, before I'd had the picture of Tom Fellows to fill my eye and give me an ideal—suppose in those days somebody had come along and offered me fifty thousand dollars flat for *any* job, even for murder?

Well, I couldn't say. I hoped that I wouldn't have taken the money except for the result of a fair, stand-up fight, but I wasn't sure. I was mighty miserably unsure, I'll tell you, just then.

"Fifty—thousand—dollar," said Whitey, mimicking, with a sneer, "is a tolerable slice of coin."

He looked at Gregor, and Gregor made a little sign, which I suppose meant that he would go to the end of any trail for his split on such a job. I hardly wondered. I didn't think the worse of him. I almost thought better!

"Fifty—thousand—dollar!" says Zip, his eyes half closed, his face looking devout and almost religious.

"And who's the big moose?" repeats Whitey.

"Fellows," says Zip.

Why should it have shocked me so much? I don't know. I'd seen Zip show his teeth before. I knew—we all knew—that he was no good. But somehow the thought of anyone bargaining for the life of Fellows made me tolerably sick.

When I got over the first rush of blood to the head, I pulled a gun for a second time, and drew a bead on the heart of Mr. Zip. But the other two were already making enough racket.

"The gent that takes a crack at Tom Fellows," said Whitey, "is gunna be hunted by every man in the county, and then he's gunna be caught, and he's gunna be burned alive, about. That's all that'll happen to him! Whatcha talkin' about, Zip? Are you crazy? Fellows? Kill Fellows?"

It warmed me a little to hear that thug talk.

Zip went over and sat down beside the fire, cross-legged,

and he stretched out his skinny hands toward it. His head jutted out. There was a thick bandage running around it, and the bandage reminded me of the terrible crack that Fellows had given him.

Zip said nothing at all.

When Whitey finished raging, big Frank Gregor took his turn, and cursed Zip, and said that he wouldn't tackle such a job for a hundred thousand, all for himself.

And still Zip didn't say a word!

What a poisonous rat he was!

Then Whitey says: "Look here. Who would pay the fifty thousand?"

"I would," says Zip.

That was another facer for the pair of them.

Gregor said: "You? You pay fifty cents! Where would you get fifty thousand dollars?"

Zip took an envelope from his pocket, and from the envelope he extracted a slip of paper, and he offered them this.

It was a small slip, but they found words on it that took them a long time to stare at.

"You take a deposit receipt like that," said Whitey, finally, "and it ain't likely to be forged." He turned on Zip again: "Even supposin' that you got fifty thousand, what would you want to have Fellows bumped off, for?"

Zip was spreading his hands to the fire again, and again he said nothing.

"It's no go," says big Gregor, shaking his head. "Fellows, he's equal to any two men in the world."

Here Zip laid a bony finger on his own breast.

"I make three!" said he.

"Holy smoke!" muttered Whitey. "The nigger is gunna go along with us, eh?"

He looked at Gregor.

Frank Gregor licked his lips and admitted that that made it different.

"You go on and step outside a minute," said Whitey to Zip. "We wanta talk this thing over in private."

Zip did not stir, made no answer.

Whitey beckoned Gregor over toward my door. I sneaked

back, fearing that they'd come right on into the room where I was crouching. If they had, they would have died, there and then, because they were point-blank, of course, and the fire behind them made them beautiful targets. I could thumb that hammer twice before they had a chance to jump. That would leave Zip, in there by the fire, and I aimed to get Zip just about as he would be jumping through the window.

But they didn't come into my room. They stopped just at the door, murmuring to one another.

"We could go and let Fellows know what Zip is trying for," said Whitey.

"Fifty thousand—that's a lot of money," answered Gregor.

"Fellows would pay us something fat for the news. He's pretty liberal with his coin."

"Fifty thousand—you don't pick that up every day," said Gregor.

"And then there'd be Fellows' friendship," argued Whitey. "You know that's worth a lot around these parts. It's better than a signed pardon in your pocket!"

"Who wants to be friends with a dead man?" asked Gregor.

"Dead?" said Whitey drawing back a little.

I could look between them and see the face of Zip. Just then he looked up and gave the pair a very faint smile. I suppose with his cat's ears that he could hear every word they were saying. They were careless with their voices, at that.

"How long will he live with that price on him?" said Gregor.

Whitey grunted, as the force of this struck home. He began to nod, and he said:

"One way of looking at it—if we don't do it, somebody else will."

"Fifty thousand—that's a good stack," said Gregor.

"Shut up!" snapped Whitey. "Don't I know that it's a good stack? And then, the nigger will help us. What's he got agin Fellows?"

"Aw, it ain't him. It's Townsend. Lefty has something agin everybody, I guess!" said Gregor.

"Yeah. Maybe you're right, at that. It's Townsend. Sure that's who it is."

"If we bump Fellows, we're solider with Lefty."

"Yeah. You're talking, now. You're making sense."

Whitey turned to Zip.

"Where's Tom now?" he asked.

"Asleep in his room," said Zip.

"Yeah?"

Zip didn't repeat his statement. He went on watching the fire with his horrible little smile, and warming his bloodless long hands at the blaze.

He was sparing his words, and he seemed to think that time would work for him, and ripen the situation. There was a brain in that narrow skull of his!

"You go with us? You show us the way to his room?" said Whitey, through his teeth. "You dirty nigger, if you tried to double-cross us, we'd mash your head in for you!"

Zip simply smiled more broadly, and made a wide gesture, with both hands, as if asking them not to be ridiculous.

Whitey turned back to Gregor.

"I guess we go," said he.

"Yeah. I guess we go. Fifty thousand—" began Gregor.

"Aw, shut up, will you?" said Whitey. "I can add as well as you can. Zip, we're gunna go with you."

Zip didn't say he was glad of it. He simply got up from beside the fire. I had both guns out, ready for quick work. If it came to the pinch, I was not going to let Fellows down. Three were a lot to tackle, but somehow I felt a sort of a glory in the thought of fighting for Tom. I said to myself, not with words, that if I could serve him like this, it would mean that I was really started on the road to being a man something like him. I guess that I was pretty simple-minded, just then.

"How're we sure that we get the money out of you after the job?" said Gregor.

Zip didn't answer this, either. He just sat down again by the fire.

Whitey and Gregor argued it out.

"He might try to dodge us," says Whitey.

"Yeah, but we got to do a *little* trusting," says Gregor.

"I don't like his look."

"I like fifty thousand, though," says Gregor. "If we do the job, we'll see that he don't slip through our hands. You can trust Frankie for that!"

He grinned like a ghoul. He was a pretty ugly boy, was Gregor.

Just then, Zip raises his head, turns it, and seems to listen, or to be getting a new idea, but he drops his head again.

"Maybe we better take the chance, then," says Whitey.

Zip slips over to one side and lays his head on his arm. It looked as though he were going to spend this time sleeping. His half opened eyes looked dreamily at the fire, which was crackling a good bit, and hissing, too.

"Zip," says Whitey, "we've made up our minds, and we're going. D'you hear me, nigger?"

He went over and stirred Zip with his foot. Zip didn't budge.

"Trying to play possum on us, you fool?" says Whitey.

He leaned over Zip, and then started, with a gasp. Out of the back of Zip he jerked something and stood up, holding it. It was one of those throwing knives that Zip had tried to chuck into me. The red was running down the blade, and coming off the point, drop by drop.

"Oh, my God!" breathes Gregor, and bolts!

CHAPTER XXXIX

WHY didn't I act, then?

Oh, it was a beautiful chance, all right. It was as perfect as anything that I could want. I could have shot that pair to death—and they would simply have been called the murderers of Zip, the servant of Tom Fellows. I had time, too, though barely time enough, because they didn't bolt through my door, or jump through the window through which that knife had been flung into Zip's heart. They veered off, and, with Whitey bolting ahead, they went through another doorway that was out of my sight, and I heard them dashing and crashing through the farther rooms.

And I couldn't shoot. I couldn't even begin to, because the shock and the horror of Zip's death had frozen up my nerves and all of my muscles. I just crouched there like a fool, and did nothing.

When I got my breath back, I left Garret's mill, and I left on tiptoe, with my poor old brain working feverishly. I wondered if my footprints would be found. I recalled the peculiarity of the sign which old Brindle left behind, and which Al had followed so easily. Perhaps I had left fingerprints around, too. Crime experts were getting too infernally clever. They made crime mighty tiresome.

Well, I got outside and found that the face of the sky was burnished bright, and I hated the brightness of it. I would have preferred that rain which I had cursed, most of the way out.

When I got on Brindle, I told myself that I had had enough. Townsend was too much for me. His arm was too long, his hand was too strong and sure. Yes, he had me fairly scared, and beaten. The way Zip died, that way I was pretty sure to drop off, one of these days.

Here I was, falling down from the high pedestal that I had been trying to climb onto. Imitate Tom Fellows? I'd imitate a sneaking coyote, for a while, and make tracks from that section of the country, and try to get the image of the dull, half-opened eyes of Zip out of my memory, if I could.

Well, I reached Brindle, again. I climbed into the wet, sticky saddle, and eased Brindle through the woods, and onto the back trail.

It would be Fellows that I had to see, first of all. A pretty bitter thing to tell him that I was giving up the work. But what had to be, had to be; and I had made up my mind—like a rock, as I thought!

So I cut across country, taking the narrow, wet trails, with even old cat-footed Brindle stumbling more than once.

So we got quickly enough to the house of Fellows. It was black and still, but I found the front door open, and went into the patio and called aloud for him.

I heard a faint answer, in a moment. Then a door opened, and Fellows came out into the court, carrying a lantern. Zip had said that he was in bed; I was surprised, therefore, to find him fully dressed. But he was yawning a little as he asked me what brought me there.

I said: "I thought you were in bed, Tom."

"I was lying down," said Fellows. "Who told you that I was in bed?"

"Zip," said I.

"Zip?" said he, with a start.

He came closer, lifting the lantern until the light of it shone against my eyes, dazzling me a little.

"Have you seen Zip, and talked to the rascal?" said he.

"I've seen Zip," said I, "and I've heard the last of his talk. He's dead, Tom."

He lowered the lantern, which he had kept high all of this while.

"Old Zip is dead?" said he. "Poor devil!"

"I wouldn't be pitying him," said I. "He was just buying Whitey and Frank Gregor to get them to come over here and help him murder you, Tom. Fifty thousand was the price he was putting on you!"

"Had he that much money put away?" said Fellows. "Poor old Zip! Yes, I suppose that he might have, because he was always a canny and a saving fellow. Poor old Zip! Poor old Zip! I'll never have a better servant, a keener or a more careful one, in many ways!"

"Keen to cut your throat, before the finish," said I. "Why, Tom, that fellow was the worst one in the world. D'you understand that he was wanting to murder you, tonight?"

Because I was amazed at this super calm of Fellows'.

"I'd used my fist on him," said Fellows, "and he was as proud as Satan. In a way, I hardly blame him. I'd knocked him down, and I'd done it before strangers. He almost had to have my blood, for that! Can't you see how he felt about it?"

"Yes, but I can see how you might feel about having him plot—besides, Tom, there's no doubt that he was Townsend's man!"

"Townsend's? Yes, I dare say that he was; which made it all the more strange that he should have remained so faithful to me, all of these years," said Fellows.

Confound him! I was half angry with him for the easy way in which he took everything. You couldn't get him to look on the black side either of people or events. Never!

Then I told him everything that I had done, since I left Kearneyville. I told him, too, how Zip had died, and the knife I described, as Whitey had held it. I tried to make the picture vivid, and he stood there, nodding now and then, but apparently almost as much interested in the showering of the fountain as he was in what I was saying. Finally I broke off, abruptly:

"I'll tell you what, Tom, I'm through with the entire business. I thought that I could do the work. I wanted to finish what Lew Ellis or his ghost would want me to do. But I see that I can't. And there's an end of it. I'm sorry. I know that it shows me up mighty weak. But I'm telling you the facts. You can laugh at me if you want to."

He didn't laugh, but he put a hand on my shoulder and said:

"You know the story about the wishing gate, Slow?"

"No," said I. I was angrier still. He had a way, which I've never described, of sometimes leading the talk away from a subject and off afield to all sorts of out-of-the-way things. I expected that he would do that now.

"You know, Slow," said he, "that the fable runs: A lad started out to find the mysterious Wishing Gate. He was told that if he worked hard enough and was patient enough, he would finally come to that gate; and, when he reached it, he could wish for anything in the world that he wanted—and it would be his. Well, this youngster lighted out through the woods—there always seem to be woods in fairy-stories—and he ran like sixty all day, or most of it. And finally he was exhausted. And he came, half blind, to a rickety old gate that barred his way, and sat down and leaned his back against it. After he had rested a while, he got up and started back home, and got there very late, and had a whipping for playing truant."

Fellows paused, smiling at me.

"Well?" said I. "What the devil does all of that mean?"

"The rickety old gate—why, you see, that was the Wishing Gate. D'you understand now, Slow?"

"I understand a little. But what that has to do with you and me and—"

He patted my shoulder with his big, gentle hand. He had a touch like a woman—or like a tiger—just as he saw fit to use it.

"The point is, Slow, that you've been wearing yourself out on this job, and daring all sorts of death and damnation, and now you're going to give up the trail at the very moment when you have a good chance to win!"

"Win?" said I, with hope rushing back through floodgates into my mind. "D'you mean that, Tom?"

"You haven't asked me why I left the hotel so suddenly," said he. "I stepped out, and left you a little up in the air, old man."

"Go on, Tom," said I. "Tell me, old son. I'm hungry to hear."

"I heard a whistle, and I knew that whistle was for me, a signal. You know, Slow, that while you've been working like a badger on this case, and while I've appeared to be sitting back and taking things easy, I've been just a shade busier than appeared. And at last I've turned up the information that I want."

"The man behind the guns?" I cried at him.

"Hush!" said he, suddenly, and glanced around about him in a startled way.

I jumped.

"It's all right," he said, "but there's no need to lift our voices. There's danger in the air, Slow, though we're going to win out. To cut a long story very short, I've been lyin' down and resting, because, in a very short time, I expect to ride out to meet our man of mystery."

"By thunder, Tom," said I, admiring him, almost ready

to cry with relief. "I might have known that while I was wandering around, sweating, making a fool of myself, you'd be quietly accomplishing the whole trick!"

"Tut, tut!" said he. "You've done some grand things. You've done some wonderful things, Slow, and the people in this part of the country are going to remember you for the way you bearded Townsend."

"I suppose it's Townsend that you're going to see tonight?" said I.

He smiled at me.

"Don't ask me for names, Slow," said he. "You know how the old people feel, when youngsters ask them for the ending of the story ahead of time? That's the way I feel, I want to give you a bit of a surprise, if I can."

"Say, Tom," said I, "you do as you please. God knows that if I come to the end of this trail, tonight, I'm a happy man. Then I can chuck away this infernal badge, and go after Gregor and Whitey, man to man. That's what would please Lew Ellis most, I think."

"You loved Lew Ellis, Slow, didn't you?" he said, gently.

"He was game, and he was my partner," said I.

"Well," said Fellows, gravely, "let me tell you this, Slow: What you've done, or tried to do, and the danger you've lived in for the sake of your friend—I don't know how to put it—but it's opened my eyes—it makes me see life in a new way, and a sharper way. It makes me wish that I were another sort of a man."

"You, Tom?" said I.

And then I laughed, rather shakily.

"My God, man—" said I, and I was about to break out with a confession of what he meant to me, as an ideal—far down the road ahead of me—when something stopped me.

He seemed to guess that some such embarrassment was ahead, for he broke off all compliments, at once, by asking me if I were ready to go along with him. I told him that I would ride to hell with him, if he wanted to go.

Then I asked him where we were going, and he took the wind out of my sails and left them flapping by his answer:

"To Garret's mill!"

CHAPTER XL

I WAS so staggered that I didn't say a word until he joined me in front of the house, riding one of his long-legged thoroughbreds, while I was sitting gloomily in the saddle on Brindle.

"Tom," said I, "did you really mean that you expect to find your man at Garret's mill?"

"Yes. Why not?"

"Why—it sort of staggers me. That's where I left Zip lying dead, you know!"

"True," said he, in his mild way. "Now, I'll tell you what, Slow. Your nerves have been shaken up a little, tonight, and I don't wonder. The thing for you to do is to stay back here, quietly. Make yourself at home. You'll find half a dozen beds; use any one of 'em that you want, and let me go along and push through this thing by myself."

Of course I wouldn't stand for that. It might be true, and it *was* true that my nerves were not so good, just then, but I wouldn't stay behind when Tom Fellows went out on such a mission as this. So off we went together, riding side by side, and the little, light sound of the golden bells at my heels made to me the sweetest music that I've ever heard. For I thought that all the rest of my way was downhill, so to speak, and easy going for me. One thing at least was certain. Fellows had said that this night he would meet the man behind all the mystery, and show him to me, and I knew that Fellows could not lie. I was almost equally sure that he could not fail. I didn't feel that I was needed. I went rather as a sort of spectator to the show.

Still, I wasn't entirely of a piece, as we headed closer and closer to the mill. The infernal place was full of horror for me. And yet there was Tom Fellows, singing softly as he rode along—Tom Fellows, almost within reach of my hand! That made everything almost all right.

I had some weird thoughts about Lew Ellis, too. If there were such things as spirits, his ghost must be riding the air close to me, now, ready to watch the business which lay ahead.

I told Tom about the wood where I had left Brindle, before, and he seemed to think that it would serve as well as the next place, though he said that there was no particular need for secrecy, now. I wondered at this, but I didn't want to spoil his fun by talking too much or by asking too many questions. He had a right to a little touch of mystery, if he cared to use it, the Lord knew!

We put up the two horses, and left them rubbing noses and getting acquainted. Then we went into the mill. I walked first, because Fellows said that he didn't know the place very well, and, also, he asked me to take him to the rear room where I had last seen Zip, alive or dead.

I found that room more easily than I could have found any other, because there was still a trace of red light coming off the dying coals of the fire that had been built there. And, stained by the rose of the flame, we could see Zip lying just as I had left him; and his eyes were still half open, and his lips were still smiling a bit, a sagging, mocking, but half weary smile.

Fellows walked over to him and stood for a moment above the dead man. He looked like a giant, standing there in that dull light. Then he said:

"Zip, good-by. As truly as I ever owed my life to you, as truly as you ever owed your life to me, I'm sorry that you're gone. I'm sorrier still that you were a fool. I would have taken care of you to the end of time, but—"

He turned away.

"We'd better build up that fire a little, old son," he said to me.

"Are we to stay in here—with that?" said I.

He took off his coat and laid it over Zip.

"It's a pity to waste the embers," said Fellows. "Does Zip bother you?"

"I can stand it," said I. "But he bothers me a little."

Said Fellows: "I rather like to be here. Zip is company for me. He was company living, and he's company dead. You know, Slow, that I've been over a good part of the world with him. He never failed me. He never let me down. I treated him as a friend and not as a servant, because he was worthy of being treated as a friend. A little too free with his knife—yes, he was that. But, after all, we all have our failings. And Zip was good to me. Mighty good to me, Slow."

He sighed, and shook his head.

I think it was the most tremendous exhibition of steel nerves that I've ever heard of. Or, perhaps one might say, the lack of any nerves at all. I was ashamed to mention my own foolish chills and fevers simply because I was in the same room with a dead body.

In the meantime, I started to build up a fire. I only objected:

"You know, Tom, that if we have a fire here it's going to attract the attention of the man you expect to meet here?"

Tom merely smiled at me.

"He won't sneak up and throw knives through the window," said he. "You really must stop worrying and leave the thing to me, Slow."

"All right," said I. "I can't make it out. Only—I'm pretty well up in the air!"

"I don't wonder that you are," said he. "But, when the thing breaks, everything will be clear to you in one second."

"It will be quick shooting?" said I.

"Quick shooting?" he said.

He seemed to ponder on this for a moment.

"No," he said at last, "if it all happens as I've planned to have it happen, I don't think there'll be any shooting—no quick shooting, at least. And perhaps there won't be any shooting at all."

I sighed.

"I sort of felt that there were more dead men in the air," said I. "That's my nerves, I guess."

He nodded to this.

"Yes," he said. "There will certainly be at least one dead man before the morning comes. Only—it may not be by shooting."

He brooded on this thought for quite a long time, sitting on the edge of the torn up floor, close to the body of Zip. He looked as big and as broad in a shirt as he did in his coat. He looked as trim and as well-dressed, too. If he hadn't been what he was, Tom could have been called a dandy.

I kept the fire up good and brisk. The warmth of it was pleasant. Why it was that that fire didn't constitute a danger to us I gave up trying to decipher. At least, I determined not to be such a fool as to doubt what Tom had expressly said to me.

But after a time—we had been there more than half an hour—I asked him about when he expected the man of the mystery.

"What time is it now?" said he.

"Eleven twenty-five," said I, looking at my old open-faced watch.

"Eleven twenty-five?" he repeated, carelessly. "Oh, well, I remember, now. We need not have come so early. He won't be here before midnight. He ought to be here at twelve, precisely."

I laughed a little, not any too steadily.

"That's sort of like part of a ghost story, Tom," said I.

"Why?" he asked me, simply.

"Well, midnight, and all of that!"

He nodded.

"It *is* like a ghost story, Slow," said he. "And, in a sense, I think that you'll find it a good deal *worse* than a ghost story. That's what I'm afraid you'll think of it. However, at twelve sharp he ought to be here." He added, as though to confirm the thought for himself: "He's one of the most punctual men in the world."

"Do you know him?" I ventured to ask.

"I know a great deal about him," said Fellows, "but I can't say, exactly, that I know him. A human brain and a human soul take a great deal of knowing, don't you think?"

"I suppose so," said I, rather embarrassed by the size of the topic and his gravity in approaching it.

"You yourself, Slow," said he. "Do you know yourself, old son?"

"Why, I've always thought that I did," said I.

"I wouldn't bet on that, if I were you," said he. "No matter if we know all the items, the sum is apt to add up differently for every man. But—oh, well, there's no use talking about such stuff. It leads one nowhere—nowhere!"

He snapped his fingers.

There was something painful to him, I could plainly see, in his last reflections.

Then he said: "What's the time coming to, now?"

"It's not quite twelve," said I.

"Well," said he, "we'll hear steps, before long."

Then we were both silent, and silence, as everyone knows, is the hardest thing to endure when there is trouble in the air. It's the hardest, the longest, and the slowest thing to endure. But Tom didn't speak. He simply sat there with the glow of the fire ruddy on his handsome face. And the only thing that supported me was the sight of his perfect calm. As for questions, like thinking, I had put them behind me.

Half a dozen times, I thought that I heard the creaking of a step, outside on the veranda, and got a sharp shiver down my spine, but I was always wrong. It was just some sound of the wind in the trees, or the wind-shaken stirrings of the old ramshackle mill building. Every minute or two, I looked at my watch, but time was standing still, like the sun in the Bible story.

However, there had to be an end to suspense—either an end to that or else an end to my heart action. It was beating like a triphammer when I heard, lightly, but distinctly, the sound of a step down the hall, coming without haste, steadily, toward us.

I stood up. Tom Fellows had risen, also. I gave him one glance and thought that his face was a little set and grim. He reached inside his coat, and I supposed that he was loosening a revolver in one of the slip holsters which he carried beneath the pit of his arms, after the fashion of the old gun-throwers.

Then I turned to face the door. The steps were almost there!

And then the shock came.

"He's here!" I whispered over my shoulder to Tom.

"Yes," said Fellows, aloud. "He's behind you!"

And, as he spoke, he caught me at the elbows with a grip that froze muscles and sinews to the bone of the arm.

Even if he had barely touched me, however, that voice of his and the words he spoke would have been enough for me. I was paralyzed.

Into the doorway, at that moment, stepped Lefty Townsend, but I hardly regarded him. I knew the incredible truth—that Tom Fellows was the man who had secured the murder of Ellis; Tom Fellows was the man who had been trying for my life!

CHAPTER XLI

TOWNSEND paused for a moment in the doorway and looked us over.

"Well, Tom," he said, "I see that you have him here. Been so doggone slippery that I kind of half thought you might not nail him."

"Come, come, Lefty," said Fellows. "You know that I'm a man of my word. And here he is for you."

"Not for me," said Lefty. "For you, boy."

He came sauntering up to me, taking a length of strong twine out of his pocket. He worked it around my wrists, standing behind me. And I didn't resist. It was partly because of the numbing power in the grip which Fellows had set upon me, and it was partly because of the sickness of heart and the dizziness of mind which still held me, and held me harder than the hands of that giant.

I had my hands lashed fast together, palm to palm. It's the best way. It gives the fingers no real chance to wriggle. The wrists have a leverage, but what's the use of that against twine? For there's no stretch or give in good twine. As I felt those cords being twisted into place, I knew that I was a dead man, and I hardly cared.

My mind was leaping back to so many other things—to the glory I had placed like a mental light around the thought of Tom, and to the many small, and gentle things he had said and done.

Well, he had been a man of his word, this night. He had lived up to his word and showed me the man of mystery. He would live up to another promise before the dawn, no doubt—that one man should die—perhaps not from a bullet wound!

Why should they use a gun on me? They could knock me over the head like a calf, or a grown ox!

Lefty Townsend was saying:

"I dunno why you should have wanted me down here, Tom. You've done all the handling yourself."

"Well," said Tom, "it's a little touch of delicacy that I can't expect you to appreciate, Lefty. This lad, you see, has had a great idea about me. He's been thinking, this while, that his battle was my battle, and I have a qualm of conscience about putting him out of the way. I pass that job over to you, Lefty."

"I don't mind," said Lefty. "What about now—and then we can have a chat?"

He stepped around to the side of me and pulled out a revolver. He grabbed it by the barrel and weighted it in his hand. One tap with that would crack my skull for me.

"Wait a minute," said Fellows. "If you drop him there, it makes *two* bodies that will have to be hauled away. Why not walk him down to the White Horse, and let the rocks eat him?"

"You've got a brain for the labor saving devices," said Townsend. "As Ma always says to me—"

"Let's forget Ma Townsend for a few minutes," said Fellows. "We might as well get on with this, though. You can find your way down the bank to the cliff with him, Lefty?"

"Sure I can," said Townsend, cheerfully. "Wait till I warm myself up a little, will you? For a little job like this, why did you have to make me ride all this way, Tom? Wouldn't Gregor or Whitey, or one of the other boys have done as well?"

"Maybe they would," answered Fellows. "But you know, Slow Joe, here, is one of the lucky lads. And it takes real brains and care to beat luck. Besides, the less known the better—the less known by anyone except you and me."

"Come, come," said Lefty. "Several of the boys know that you're gunning for him."

"Nobody knew," said Fellows. "Only Zip. Zip handled everything for me."

"Then why didn't he handle this?" asked Lefty.

"Because he's lying there under that coat," said Fellows. Townsend went over and lifted the flap of the coat and looked.

"Well, well," he said. "How did it happen? Slow Joe, again?"

"No. I didn't know Slow was here. But I knew that Zip was on the loose to get me. I spotted him this evening. Spotted him by leaning out from a hotel window, Lefty!"

"Oh, you're the boy with an eye, Tom," said Lefty. "I always knew that!"

"So I trailed him up here, half thinking that I might be able to talk him out of his foolishness. But I wanted first to see how far he would go. He'd already tried to shoot me through a window of the Guernsey Hotel."

"The fool must of been crazy," said Lefty.

"Only proud," said Fellows. "The fact is that I'd had to knock him down, the other day. He was about to throw a knife into Joe. I wouldn't have minded that, but the girl, Al, was there, with a drawn gun. She would have made everything difficult."

"Yeah, and that's a true thing," said Lefty. "She made

things a mess for me, too, after Zip had come up and said that you wanted the kid bumped off."

He added, directly to me:

"You know, Slow, that if you'd taken my offer, and joined up with us, there never would of been no more trouble for you. I would of stood out for you agin Tom, even, long as him and me have worked together. But I would of valued you, Slow, and made a man of you, and got you famous, and rich, too. I took a likin' to you, and so did Ma. She really laid herself out to like you, Slow. But you was proud, and pride is a terrible thing. It gets between a terrible lot of men and their business. Am I wrong, Tom?"

Fellows shrugged his shoulders.

"Are you warm enough now, Lefty?" he asked sharply.

"Don't get nervous, Tom," said Lefty. "I'm gunna take him out and give him a swim in the White Horse, all right. But don't you go and get all excited about it. There ain't any good in that. Besides, I'm kind of dampish. I been rained on a good bit, tonight." He added: "Where's that hell-cat of a kid? It's a wonder that she ain't had her claws in this!"

"She's taken care of," said Fellows. "She's enjoying a little rest."

"Have to tap her over the head?" asked Townsend, indifferently.

"I hope not," said Fellows. "I don't know just how the boys managed it, but I hope that they didn't have to slug her. A bright youngster, Joe," he added to me.

I hadn't been able to speak, up to then. Sickness of heart had choked me and stopped me. Now I said:

"Tom, she's the girl you wanted to marry. Or was that only lying, too?"

"Listen to him," said Lefty, pushing his detestable face close to mine. "Doggone me if the kid ain't got tears in his eyes, besides that wobble in his voice. You've gone and hurt his feelings, Tom! That's what you've done."

Fellows did not smile, and he met my eyes with a perfectly level and steady glance. His color had not altered. No, it was not a question of perfect nerves. It was a matter of no nerves at all! I could see, as through the sudden opening of a door, why he had seemed like a god to the rest of us. It was because of the man's superhuman calm. But what we thought was resolved gentleness and humanity was the utter lack of either. He was never troubled because the pain of others meant nothing to him!

To think that already, this night, he had been at the mill, committed a murder, and returned to his house to wait —no doubt in the hope that I would have to look him up before it was time for him to keep his appointment with Lefty. No, it must have been more than hope. He banked on my coming to him, when I found out that Al had disappeared. The letter she had left for me? That would be a simple bit of forgery, of course. And I didn't know Al's handwriting very well.

So now he was able to meet my eye, without shame.

"I wanted to get her away from you, Slow," he explained to me. "If I could substitute, in your place, another interest that would occupy her mind, if in any way I could cut her off from you, I knew that you'd soon be in my hands. Already, it had only been the girl who saved you, several times."

"Yeah, I know the times," said I. "It was only a play of yours, then?"

"Only a play," he admitted.

"Tom," said I, "will you tell me what made you want to kill Ellis?"

"I don't mind telling you," said he. "Ellis was growing a little too ambitious on the frontier. Lefty and I have widespread interests, you see, and some of our interests have to do with smuggling of various kinds—"

"Hold on, big boy!" said Lefty. "There ain't any need of telling him everything."

"Lefty," said Fellows, "the desire to learn, even at the point of death, is one of the most admirable passions in the world. There was Socrates who—"

"This one ain't dead yet," said Lefty.

"No," agreed Fellows, "but he's dying."

"One more thing, Tom," said I. "Ellis wasn't enough. You had to start on me, too! What had I done to you?"

"You were on my trail, you fool," said Fellows, with a touch of contemptuous emotion, the first that he had showed.

"I wanted to brush you aside, gently, but you wouldn't be brushed. You and your golden spurs!"

He looked down at my heels, openly sneering. I felt what he had called me, a fool. He was not a man. He was simply a devil. There was not even mystery about him, except the mystery that his handsome face showed none of the evil in his heart. But was even that strange? No, I think not, because evil shows in the face only when it is recognized in the heart. He added:

"I would have done away with you before—but there was something touching in the doglike devotion you were showing for me. I'm sorry, Lefty," he said, "but you must admit that I've never troubled you with this sort of a thing before."

"No, big boy, no," said Lefty, cheerfully. "Always been willin' to wash your own dirty clothes, before this. But I don't mind. Shucks, what's a friend for?"

"Then take him out of my sight, will you?" said Fellows. "I'm tired of the sight of his crooked jaw!"

And he stepped back, and made a little, passionate gesture of disdain and disgust.

I was really amazed, not now by what he said, but by the real emotion that was in his voice and in his action.

"Well, Tom," said I. "So long! If you've hurt Al—well, may you burn an extra while in hell."

"Take him away—take him away, Lefty," said Fellows. "In another moment, he'll be forgiving me, and I don't want that to happen. I'll wait for you here, and when you come back, we'll take Mr. Zip down the same trail. So long, Slow."

And so I was led away from him, and into the darkness of the hall.

CHAPTER XLII

LEFTY rested the muzzle of a gun in the small of my back. It was the easiest way of keeping in touch with me. In his other hand, he held an end of the cord that was lashed to my wrists.

"It's all right, Lefty," I said. "Don't worry. I'm not going to make you shoot early and then have a long trek with my body."

"Slow," said Lefty, "you got nacheral manners, that's what you've got. I always admire to see the way that a well brought up young feller acts. Mostly, they ain't raised, nowadays. They ain't no care put into their training, and that's a mighty pity. But you been raised proper. Yeah, and a pity and a cryin' shame that you didn't join up with me, before that Zip come along with the word from Tom. I would have stood up for you, even agin Tom, as I was sayin', once you was on the inside. But you wouldn't! Howsomever, that's over, and ended. But a mighty lot of use we might of been to one another, all said and done. But I took it kind of hard that you would of sent Wallie Blue after me. That seemed kind of downright mean, young feller. But there ain't any meanness in my nacher. I forgive you, right enough. Free and clean I forgive you."

He chattered along in this manner, while he forced me down the narrow path that passed along the verge of the river. The bank began to grow deeper and steeper. Ahead of me I could hear the roaring and the chanting of the White Horse; and, though it was dark, I felt that I could see the bright leaping of the waters as though a summer sun were sparkling above them.

Nothing human, nothing that was I, would pass through that terrible flume.

I don't think that I was afraid. The walking, and the talk of the strange fiend behind me benumbed my brain. Perhaps I'd had too many shocks, all piled together, to be able to register any new emotions, or any great ones.

At any rate, we were already at the beginning of the cataracts, and the thunder of them was shaking the cliff, when I felt a sharp jerk on the cord, fastened to my wrists and the next instant the pull relaxed entirely.

I whirled about, wondering if God Almighty had made Townsend stumble. And then I saw him lying on his back, his arms thrown out wide, and, stepping across the fallen body, to me, was a slender form that I knew right well.

"Al!" I shouted at her.

She had the clubbed revolver still gripped in her hand, and her voice was a screech as she called back to me above the roaring of the water:

"Have I killed him, Slow? See if I've killed him!"

She had a knife out at the same moment, and cut the cord that held my hands together. She offered me her own weapon. I didn't need it. They hadn't bothered to remove my own Colts, and one of them was poking into the stomach of Lefty as I kneeled beside him.

Instantly I felt the beating of his heart.

"He's all right," I said. "He's alive. Only stunned. Pick up that gun at your feet. D'you see the glint of it? We'll bring him back to Kearneyville alive and see what—"

That was as far as I got.

A staggering blow clipped me across the point of the chin, for he had jerked his elbow across his body and the sharp bone clipped me cleanly on the "button."

I sat down hard and fast as Al yipped like a frightened wolf and leaped aside, swinging up her gun for a shot. I don't know that she would have had time to use it before Townsend's bullet found me, but, as he rolled over and leaped to his feet—agile as a cat in spite of his hardy years—he miscalculated one thing, his nearness to the brink of the cliff. Or was it that he was still half stunned from the effects of the blow that Al had given him?

Anyway, suddenly he slipped and toppled backward. He threw out both hands to regain his balance, but toppled still farther out, the gun dropping from his clutching fingers.

It was a frightful thing to see. It cleared the mist out of my badly jarred brain; and, flinging myself forward, without getting to my feet, I reached for him.

My hand closed on nothing but the flap of his coat as he shot downward, and that coat was so loose and sloppy of fit that it peeled off in my hands.

Townsend shot down out of our ken, with a frightful screech that I shall never forget.

And there we were—I prostrate, and Al kneeling beside me—looking into the starlit dimness, the hell of that seething water beneath us.

The world would see nothing of Lefty Townsend again, not a vestige, not a shadow of him.

I got to my feet. I grabbed Al by the shoulders, and shook her.

"It's once more, Al!" I said to her. "And this time it was sure-fire finish for me."

I tried to kiss her. She put the heel of her palm under my chin and pushed herself away from me.

"Lefty was out of luck with you," says she, trying to be light. But her voice shook a lot.

"There's one more left, Al," said I, with misery rising up in me.

"One?" said she.

I hurried her back down the path; the roar of the White Horse grew dimmer behind us.

"Ay," said I, "the man behind, the worst of them all—the—"

I stopped walking; I stopped talking. It was a thing, somehow, that I didn't want to talk much about. I didn't have the words, or the heart, to speak about him.

"Fellows!" she gasped at me. "It's Tom Fellows that you mean!"

"Were you there, Al?" said I. "Were you out there on the veranda at the mill window?"

"No," she said. "I picked you up after you left Tom's house, and I followed you in, just out of your hearing distance. You two didn't look around once! Then I waited around outside of the house. It was pretty bleak work. But when I tried to cross the veranda and get at the window, I saw that the boards would creak."

She had been waiting outside all the time! How I admired the patience of that little cat of a girl!

"And then, Al?"

"Then I saw you come out with Lefty Townsend. That's all. I just followed along, sneaking from bush to bush—pretty scared—because Lefty *did* look back!"

"What made you think of Fellows?" I asked.

"Who else is there in the mill?" said she, simply. "Besides, I knew he wasn't what he seemed."

"How did you know that?" I asked her, amazed.

But then, I don't suppose that she could ever have really surprised me with her knowledge and her insight. I was getting too used to it.

"I knew it," she said, slowly and carefully, "when he began to talk as though he were fond of me. Because I knew that he really couldn't be. There was a difference. I wasn't important enough to attract Tom Fellows. He was lying. I knew he was lying, but I couldn't tell why. I just guessed that he wasn't as simple as he seemed. I wanted to tell you. But I was afraid. Besides, I wasn't *quite* sure."

I said:

"He's the man behind the gun. He's the fellow who sent Gregor and Whitey Peyton to kill Lew Ellis. He's the devil himself, and he's back there in the mill—and I'm going to get him, or kill him! You stay here."

"I'll come along," said she. "I've earned a right to have a hand in that."

I got her by the arm and held her hard. I said:

"Listen to me, Al. Other things you could help me with a good deal. But you can't help me with this. I've loved him. I've worshiped him, just about. Now I'm gunna see if there's a God. I'm gunna go back and face him. I'm not afraid. Not a bit. I'm going to fight him. If there's a God, I'm going to down him. It's not for any other human to step in between us. It's God that'll decide."

Well, I felt that way, though the words look funny as

I write them down. I mean, it seemed pretty impossible that anything as evil as Tom Fellows could live, and keep right on flourishing in the world. There was a justice somewhere.

Al began to whimper. She said:

"He'll kill you, Slow!"

"Maybe he will," said I. "But I don't think so. I think that he's gunna drop. And if he does, I'm gunna change and reform—"

"Wait a minute, Slow," said she. "Don't you be promising too much."

I remembered, even then, what the marshal had said to me in San Whiskey, and I could have laughed, except that there was no laughter inside of me.

"You stay here. Don't you dare to come in," said I. "Don't you sneak in behind me."

She said nothing. She just stood there, and I walked on back to the house, and down the hall of it, and into the room, where Tom Fellows was still sitting by the fire, near the dead man. He didn't look up.

"Well," he said, "we'll have to get rid of this carrion now, Lefty."

When I didn't speak, he looked up, and saw me. Then he stood up. He looked at me. He looked at my hands.

"I didn't hear your spurs!" said he.

"I stuffed grass in 'em," said I.

It didn't seem strange to me that he should speak about the bells of my spurs. They meant something to me, too. They were still a sort of a symbol. Then I said:

"You've got guns on you. Make your move, Tom. Make your move first."

"Slow," said he, "you're a brave fellow. I really always liked you. You could have potted me at your leisure through the doorway. I hope that I don't have to kill you now. I'll try to let you off with a broken leg, or a smashed shoulder. You're bringing this on yourself. I don't really want to do it."

I could look him back in the eye; and, for some reason, I was as sure of myself as I am that a clock ticks.

"I'm going to beat you, Tom," said I, "because there *is* a God, somewhere!"

He started to speak, changed his mind as though he were gagging, and suddenly his face froze in ugly lines. His hand flashed inside his coat for the draw.

It was a beautiful move. It was as fast and sure as lightning, and even as my own hand jumped for my gun, I knew that I'd never beat his draw. I didn't. I was a whole tenth of a second behind him, which meant that he had fired twice before I dropped the hammer on my first cartridge. I felt the whir of his bullets past my head: he wasn't playing for the body after all. It was my death, in the pinch, that he wanted. But he missed! Something put a quiver in that rocklike arm of his. He missed, and my first shot dropped him to the floor of that room.

CHAPTER XLIII

AL came with a white face. She had followed me, in spite of my commands. She would! When she saw me standing there, looking stupidly at the great form on the floor, she ran past me, and bent over him; before I knew what she was about, she was tying those terrible hands of his behind his back, tugging and wrenching to make the cords fit tight.

For he wasn't dead! No, he was living, and the blood that reddened one side of his face came from the furrowing of the bullet as it scraped along the side of his skull. He was stunned; that was all.

In a moment he sat up, moved his arms, felt the cord hold his hands, and was still. He didn't speak while we tied up his wound. He didn't speak when we mounted him, his high-stepping horse tied to the pommel of my saddle. He didn't speak all the way back to Kearneyville. He didn't speak as we came into the town in the early cold and gray of the dawn. He wasn't sullen. He wasn't gloomy. He wasn't afraid. He was simply his old steel-nerved self, composed and quiet.

We went to the house of Wallie Blue. I hollered for him. A window was thrown up. Wallie leaned out.

"I have Tom Fellows here with me," I said.

"Well, he oughta be able to take care of you," said Wallie. "What do you want me to do?"

"Keep him in jail till he's hung," said I.

That brought Wallie out of his house. It took about an hour to make things clear to him, and even then I think he would have called me a fool and a liar except for the bloody bandage around Tom's head, and what we found in the coat of Townsend. Because Ma Townsend was wrong. Lefty didn't carry all of his accounts in his head. He carried them in a big, fat notebook, fully annotated. There were twenty years of accounts in that book, and the name of Fellows was spelled out a hundred times. Before we got through reading in that book, we knew enough to hang Fellows twenty times. And he was put in jail and loaded with fetters, and then three men were put on duty sitting with riot guns outside of his cell. That satisfied even me. I was sure that the finish had come for him.

So I went back to the hotel, and got a room for Al, and kissed her goodnight, and went up to my own room, feeling like an old man. The face of big Fellows was bright in my mind. And two other faces were loading down my memory, too. Gregor and Whitey Peyton.

After all of my efforts at them, they had been jailed by mere chance. When they came back from the mill, they went to the Kicking Mule, braced themselves up with too much liquor, began an argument, and pulled guns. They broke a lot of glass with their bullets before they were tapped on the head and taken to the jail, not on a serious charge, but simply to keep the peace.

Well, Townsend's notebook would hang them, too.

So I got to my room, and opened the door, and lighted the lamp, and as I turned around from it, a voice said:

"Hullo, Hyde. I've been wondering when you'd come back."

That was Marshal Werner, sitting up in one of the beds, looking fit, though his hair was all tousled from the pillow.

I gave him a good long look. Then I took out the badge —the neat little steel shield that had his own signature scratched on the back of it. I threw it onto his bed.

"That's a present back for you," said I.

I flopped on the other bed, grabbed the quilt, and gave myself—mud and all—a roll in it.

"You want to give up the job?" says the marshal. "You prefer jail to this sort of work, man?"

I didn't explain. I just shut my eyes. Nobody needed to sing me to sleep. I heard him talking, still, getting a little angrier as he went on. That was the sound that I went to sleep hearing.

When I woke up, it was broad noon. No sun was entering the room, except a hot fringe through the south window. The marshal was standing in the middle of the room, watching me; and as he stood there, looking so spic and span, and efficient, and sort of like an army officer, I couldn't help sitting up in bed and thumbing my nose at him.

He didn't flinch. He didn't budge. He just stood there and watched me get up and go into the bathroom. I shaved and bathed, and came out with a clean skin. But there was no joy in me, not even when I saw Werner standing just where I had left him before. Then he said:

"Slow, I underrated you about a thousand per cent."

"You didn't," said I. "I would have been a dead man ten times, except for that girl, that Alicia Doloroso. She saved me last night. She picked me out of the White Horse, as you might say. You can take all your praise and go to the devil with it. Or else, take it to her. She did everything. What's the noise ouside?"

"They're making up their minds to try to lynch Fellows and his two friends," said Werner. "But they won't. A Kearneyville crowd hasn't it in them. Besides, Blue will stand by me, and I'll get all three of them into a Federal court. This is going to be a great case, a grand case. It's going to be the making of you, Slow. You're going to be a great man in the service."

"As a marshal?" said I.

"Yes," said he. "As a marshal, and a great one."

I went over and tapped him on the chest, sort of familiar.

"Werner," said I, "I'll tell you the service that I'm going into. I'm dirty. I'm dirty inside. I'm gunna get clean by going into the cow-service. I'm gunna be nursemaid to a herd of long-horns, and personal valet to a caviya of bright little mustangs, strung on a chain of hell-fire. That's gunna be my career, at thirty dollars a month, till I feel decent again. Don't talk about your damned law. I don't want it."

He stood the shock of that pretty well.

"The law's done better than you think," said he. "It's turned loose a friend of yours. He's waiting to see you in San Whiskey."

I got pretty weak in the knees, all at once. I grabbed his hands.

"It ain't Dick?" said I.

Suddenly he grinned at me, and I knew that he'd done it himself. I saw that he was white. A real white man, and it knocked me all in a heap. I had to go over and stand at the window, for a minute, getting air, and while I was standing there, a lot of fool cowpokes that were riding down the street seen me, and they started throwing up their own hats, and shooting holes in 'em, and yelling their heads off, like I was running for a political office and needed votes. I gave them a good, silent damning, and turned around—and the marshal wasn't there.

No, he was gone, and I was gone too, in a minute, because trouble busted in Kearneyville, just then, with a roar of guns. I started sprinting, but I sprinted too slow. When I got to the jail, the mischief was done.

What had happened was pretty simple. The three guards had sat on their chairs, fine and steady, until the crowd begun to pack around the jail, thicker and thicker, and threatening to rush the place. Then those guards got scared. They were willing to fight to keep the crooks from getting out, but they weren't willing to die to keep the crowd from getting in to lynch the rascals. So when it looked as though that crowd would make the rush, the guards just slipped away.

A minute after they were gone, big Fellows dropped off his shackles and picked the lock of his cell door, and then turned loose Gregor and Peyton. The three of them made the break. While that crowd was yelling and howling and trying to get up its cowardly soul, the way that a crowd will, through the back door of the jail, three men came in a flying wedge, with Fellows at the point of it.

They clove right through that mob, and they got to horses, before much was done; but, when the three of them mounted, they made pretty good targets, and a rattle of shots dumped Gregor and Peyton on the ground.

Wouldn't you know it? The two underlings went down, dead. I saw their white, peaceful faces, as they lay, now stretched out on the steps of the jail, a bit of tarpaulin drawn over them. But Tom Fellows got away.

Not clean, though. He dripped blood for three miles. And then the pursuit lost him.

Well, somehow that didn't seem so very important to me, for when I walked down the steps of the jail, from looking at the dead men, I was seeing, again, the way Lew Ellis pitched from his chair; and I was listening to the faint chiming of Lew's golden spurs. I wasn't happy. I simply felt new—clean, different.

Down at the bottom of the steps, I nearly ran into somebody that didn't move out of my way.

"Give your eyes a rub, Slow," says Al.

I hooked my arm through hers.

"We're gunna eat, Al," says I.

"I've eaten," says she.

"You'll eat again," says I. "Or you sit and watch me feed."

"I've seen that pretty picture before," says she. "I don't have to repeat, Handsome!"

"Then you come and just think about school," says I.

"Are you gunna send me to school?" says she.

"No," says I. "You're gunna teach. And I'm the pupil. One of these days, maybe—when you get a lot younger—whatcha think, Al?"

"Listen," says she, "you're not getting sentimental, are you, Slow?"

"I wouldn't be such a fool," says I.

"Jiminy!" says she. "I'd hope not."

"Come on," says I. "Let's go."

"Yeah, let's go eat," says she. "I haven't had a square meal in a month!"

That's the way we started down the street. And it wasn't to end there.

END